ACCUMULATION

buan boonaca

ISBN 978-90-826859-1-6
ISBN 978-90-826859-0-9(ebook)

*"All the world's a stage and once in a while some
of the players forget their lines."*

A dead English guy

FROM THE RUBBLE of their fallen predecessors, the mega-hotel/casinos rose up, towering higher and higher over either side of the boulevard—glittering amnesiacs with the memories of what had come before hidden deep within their foundations. Cam was on an upper floor in one of these enormous structures looking down at the awesome view of the Las Vegas strip from the room's bank of floor-to-ceiling windows. Miniature cars in a rush to get to the next club or casino inched forward along the boulevard, their way blocked by all the other miniature cars in a rush to get to the next casino or club. The herds of people that filled the sidewalks did not seem to be in any hurry to get anywhere, but still beat the occupants of the miniature cars to the next club or casino.

Individuals were barely distinguishable at this height, but it didn't stop Cam from trying to pick out the beauties from the beasts. A couple of blondes looked promising, but the lack of detail became too frustrating and he gave up the pursuit. A casino across the street had large video screens advertising its dancing magicians and topless comedians. Cam was briefly entranced by the moving images and the way their light altered the color of everything in their radius. In fact, the video screens were the principle source of illumination in his room—changing it from red to green to blue and then back to red.

The awesomeness of the view soon lost its novelty and a much more interesting view, the transparent reflection of himself in the window, took its place. He didn't want to take in the whole scene at once; there were too many separate sections worth taking a closer look at. He started with the hair. It had the appearance of being purposely left uncombed, but the reality was the complete opposite; the hairs were carefully gelled into a controlled chaos. A few of these hairs had fallen into place and Cam had to return them to their forced state of apathy. He turned his face side to side and saw he had the perfect amount of stubble; he'd stopped shaving two and a half days ago. Three full days just looked sloppy and anything less than two and a half didn't do his jawline justice. His t-shirt, which was imprinted with an obscure line from one of his favorite cult comedies, was tight enough to show off his muscular chest, but not tight enough to seem like he was showing off. The problem was that after so many repeated wearings, it was becoming a little too loose. He turned sideways and saw that the contours of his pecs were still visible, so he shrugged off his concern. There was a similar issue with his jeans. They had to be somewhat baggy, but not to the point where his ass was completely hidden.

Twisting his neck as far as he could over his shoulder, he attempted to get a good look at his behind. Cam readjusted his belt so that the waistband fell around his hips at just the perfect spot to where the curve of his buttocks subtly protruded through the denim. Turning back around, he faced himself in the glass. His transparent figure turned blue, red, green, and then back to blue. Staring into his own eyes, he could see the city behind them.

A second, better-dressed figure appeared in the window, breaking Cam's gaze.

"You ready?" T held a pair of glasses as he approached the bank of windows.

"Yeah, what about you? I've been waiting here forever." Cam had been enjoying the views for approximately twelve minutes.

"I can't decide if I should wear my glasses or not." T put the glasses on and took them off a few times, using the window's reflection to judge his appearance.

"It doesn't matter dude, you're ugly either way. But at least the glasses hide a little more of your face." As far as Cam knew, T's face had never been a hindrance with the ladies. The roadblocks were put in place by the things that came out of the face.

"I'm not gonna wear 'em. Your face looks better out of focus, but not by much." Glasses made him seem smarter, but at the same time older. The kind of chicks he was on the hunt for tonight probably wouldn't care about his intelligence or age, so looking younger wouldn't hurt. Plus, he didn't want to get drunk and lose them; the frames weren't cheap.

"Let's go then, I want to get out there and kick this city's ass." Cam's fantasies of instant wealth and free-flowing alcohol and vagina accompanied him as he and T began their Vegas adventure.

The awesome view of the Strip remained in the empty room, now with Cam and T as part of it.

Rubber hit rubber as the wheel of a stroller slammed into the back of Cam's foot, causing him to involuntarily hop around for a few seconds. Oblivious to this minor obstacle, the stroller continued on its way. Smoke from the pusher's cigarette trailed behind, and a small boy was trying to keep up by running after the dissipating wisp. T was luckier and narrowly avoided the wheelchair charging towards him. The occupant, an ancient man hooked up to metal canisters, had no control over his conveyance. It was being pushed by a woman with her eyes glued to the dancing water in the distance.

A camera flashed, temporarily blinding Cam and T. The photographer had been aiming at a group of Japanese tourists posing next to an exact replica of a European landmark. When Cam and T regained their sight, they found themselves being handed pornographic pamphlets by a long line of Latino men. Brochures were piling up in their hands as they passed through this gauntlet of smut. Without even looking at them, they dropped the brochures in the street, adding to the already existing heap of erotic litter. A couple of pre-teen boys trying to keep their distance behind their guardians quickly grabbed what they could off this heap and shoved it into their pants. Cam had to stop himself from shouting an obvious masturbation joke. Instead he chuckled at the hilarious comment he would've made.

Waddling at a leisurely pace, two morbidly obese women filled the entire sidewalk in front of Cam and T. Squeezing in between them was impossible. On the left was a wall and on the right, the boulevard—filled with traffic barreling towards the next red light. They tried the left, but there just wasn't enough space between the fat and stone and the right was too dangerous an option. They danced from left to right, trying to find some space to pass the impassable, but realized that without a bucket of grease and a crowbar, they weren't getting through. The flow of people was rapidly building up behind them. Now trapped on all four sides, they had to act fast. Carefully watching the street, they found a small window of opportunity in which there was a lull in the traffic and took a chance. They ran into the street and were able to pass the women and jump back onto the sidewalk just as the onslaught of cars resumed, barely missing them. Free at last, they continued unhindered to their destination: the casino six yards in front of them.

Cool, fresh-perfumed air embraced Cam and T as the glass doors of the casino parted for them. Siren songs of familiar game show and sitcom themes lured them into a labyrinth of gaming machines. Their way was strewn with the victims of this devious maze, elderly women whose semi-conscious bodies were attached to these machines by curly plastic cords. It wasn't clear if they were giving life to the machines or if it was the other way around.

After making a series of wrong turns and nearly losing hope of ever finding a way out, they finally made it to the center of the casino. Instead of encountering an awaiting Minotaur ready to devour them, they discovered something else, the gaming tables. Cam and T surveyed the scene spread out before them.

"Well, what do ya think?" Cam was anxious to get to a table, make his fortune, quit his job, and retire.

"I see way too many Asian dealers here. I never play against Asian dealers." T put his hand in his pocket and held onto his wallet.

"All these years I've known you and only now I find out you're a racist. I'm shocked."

"You know I'm not a racist. Don't you remember for a while I would only go out with Asian chicks?"

"Did you ever get any?"

"What are you talking about, you know I did. You remember Mia, don't you? I went out with her like three times."

"I'm pretty sure Mia's dad is white."

"Whatever, the reason I don't play against Asian dealers is because they're like machines. The casinos program them to always win. I've never, ever won playing against an Asian dealer."

"Have you ever won against any dealer?"

"Come on, let's go find a table." T was also anxious to make his fortune, but he was realistic about it. He only needed to win enough to start an aggressive investment portfolio which would earn him enough in dividends to get into the property market where all the real money was made. He saw his opportunity for riches open before him. "It looks like there are a couple open spots at that table, the one with the chubby white dude dealing."

Suspicious eyes followed Cam and T as they climbed into the blackjack table's two empty chairs. Each of them theatrically threw their cash onto the table for exchange. From behind his fortress of chips, a middle-aged giant looked over at the cash littering the table. "Hey, could you guys wait until this deck is finished before jumping in? We're all doing pretty good here and we don't want to mess up the luck."

Cam didn't feel like getting his throat crushed by the giant's massive hands. "I guess so." He looked over at T. "We're gonna wait until the dealer finishes this deck before we start."

T had already begun mentally building his investment portfolio. "Really? I wanted to start playing."

"Show the table some courtesy, man." Cam said it loud enough for the giant to hear, hopefully getting in his good graces. He and T took their money off the table.

"So what do we do now, just sit here with our dicks in our hands?" The sooner he made the money to start his portfolio, the faster T could become a property magnate.

"If you think that will bring you luck. I'd rather have a drink than rub one out in a crowded casino." Cam thought some alcohol would grease the gears in his head and help him play better. "Look, I think that cocktail waitress is coming over here."

Large breasts spilling over the top of a sequin-covered

corset were easy for Cam to spot across the casino floor. In fact he followed them until they were directly in his face.

"What can I getcha?"

"I'll have a rum and Coke." T answered first as the waitress' question took a few seconds to pass over her breasts and register in Cam's brain.

Cam's brain got the message and commanded his mouth to spit out a clever drink order. "I'll take a Caucasian."

"A what?" The waitress was only a couple hours into her shift and her feet were already starting to hurt. She wasn't looking forward to another six hours carrying around drinks in ill-fitting heels. This guy's stupid order wasn't improving her mood.

"A Caucasian." Cam enunciated the drink's name as he repeated it.

"What's that?" She heard him the first time, but it didn't make it any less of a stupid order.

T jumped in before Cam's stupid order caused the waitress to leave without getting either of them anything. "Just get him a White Russian."

It took a moment or two for T to regain his annoyance with Cam's drink order as his attention was temporarily occupied by a beautiful sight. When the cocktail waitress turned to leave, her marvelous ass revealed itself. Two plump round cheeks covered only in a narrow bikini bottom over shear black tights.

"Seriously, why do you have to do that?"

"What? That's what the drink's called." Cam didn't see any problem with his drink order.

"When you're with me call it a White Russian, OK? You always embarrass me with that Caucasian shit."

"I like testing the cocktail knowledge of my server."

"And if any of your servers happen to know what a Caucasian is, do they win some sort of prize or something?"

Cam flashed his most charming smile. "Yes they do, the chance to get a shot at this." He gestured towards his crotch.

"Goddamn, you're such a prick."

The dealer began to shuffle the cards, which was the signal for the boys' cash to be thrown back onto the table. It was done without the theatrical flair this time. After the cards were well mixed the dealer made the exchange and pushed small stacks of chips to Cam and T. Cam read the white plastic rectangle attached to the dealer's shirt. It said: 'Kyle from Florida.' "Are you gonna be good to us, Kyle from Florida?"

Kyle from Florida's sheepish grin was his only response. He knew better than to make a guarantee that mathematical odds would eventually nullify. Cards flew from his hand, shrinking the deck held in his other. This in turn caused the shrinkage of all the players' piles of chips. Kyle from Florida removed another of Cam's chips from the red imprinted circle on the green felt. He replaced the missing chip with one from his withering pile. "Take it easy Kyle F. F., we just got here. At least give us a chance to get our expensive free drinks before you take all our money."

Kyle F. F. raised his eyebrows and motioned with his head to the cocktail waitress who had finally arrived. With exaggerated care, she set Cam's drink in front of him. "Your Caucasian, sir."

Cam winked as he set a tip on her shiny metal tray. "Thanks babe."

T's embarrassment and annoyance returned yet again as he received his drink. He had an overwhelming urge to slap Cam's unshaven face, but it wouldn't look cool if he lost his cool, so the urge was buried along with all his other uncool urges.

Cam picked up his glass and made a toast regarding some surprising news he'd only recently received. "Here's to Blocko. I can't believe that dirty son of a bitch is going to have a kid."

Their glasses clinked and as the rim touched T's lips, he stopped. "What a minute, did you just call your mom a bitch?"

Cam stopped mid-sip. "Oh shit. OK… here's to Blocko, that dirty son of a nice lady."

After the re-clinking they at last got the heavily diluted alcohol into their bellies.

"Is he going to marry that chick or what?" T was a little old-fashioned when it came to children and marriage. If a guy was dumb enough to get a girl pregnant then he should have the decency to continue his stupidity and also marry the girl.

"I have no idea. I never thought he'd even have a kid. My mom gave up on him a long time ago. She was pinning all her hopes on *me* knocking up some girl."

"I can't imagine you having a kid—you can't even keep your own stinky ass clean."

Cam took another sip of his Caucasian. "You never know. Crazier things have happened."

"What? Is Crazzee dropping hints?"

"Once in a while she says some stuff. Why do you think I got her a puppy? That little guy keeps her busy and her mind off kids, for now. Plus I got one of the best BJs ever after I gave her that furry bastard."

Kyle F. F. beat the entire table again. The giant in his diminished fortress looked over at Cam and T with accusing eyes. Cam looked down at his two remaining chips in disbelief. "What the hell are you doing to us, K. F. F.? I've only taken a couple sips of this watered-down excuse for a Caucasian and my money is almost gone."

T tapped Cam on the arm and leaned over to give him some advice. "Let's try another table—he's way too hot."

"No! You're the one who wanted to play here, so we're going to stay and win our money back. Right K. F. F.?" Cam slammed down another bet on the table.

K. F. F. glanced up as he was finishing the shuffle. "I'll see what I can do."

The first card Cam received was a five, which was met with an audible sigh. He was dealt another five and nodded his head in approval. A ten wasn't a bad start. Cam smiled as he saw K. F. F. had given himself a six, the worst possible card a dealer can have showing. Cam slid his last remaining chip next to the other chip in the red felt circle. "Double down!" he shouted.

K. F. F. placed a Jack of Spades on Cam's two fives, giving him a respectable twenty. "Nice!" Cam smacked his hand down on the table in joy, causing a tremor that disturbed the walls of the giant's fortress. The giant didn't look pleased as he repaired his fortifications.

K. F. F. exposed the card that had been hiding under his lousy six. It was a five. In chorus, the players gasped at this revelation. The odds of K. F. F. getting a ten and making twenty-one were very high. Luckily the next card was a four. The chorus became a sigh of relief. The odds of a ten coming were still high, which would give K. F. F. twenty-five, cause him to bust and make every player at the table a winner. Then all the laws of probability were defied when K. F. F. dealt himself another six. He looked down almost apologetically at his unlikely twenty-one and with great solemnity, swept the table clean of chips.

Cam stood up. "Thank you Florida, thank you for taking all my money."

T grabbed his last chip and joined Cam's exodus.

After his first step away from the table, Cam turned back. "I hope when you go back to Florida you fall in a swamp and an alligator bites your hand off like that Mexican general in *Romancing the Stone*. Then you'll never be able to deal again and screw people out of their money."

Hearing much worse on a daily basis for years, Cam's words bounced off the calloused shell Kyle from Florida had grown as a necessity for his chosen profession. The cards flew from his hand unabated.

As T led Cam away from the scene of defeat, he shouted to no one in particular, "Yeah! Vegas baby!" It was only the beginning of his tirade. "I bet that fat fuck thinks the chips are barbeque flavored. The more he wins, the more he gets to eat after work. Have you ever noticed that eighty percent of stories in the news about scummery or white-trash hijinks come out of Florida? Those rednecks shouldn't be allowed to leave the state."

T put his arm around Cam's shoulder. "Dude, calm down. Let's go get some more drinks and chill. By the way, that general in *Romancing the Stone* was Colombian."

Cam pulled his wallet out of his pocket and took a

long look inside. "Damnit! I don't think I can even afford to get drunk now."

"I have an idea, let's go play some slots. That way we'll be able to get at least a few free drinks, if we play slow enough." T hadn't given up on his quest to become a tycoon. Some of the slot machines had huge jackpots—big enough he could skip the investment portfolio and jump right into property market.

"Whatever, as long as I can get another beverage." Cam just wanted to get buzzed enough to forget about his crushed dream of early retirement.

Tucked in between the bathrooms and a bar seemingly forgotten by the rest of the casino, was a row of lower-denomination gaming machines. Cam and T sat drinkless at a couple of these lonely machines. With every push of the blinking button Cam would whirl around on his stool searching in vain for a cocktail waitress. "Where the hell is she?"

T was actually concentrating on the screen, hoping the symbols would line up and he would win the jackpot or at least some of his money back. "I have no idea. Keep playing as slow as you can and try to make your money last."

"I'm trying, but this is boring as hell. How do people get addicted to this crap? Watching these little symbols constantly spin around is really getting on my nerves, plus I'm thirsty as fuck." Cam pressed the button again. The machine froze. Loud beeping noises began to blast from it and the orange siren that sat atop the machine lit up and spun around. Cam tried pressing the button again and again, but nothing happened.

The sudden commotion startled the crap out of T. "What the hell did you do?"

"Nothing, I just pressed the button and the thing started going nuts."

T looked around and saw no one had noticed the disturbance yet. "Maybe we should get out of here. I don't want to get busted for breaking one of these machines."

Cam started looking for the quickest escape route when he saw two casino employees walking in their direction. An older woman who had an obvious lifelong love of cigarettes was joined by an extremely overweight Pacific Islander. He was struggling to keep up with her brisk pace.

"Shit! It's too late, here they come." Cam thought about making a run for it, but then realized he had no clue in which direction the exit was located. He was trapped.

"Tell 'em it was an accident." T knew he had nothing to do with the damage of casino property and hoped the casino would also see it that way. It was all Cam's fault.

The large Pacific Islander was now near enough that Cam could hear his labored breathing. The man reached for his belt. "Excuse me."

Cam jumped off the stool. "I swear I didn't do anything to break it. I just pressed the button and then the thing started going crazy."

The big man used his native intuition to choose the correct key from the dozens of others on his massive keyring and with it, brought calm back to the machine. Seeing the obvious fear in Cam's eyes, the older woman smiled at her colleague. "You didn't break it hon, you hit a jackpot.

See." She pointed at the rows of identical symbols flashing across the screen.

Cam inspected the symbols, but couldn't interpret the strange language used by the gambling culture. "No way, you're messing with me. How much do I win?"

Her tar-coated voice box produced the sweetest words he'd ever heard. "Thirty-nine hundred dollars."

Cam turned his head towards T in disbelief. Eyebrows rose, dopey grins formed, and the dam burst. Jumping, air-punching, and skin-stinging high fives followed. "HELL YEAH!"

The crisp fresh texture of new one-hundred-dollar bills massaged the surface of Cam's fingers. He held the small pile of cash to his nose and inhaled deeply. "My god that's good. I wonder if they make cologne that smells like this. If they don't they should." He extended his index and middle fingers towards T. "Do you want to smell it?"

T smacked the fingers away. "You have to take that money back to the tables. Do you know how much we could turn that into?"

"Yeah, back into nothing." The thought of parlaying his windfall into the fortune needed for his dream of early retirement had crossed his mind, but then an image of that fat Floridian fuck taking all his money from him popped up and overruled the first thought. "Listen, we always talk about coming to Vegas and partying like rock stars, but what do we usually end up doing? Losing all our money, getting drunk on cheap booze, and aimlessly wandering around the Strip hoping to find hot chicks to come back to our room with us. With this much cash we really can party like rock stars." Cam flipped through the stack of bills. "Let's get nuts."

The boys plopped themselves down in the back of a taxi. Cam spoke to the back of the furry head in front of him. "Hey man, what's the hottest club in town right now?"

A pair of dark eyes stared back at him in the rearview mirror. "Press Huur."

Cam turned to T. "Press her?" He looked into the mirror. "No, we don't want to go to a place like that. We just want a normal club, you know, where we can dance." Cam performed a little backseat dance for the set of dark eyes.

The eyes responded. "Yeah, dancing. I take you to Press Huur OK."

T took the initiative and gave the eyes the go-ahead. "Cool, let's go." He leaned over and spoke into Cam's ear. "He's saying Pressure. I've heard about that place, it's supposed to be off the chain."

"Off the chain huh? I don't know. If it was off the hook or even off the rails I'd check it out, but off the chain?" Cam's smile was met with a hard punch to the arm.

The taxi deposited them in front of a huge concrete cube, its top rimmed with red neon and its bottom rimmed with people. The line to get in wrapped around three sides of the structure. This particular feature of the building didn't impress T. "Goddamn it! Look at that. I don't want to waste my night standing in a fucking line."

Cam reached into in his pocket and retrieved one of his newly acquired hundred-dollar bills. He began to fold it into a palm-sized square. "Don't worry about it, I've got our VIP pass right here."

"Think it'll work?" T was skeptical. He thought things like that only worked in movies.

"Why wouldn't it work? How do you think these chump-filters make their money?" Cam once watched a documentary about bouncers on TV.

With their best imitation cocksure attitude, Cam and T bypassed the desperate rabble waiting to be let in and approached the bouncer holding the clipboard containing the names of those deemed worthy to enter without delay. Every contour of the guardian's over-pumped torso could be seen beneath his skintight black t-shirt, including his colossal pecs—bigger than the breasts of the majority of the females waiting in line. Females who thought their big boobs would mean automatic express entry inside.

Cam got as close as he could to the sacred list attached to the clipboard. As he gestured at the holy document, a little green square fell from his hand. "I think we're on the list."

The black t-shirted clipboard holder looked at the green square sitting on his list. He looked Cam up and down and unhooked the otherwise impenetrable red faux-velvet rope. The boys proceeded to enter to the club. Cam passed without incident, but T was stopped with a muscled palm. "I don't see his name on my list."

Cam retrieved another bill, folded it, and repeated his previous performance. "He's right there."

The palm withdrew and T was free to enter.

"Fifty."

"What?"

"The cover's fifty." The girl behind the counter didn't look up from her phone as she spoke. Yet another bill had to be retrieved, but at least this time he didn't need to go through the trouble of folding it. Cam waited for his change, but it never arrived. Fifty dollars was the price each man had to pay to achieve entry into this exclusive paradise.

Angry beats pounded on the steel door in front of them, violently trying to escape the Eden they were an integral part of. A few beats managed to gain their freedom upon the opening of the door, but immediately missed their brothers when the door slammed closed again, cutting off the escapees from their family. The beat's entire family of deep house steptronic ripped through Cam and T at maximum velocity once they were on the other side of the door—vibrating their internal organs.

Recovering from the initial shock of sound, they found the music wasn't the only thing thickening the internal atmosphere. A tropical climate had developed in the middle of the desert, fueled by the heat and moisture being given off by the solid block of the few thousand fortunate ones allowed in.

Navigating through this jungle of limbs took skill and patience. A machete would have made the journey a lot quicker, but since that wasn't a viable option, it was necessary to flatten oneself and squeeze between the individual bodies. Sweaty bare arms helped with this by lubricating several stretches of the path. Occasionally Cam would have to stand on his tiptoes to rise above the canopy and make sure he was heading in the right direction, towards the bar. He also had to keep looking back to see if T had gotten himself lost in the wilderness or if he was still following the trail Cam was blazing for him. He was doing just fine; T had a lot of experience traversing the great indoors.

"THIS PLACE IS AWESOME."

"WHAT?"

"THIS PLACE IS AWESOME."

Communicating in this type of environment was a delicate balance of yelling loud enough into the listener's ear so as to be heard, but softly enough as to not cause permanent damage to the listener's eardrum. Ordering a drink required none of this balance; the only thing required was being obnoxious enough to get the bartender's attention and shouting over the other patrons trying to place an order. Getting the drinks safely away from the bar without spilling a drop was a skill in itself. Shaolin masters used a similar challenge to test the concentration of their students. Getting away from the bar with the entire drink intact wasn't the end of the story. Each time the beverage traveled from the hand to the lips, it had to avoid a constant barrage of elbows and shoulders. Cam and T felt a sense of accomplishment as they sipped their hard-earned cocktails.

"I'M STILL SURPRISED THEY LET YOU IN." T was doing his best to look suave and sophisticated despite being shoved around by the never-ending stream of bodies flowing back and forth from the bar.

"WHY? I GAVE THAT GORILLA AT THE DOOR ENOUGH FUCKING MONEY." Cam was nearly offended. If it weren't for his big win, T would've never gotten into this amazing club and would probably be drinking a shitty cocktail with the rest of the losers walking up and down the Strip.

"LOOK AT YOU, YOU'RE DRESSED LIKE SHIT. YOU'RE WEARING YOUR FUCKING BASKETBALL SHOES FOR CHRIST'S SAKE." T was nearly offended. He put so much effort into finding and putting together his outfits while Cam probably just threw on whatever clothes hadn't made it into the hamper yet.

Cam shrugged and looked at his shoes. Shoes he spent a lot of effort finding and a lot of money purchasing. "WHO CARES WHAT KIND OF SHOES I'M WEARING? NO ONE EVER NOTICES YOUR SHOES. HAVEN'T YOU SEEN *THE SHAWSHANK REDEMPTION*?"

"I'VE SEEN *THE SHAWSHANK REDEMPTION* LIKE TWENTY-FIVE TIMES AND YEAH, OTHER DUDES DON'T NOTICE YOUR SHOES, BUT IT'S THE FIRST THING GIRLS NOTICE WHEN THEY MEET YOU." T was wearing his most recent acquisitions—a pair of shoes which all the men's magazines agreed was the in thing right now.

"IS THAT WHY YOU HAVE LIKE THIRTY PAIRS OF SHOES?" Cam glanced down at T's boring shoes that looked exactly like all his other boring shoes.

"ACTUALLY I HAVE CLOSER TO FORTY. IN THIS WORLD HOW YOU LOOK IS EVERYTHING." T knew he made a true and profound statement and hoped Cam would follow his lead someday and put some effort into his appearance.

"WELL, I DON'T NEED A PAIR OF SHOES TO GET ME LAID." Cam gestured to a couple of girls leaning on the railing separating the dance floor from the regular floor. Both of them were wearing miniskirts and shiny tank-tops and each girl was holding the remnants of a long-finished cocktail while attempting to dance in the limited space provided. The railing was most likely being used for balance as the combination of high heels and alcohol made standing difficult. "SEE THOSE TWO CHICKS."

"REALLY? THOSE TWO CHICKS LOOK SO DRUNK THEY WOULDN'T EVEN NOTICE IF YOU WERE WEARING FLIP-FLOPS. BUT FOR SKANKS, I GUESS THEY'RE KIND OF HOT." T was going through a bit of a dry spell and either one of the girls would be a much-welcomed oasis.

"THIS IS GOING TO BE LIKE TAKING CANDY FROM BABIES IN A BARREL." Cam felt kind of bad going after such easy prey, but how could girls like that regret being with a guy like him, even if the decision was made with diluted judgment?

Cam and T squeezed their way through the barrier of bodies separating them from the girls.

"HEY, YOU GUYS LOOK LIKE YOU COULD USE A DRINK." Cam's opening line caused the girls to notice that their glasses only contained pieces of melting ice. They smiled and nodded, impressed with Cam's powers of observation. Four fresh cocktails were obtained and the introductions began.

"SO, WHAT ARE YOUR NAMES?" Cam thought it would be helpful if the girls had labels.

"I'M KAITLIN AND THIS IS KELLY." The one with the slightly blonder hair threw her arm around the one with the slightly less blond hair.

"WHAT'RE YUR GUYSES NAMES?" Kelly, the one

with the slightly less blond hair, asked because Kaitlin, the one with the slightly blonder hair, had just turned all her attention to getting the elusive black straw protruding from her glass into her mouth.

"I'M T AND THIS IS CAM." Up close they weren't so bad, T thought. They were doable.

"OH, LIKE VINCE VAUGHN IN THAT MOVIE *SWINGERS*. I LOVE THAT MOVIE." Kelly had to answer again as Kaitlin had achieved her goal and was sucking down her cocktail.

"FUCK THAT MOVIE, I WAS CALLED T WAY BEFORE THAT SHIT CAME OUT." In kindergarten when all the children were learning to write their names, T only managed to write the first letter of his name—the other letters had too many curves and squiggles. His teacher tried to get him to write the rest of the letters, but T was stubborn. As a punishment his teacher decided to call him T until he wrote the rest of his name out. The class forgot his real name after a while.

Cam was grateful a good-looking girl mentioned *Swingers* and not some guy or else T would've really gone off. "DUDE, IT'S OK. LET IT GO."

It pissed T off that people thought he named himself after a character in a lame movie. "I JUST HATE BEING ASSOCIATED WITH THAT OVERSIZED BAGGY-EYED PRICK. IF I EVER MET HIM IN PERSON I'D SAY—HEY BRO TAKE A BREAK FROM MAKING ALL THOSE SHITTY MOVIES AND GET SOME SLEEP. I DOUBT IT'S THAT HARD PLAYING THE SAME CHARACTER OVER AND OVER AGAIN ANYWAY."

Kaitlin and Kelly thought T was joking and giggled

during his little rant. Kaitlin then whispered something into Kelly's ear, which caused her to look at Cam and smile. Cam noticed the smile and was relieved T didn't scare them away. "SO, WHERE YOU GUYS FROM?"

"FARGO, YOU KNOW LIKE IN THAT MOVIE *FARGO*. AND YOU GUYS?" Kelly answered again. Kaitlin decided she would be the shy one.

"WE'RE FROM ORANGE COUNTY, YOU KNOW LIKE IN THAT SHOW *THE O.C.* WE WORK IN FINANCE OVER THERE." T jumped in to answer and hoped giving them the idea that he and Cam dealt with large sums of money would make them forget about his outburst.

The girls looked at each other and smiled, seemingly impressed by the answer. T and Cam then gave each other a look; the time had come. They spoke in unison. "WHO WANTS SHOTS?"

Kaitlin and Kelly jumped up and down, each with a raised arm. "ME, ME."

"Sweet," Cam said in his non-all-caps voice.

Calling it dancing would be using the term in the loosest sense of the word. The four of them were on the dance floor together each in their own square foot of space, swaying their bodies and moving their arms, but the feet were firmly planted. At one point Cam decided to throw some flair into his dance routine and added a couple of steps, but it violated his allotted square foot of space and caused him to bump into a nearby body. That nearby body bumped into another nearby body, which triggered a domino effect of bumping bodies. The final bumped body spilled his drink on the body next to him. These two bodies became involved in a minor altercation, which the bouncers were more than happy to solve.

"WHEW, I'M EXHAUSTED. DOES ANYBODY ELSE WANT A NICE REFRESHING BEVERAGE?" Cam prayed his dance perspiration didn't alter the delicate chaotic balance of his hair. He was anxious to go look in the mirrors behind the bar to check if his hair was still out of place.

"WE DO!" the girls said in unison.

After another round of cocktails the four of them were back out on the dance floor, but any attempt at dancing had been given up. T and Kaitlin were holding each other and groping to the beat. Cam and Kelly were enmeshed in a sloppy make-out session, ignoring the beat altogether. Kaitlin took a break from her tactile exploration of T's well-dressed body and tapped her friend on the shoulder. Kelly dislodged her tongue from Cam's mouth. "WE HAVE TO GO TO THE LITTLE GIRL'S PEE ROOM. I MEAN WE HAVE TO GO PEE IN THE ROOM.... WE'LL BE RIGHT BACK."

Cam and T decided to be gentlemen and followed the girls to the bathroom and waited patiently for them outside. They didn't want the girls to forget about the nice boys who had gotten them wasted and have a couple scumbags swoop in and take the credit for all their hard work.

"It looks like we got a sure thing here bro." T was super anxious for his dry spell to end.

"I think so my friend." Cam wasn't as anxious, but it didn't stop him from returning T's high five.

T looked at his watch. "What the hell're they doing in there? Are they taking dueling dumps or what?"

"Oh nooo." Cam saw Kelly and Kaitlin finally make their grand stumbling exit from the bathroom. On closer inspection Kaitlin wasn't actually stumbling, she was being dragged along by Kelly. Her neck had the muscle strength of a newborn; it couldn't support the weight of her head. In keeping with her infant theme, Kaitlin also had a whitish vomit stain on the front of her shiny top. Kelly had done her best to clean it off, but vomit was hard to get out and her laundering skills were somewhat impaired.

"Kaitlin doesn't feel so good." The words dribbled out of Kelly's mouth.

"I threw up." Kaitlin told the front of her shiny top.

"Can we sit down for a sec?" Kelly's newfound career as Kaitlin's crutch was short-lived. Her strength gave out and both their bodies slid down the wall behind them.

Cam turned to T. "Dude, those two are completely shit-canned."

"So? We can still take 'em back to our room." T didn't want his oasis to turn into a mirage.

"Seriously, look at 'em. I don't want to take care of a couple of drunks the rest of the night."

"The plan would be they'd be taking care of us, if you know what I mean." T raised his eyebrows to emphasize his point.

"Of course I know what you mean prick, but they'll be like completely passed out before we even get to the room."

"So what, we can still have a good time with 'em." T didn't care if his oasis was filled with tainted water, he was dying of thirst.

"I don't know dude, that sounds pretty weak." Cam didn't have a problem going for the easy catch, but what was the fun of getting into a boat already filled with dead fish?

"You're such a pussy. What should we do then, huh? Just leave 'em there on the floor? What a waste. The club is closing, so now there's no time to find replacement chicks."

"I have an idea." Cam put his arm around T's shoulder and led him away from his polluted oasis. T looked back longingly at the two heaps of female.

"Now isn't this better than banging a passed-out drunk chick covered in her own vomit?" Cam inquired as a bare-breasted woman rubbed her ass on his crotch.

"I guess so." T's reply was muffled by the large pair of surgically enhanced naked breasts that covered most of his face.

The girls removed themselves from the guys' laps as soon as they heard the last note of the song they'd been grinding to and replaced their tops. It was done with so much speed that Cam and T's erections had no time to subside, forcing them to squirm in their seats in awkward attempts to disassemble their trouser tents.

Verbal intercourse wasn't the sort of intercourse on the boys' minds so they filled their mouths with beer instead, while the ladies sipped their champagne. Knowing any lull in conversation could cause the customer to lose interest and result in lost profits, Cam's companion began to stimulate his other erogenous zone, his ego. "I like your shirt."

Cam looked down at the film quote written across his chest. "Oh yeah? Thanks."

"I think I've seen that movie like fifty times, it's fucking hilarious." Zonda had only seen the film once and didn't find it hilarious. Three or four guys a week came in wearing the same shirt, so it felt like she'd seen the movie at least fifty times, having to feign interest in it so often.

"That's cool. Most girls have no idea what this shirt even means." Cam was impressed—she had beauty and brains.

"I guess it means I'm cooler than most girls." She moved a little closer. "Don't you think?"

"Yes, you are definitely cooler than most girls." Cam lowered his voice. "I want to know your real name though. Zonda sounds like the name of some super-villain's girlfriend and trust me, I'm not a bad guy."

Zonda giggled, looked around, and whispered in his ear. "It's Lisa, but don't tell anyone, OK?" Her real name wasn't Lisa; that was just her standard answer. The 'what's your real name' question was asked all the time and giving her customers the secret answer made them feel special.

"Lisa. I've liked that name since I was a little kid and saw *Weird Science* for the first time." Cam spoke in a half whisper, but T could still hear him and shook his head with disappointment.

"I've heard of that movie, but I've never seen it. Who's Lisa?" Lisa/Zonda asked.

"She's the dream girl of these two nerdy teenagers and

they find a way to create her in some crazy experiment using an early version of the Internet during a lightning storm." After hearing himself giving the brief synopsis, Cam knew it made him sound very uncool, but he blamed it on the alcohol and forgave himself.

Lisa/Zonda looked at her body, then into Cam's eyes. "Am I *your* dream girl?" She put her hand on his thigh.

"You are right now." Cam's conversation was entertaining T more than the bored girl quietly sitting next to him.

Lisa/Zonda noticed the eavesdropper and stood up. She extended her hand to Cam. "Let's go somewhere a little more private."

Cam allowed himself to be led away, but T stopped him. "Hey, wait a sec. I lost most of my cash back in the casino and you know I never bring my debit card out with me when I gamble. I don't wanna have to nurse this beer until you come back, so do you think you could help a brother out?" T had sufficient cash on him, plus his debit card.

Cam slipped him a hundred. "Make it last."

"Thanks man, have a good time back there." T added the hundred-dollar bill to the others he had in his wallet.

Cam entered a private room with Lisa/Zonda where he eventually received a hand job, but only after buying a lot more lap dances and an expensive bottle of cheap champagne.

With a bit of gentle persuasion, Cam and T were led out of the club and staggered into the borderland between night and morning. A washed-out purple light bathed the empty the parking lot in front of them.

"Why are they closing? Nothing's supposed to close in Vegas." Cam tried to go back into the club. "Hey! You can't close, don't you know where you are… ? Twenty-four seven, that's what the commercials say. I'm calling the Chamber of Commerce." Cam patted his pockets. "Where's my phone?"

T intervened. "They're not going to be open."

"Twenty-four seven! They have to be open, everything has to be open. We were just starting to have some fun. I don't want this night to end yet."

"Me neither, but I doubt you can call anyone to stop that." T pointed towards the horizon.

Dawn became the enemy and Cam began to pace back and forth, formulating a plan to defeat it.

"Dude, dude… let's go, if we stand out here any longer, the bouncers will think we're those creeps who wait outside the club for the strippers to leave." T didn't want to end his night with a beating from a security guard looking for an excuse to release some of his pent-up roid rage.

"I got it! I know how we can make this night last forever, c'mon." Cam led the way through the empty parking lot towards his imagined destination. It was fortunate a taxi on the lookout for drunks to rip off found what he was looking for and picked them up or else Cam and T might've ended up doing something they would regret.

The buzzing of metallic insects filled Cam's ears as one of the noisy creatures spit its black ink into his body. He was lying on a padded table, his left pant leg was rolled up, and the sock and shoe were gone. Cam only had a partial view of the attack taking place on his outer ankle. The rest of his view was blocked by the assailant's black overcoat and the long black hair that hung down around his face. On the other side of the table T stood shirtless in front of a full-length mirror. With his back facing the mirror, he was peering over his shoulder trying to get a good look at his new tattoo—a small green dollar sign on the upper right part of his back.

"Let me see." Cam wanted a closer look.

T proudly displayed his new addition.

"Why did you get *that*?"

"Because I'm so fucking money and now wherever I go the cash will follow." T glanced over at Cam's ankle. "What're you getting? I forgot."

"Oh just a little tribal symbol I saw in that book on the counter over there. I don't know, it looked kinda cool and I couldn't think of anything else to get." Cam noticed the buzzing at his feet had ceased. He saw a pair of black rubber-gloved hands wipe away the excess ink from his skin. "Are you done?"

Long strands of black hair swayed back and forth as the head underneath nodded.

"I didn't feel a thing."

A black hand gestured towards the mirror. Cam spun around and hopped off the table anxious to see how his ankle now looked. Groups of curves and sharp lines intersected to form what Cam saw as the vague shape of a man standing over a weird fish. He studied the design from all possible angles, finding new interpretations each time. "Looks good, almost like it's supposed to be there, you know?"

T only saw a mess of black lines. "Let's see if you feel the same when your ass sobers up and you're like 'what the fuck is that thing on my ankle?'"

"Hey, at least my tattoo…" Behind him, reflected in the mirror, Cam saw the figure in black pick up a bag and rush away. "What the hell? Don't we have to pay that guy?"

"Seriously? Damn, you're more trashed than I thought. Dude, we already paid him. Remember? He only agreed to tattoo our drunk asses if we paid him up front, probably way more than we should've."

"Shouldn't he at least bandage our tattoos up or somethin'? I don't want this shit getting all infected." Cam found his missing sock and shoe. He sat down, sock in hand, and weighed the pros and cons of covering his newly inked ankle with the stinky cotton tube dangling from his fingers.

"Maybe he was in a hurry and forgot. Don't worry, it'll be fine."

"I hope so." Without his knowledge, someone put Cam onto a carousel. The room began to spin around him. The centrifugal force must have been great because Cam found he wasn't able to get off the carousel. All he could do was close his eyes and hope it would stop.

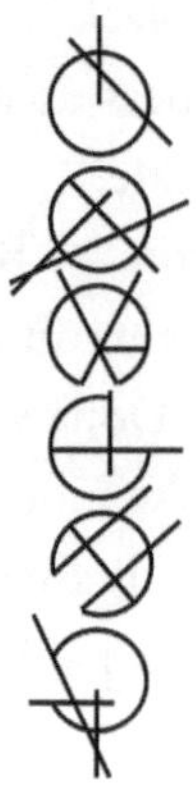

CAM OPENED HIS eyes the moment he heard the obnoxious repetitive screaming of his alarm. He reached over, pushed the button to make it stop, and fell back to sleep. The screaming resumed, so he pushed the button again and fell asleep. More screaming—it refused to be ignored. Cam was tempted to fight on against the screamer, but it was a battle he lost every time, so he got out of bed and went into the bathroom attached to his bedroom. Once inside, he began his strictly followed morning routine.

1. Piss. He always peed before going to bed, but for some reason his bladder was full again every morning. As a child he asked his mother about it. She told him it was the work of the pee fairies.

2. Examine face. The time this took varied wildly day to day. It depended on how many imperfections he found

and had to remedy. On this particular morning he found a few stray eyebrow hairs that needed plucking and a pimple on his chin that needed a squeeze.

3. Brush teeth. If he did this early enough the tooth-paste flavor in his mouth would subside and wouldn't taint the flavor of his breakfast and coffee.

4. Shower. This was done almost every day, except on days when he refused to surrender to the screamer and prolonged the inevitable defeat too long or if the fates had cursed him with a plethora of imper-fections he had to correct, thus extending the time it took to complete step 2 on the list. (Needless to say, he washed his face with an expensive exfoliat-ing cleanser regardless of taking a shower or not. His pores weren't going to unclog themselves.)

5. Shave. His two-and-a-half-days-of-stubble look was only for special occasions, but Cam thought shaving every day was bad for the skin so his com-promise was to shave every other day.

6. Dress. Cam always laid his clothes out the night before so he didn't have to waste time in the morn-ing deciding what to wear. His outfits were carefully chosen to seem thrown together at the last minute.

7. Apply moisturizer. Cam had been doing this on a daily basis for a number of years. He wanted his skin to look as young as possible for as long as

possible. It's easier to prevent wrinkles than try to get rid of them later on.

8. Style hair. His hairdo on workdays was less anarchic than on the weekends, but he still put enough effort into it to make it look as if no effort was put into it at all.

9. Hide imperfections. The time this took varied according to how many imperfections needed concealing. Cam had a little bottle of makeup he used to cover any pimples or red remnants left behind by old pimples. He used as little as possible because he hated running out of it; buying more was very embarrassing. Almost as embarrassing as anyone finding out he performed this step every morning.

10. The once-over. After all of the above had been completed, Cam reexamined himself. First each individual section—hair, face, skin, clothes—and then how each section fit together as a whole. If needed, he made any necessary adjustments.

Satisfied with his appearance, Cam left the bathroom. One little skin problem he did fail to notice during his morning routine was the vertical series of six small black circular shapes tattooed on the back of his left arm.

T was eating a Pop Tart over the sink when Cam walked into the kitchen to grab a granola bar out of the pantry.

"I'm taking off as soon as I finish this." Crumbs fell from T's mouth onto his freshly ironed work shirt.

"Yeah, I'm leaving now too." Cam never wasted time eating breakfast at home on workdays. A granola bar on the way was enough and the coffee at work was free.

They exited the apartment together and walked downstairs to their respective vehicles. T to his oversized white Ford pickup and Cam to his late-model silver Toyota Camry. He didn't buy the Camry because its name was similar to his own; it was only an unconsciously planned coincidence.

"See ya." T hopped into his truck and slammed the door.

"OK, later." Cam got into his car, unwrapped his breakfast, and shoved it in his mouth. He followed T's truck to the parking lot's exit. When the automatic iron gate slid open, T made a left and Cam turned right.

Cam's route to work was carefully thought-out and immaculately executed. The street under his late-model Camry's tires was blemish free, not a pothole or crack in sight. It was split into two perfectly symmetrical sides by a birch-tree-filled divider. Birch trees were chosen as their white trunks evoked feelings of cleanliness and freshness. Each tree was planted exactly ten yards apart from each other and they were all kept the same exact height. Wide white sidewalks ran parallel to the street and were buffered from the street by florescent green grass. Sprinklers were precisely timed to coat the grass with fine mists of water in the early mornings and late evenings. It prevented daytime evaporation and kept the grass its unnaturally natural color. Nothing was in walking distance, so the sidewalks stayed empty and clean, free from the discoloration dirty-shoed pedestrians cause. On the other side of the sidewalks were matrices of shrubbery and flowers, mathematically formulated into random and therefore natural patterns. Four times a week a small army of landscapers invaded and attacked any unplanned growth.

Beyond the shrubbery and flowers were the high walls, which shielded the residential areas from the non-residential world. A sea of Spanish red-tiled roofs peeked over these high walls so only hints of the homes underneath could be seen from the street, homes which were painted one of the five approved shades of umber. Across the street from one section of wall was a lake. It was built as a scale model of Lake Superior and its far end was ringed with Spanish red-tiled-roofed homes each painted an approved shade of umber. A little past the homes and the lake was a shopping center and under its Spanish red-tiled roof and behind its approved shade of umber walls could be found all the goods and entertainment needed to survive the demanding modern world.

In total, Cam's commute took him past five miles of high wall and sidewalk, a Great Lake (Superior), a shopping center, four more miles of high wall and sidewalk, another Great Lake (Michigan), and two more shopping centers. Just beyond the last shopping center began the acres of office parks. Each office park was set in a palm-tree-ringed parking lot; the office buildings themselves were built of approved combinations of glass and stone. Cam made a left into the second palm-treed parking lot and pulled into a spot next to T's truck. T was already out of his truck and was about to head into work, but saw Cam and waited. "I always tell you that you should take the freeway, it's faster, but you never listen."

"I like the scenic route."

Together they walked down a concrete path between parallel rows of palm trees and entered a glass and granite structure. Their steps on the black and white imitation marble floor echoed throughout the lobby. An elevator opened and brought them up to the sixth floor where they were greeted by the sight of a young and very attractive blonde. She was sitting behind a blue neon-rimmed counter. Behind her emblazoned on the wall was the company's logo, a refresh icon fashioned into a whimsical shining sun. Underneath it in a friendly but professional font was printed the company's name—Reboot Financial. Under the name was the company's slogan—'Does your credit need a reboot?'

Glancing up from her computer screen, the blond receptionist mumbled a forced "Good morning."

"Good morning," said Cam and T almost in unison as they entered the main office.

"She's definitely hotter than the last one," Cam remarked as soon as the hot receptionist was out of earshot.

"Yeah, but the last one wasn't such a bitch. She actually made an effort to learn our names." T thought a receptionist, despite her hotness, should do her job properly and flirt with every guy who walked in.

"You just liked her because you thought you had a chance with her, unlike this new one who you have absolutely no chance with at all."

"Like you do."

"Maybe, maybe not. We'll never know because I'm already taken." Cam gave T one of his charming guy smiles.

"Get to work prick." T turned left.

"Later." Cam turned right and then left into a cavernous room filled to capacity with large desks. Each desk was split in half with low dividers, four people per desk and two work stations per side. Cubicles were not permitted here; it was a modern open office, nothing to hide and nothing hidden. Managers, associate managers, assistant managers, executive supervisors, supervisors, team leaders, deputy team leaders, and senior administrators sat among their minions to give the impression of equality. Cam's desk was in the second row, fourth from the end. His person-of-size deskmate had already arrived and was enjoying her breakfast diet soda. "Happy Monday."

"Yeah, you too." Cam sat down, pressed the big button, and stared at the blank screen while he waited for his computer to boot up.

"Sooo… how was Vegas? Whatcha doo?"

"Oh you know, the usual, hookers and blow."

Cam's deskmate had grown accustomed to his off-color humor and despite her best effort, was never able come up with any humorous off-color comments of her own. "Did you win anything?"

"Didn't you just hear what I said? How you do think I paid for the hookers and the blow? They don't come complimentary with the room. I think you have to stay in the penthouse suite to get that kind of service. This stupid thing is taking forever to boot up. I know retro-tech is all the rage right now, but having to work on an old piece of crap computer every day doesn't really make me feel that cool. I'm gonna grab a coffee, want one?"

Cam's deskmate couldn't answer the question—her phone had just beeped and her attention had shifted to the customer speaking into her ear. Cam knew she didn't drink coffee, but he always asked her anyway so she wouldn't complain about how long he lingered in the break room. The lingering wasn't entirely his fault; he was usually cornered by some small-talking co-worker, if he was lucky. Today he wasn't lucky. The Coug snuck up behind him as he poured his coffee.

"Hey handsome." The Coug could have been anywhere between the ages of forty and sixty. She dressed so young and wore so much makeup it was difficult to determine; only the girls in HR knew her real age. Cam and his co-workers assumed she was in her early fifties; the younger you tried to look, the older you probably were.

Cam flinched and turned around. "Oh, hey."

"How was your big Vegas weekend?"

Cam always tried to say as little as possible so not to encourage her, but it rarely worked. "It was alright."

"I remember the time Todd Bridges, you know, Willis on *Diff'rent Strokes*, took me to Vegas. Back then interracial couples weren't as accepted as they are now, but since he was so famous people didn't really give us too hard a time. We were at the craps table and he was on a winning streak, people were shouting, whatcha talkin 'bout Willis, whatcha talkin 'bout Willis, every time he threw the dice and as the dice flew out of his hand he would yell 'you know what I'm talkin 'bout!' He usually hated it when people said that whatcha talkin 'bout line to him, he heard it every time he left the house, but all the cash he was winning put him in a good mood. So, later that night we used his winnings to go see the *Siegfried and Roy* show. During the show we snuck off to the bathroom together to do a few lines and you'll never guess who burst in on us… Dana Plato! You know, she played his sister on the show. They used to date but he broke it off and she didn't take it well and had been apparently stalking him. They got into this huge argument. She accused him of owing her money for all the coke she bought for them. He said he always paid his share. All the commotion caught the attention of security, but luckily I finished the last of the lines just as they came in, so we didn't get busted. But they did ask us to leave, so I never got to see Siegfried and Roy's big finale with all the white tigers. I always regretted that."

"Well… I got to get back to my desk. Talk to you later." Cam was forced to edge by her since she had him practically pinned against the counter.

"OK, bye." The Coug's longing stare followed Cam as he returned to his desk.

While he was away, Cam's computer had finally finished booting up and as he was about to log in, an extremely well-dressed and obviously homosexual man approached his desk. "I heard you boys had a pretty wild weekend. I hope you weren't too naughty."

It was Cam's super-supervisor, so he had no choice but to participate in the playful banter. "It depends, what did you hear?"

"I don't think we can talk about that in the presence of a lady." The super-supervisor gestured towards Cam's desk-mate, who was busy checking if anyone had commented on her new profile pic. "I just hope you're not too hungover to work today. It's almost quarter-end and you know what that means."

"Free booze?"

"Yes it does… if we meet all our targets."

"You know I'll do anything for free booze."

The super-supervisor raised his eyebrows. "Anything?"

Cam gave him an exaggerated wink.

"Get to work." The super-supervisor sauntered off to harass some more of his underlings. Cam was never sure if his super-supervisor did anything else during his work-day but harass underlings. Some people in this office did have some real work to do though, so Cam put on his wireless headset and set his status to ready. As soon as he did, he heard a long low beep, the terrible sound which would sometimes invade his dreams and wake him from his sleep. It meant a customer was on the line waiting to speak with him. The little pit of dread in his stomach came alive, which was the signal that his workday had truly begun.

"Reboot Financial, how can I help you to reboot your credit?" Cam spun his chair around, looked across a couple rows of desks to the window. He could see a piece of sky above the grey stone of the building next door. A little white fluffy cloud was floating across the sliver of blue. He watched the cloud as the client in his head gave him her credit sob story. Cam spun back around and punched her info into his database. "I can help you to reduce your debt by almost forty percent."

The long low beep came again through the headset. "Reboot Financial, how can I help you to reboot your credit?" Cam's right leg began rapidly bouncing up and down as he listened to the next heartbreaking story. "If you work with us, we can get you debt-free in less than six years."

Cam was throwing a little foam basketball from hand to hand when the long low beep shot through his ear, catching him off guard and causing him to drop the ball. "Reboot Financial, how can I help you to reboot your credit?" He picked up the ball and began to squeeze it as he listened to the client. "You will definitely have lower monthly payments, so yes, you'll have extra money every month to spend however you like."

He stood up and tried to get a better view of the window. The sky had lost its deep blue and was now a pale, almost white-blue with just a hint of orange. Cam was contemplating the great variety of colors the sky could possibly turn when the long low beep forced itself into his head. "Reboot Financial, how can I help you to reboot your credit?" He paced around and fell back into his chair when it was time to enter the gentleman's info into the database. The client's story was longer and more pathetic than usual. It caused Cam to roll his eyes and pantomime-choke the client. "We all make mistakes, sir. You shouldn't have to pay for them for the rest of your life… ." "No need to thank me sir, we're here to help you."

Cam threw his headset onto the desk at the end of the call and put his head down.

His deskmate attempted to lift his spirits. "Only four more days 'til Friday."

Without raising his head he responded with an unenthusiastic "Yep, can't wait." The vibrating in his pocket gave him a reason to raise his head from his desk. He pulled out his phone. It was a message from Crazzee, '*meet me at the station*' followed by the usual winking smiley face emoticon. Cam answered, '*OK, b there at 6*' but refrained from inserting an accompanying emoticon. He checked the time, another hour to kill. Couldn't go to the break room—the Coug might be lurking around. Couldn't go outside—don't smoke. Couldn't go to the bathroom—just went forty minutes ago. Couldn't fool around on the Internet—gotten too many warnings already, might as well put the headset back on and work. The low long beep once again traveled through his ears and into his head. "Reboot Financial, how can I help you to reboot your credit?"

The Station was a music and movie store resurrected in what was previously a music and movie store. The former tenant was a part of a nationwide chain that had gone out of business. The new tenant hadn't changed much of the former's décor, but had made a half-hearted attempt to give it a train station theme. A large old-fashioned clock was hung above the cash registers, antique-looking benches were scattered throughout the store, video monitors displayed lists of destinations and next to all of these destinations was written: Cancelled. Encircling the upper rim of the interior was a miniature train track, but the miniature train was nowhere to be seen.

Cam entered the Station and began to search for Crazzee, but it was only a casual search. Being easily distracted by the world around her, Crazzee was never on time for anything. Cam browsed the store's selection of basketball DVDs while he waited. The selection was quite limited and he was about to browse through a new category of DVDs when he noticed a tall man dressed in a long black coat and with long black hair. He was standing a few aisles away, with his back towards Cam. The uncertain familiarity of the man piqued Cam's curiosity. He made his way towards the aisle containing the man. Cam never reached his destination though; a pretty orange-tinted face suddenly appeared in front of him. The thin body attached to the face jumped into Cam's arms. He easily caught her and returned the hug.

"Hey baby, I missed you." Crazzee gave him a big kiss on his lips and jumped back down onto the floor.

"I missed you too," Cam replied with as much enthusiasm as he could muster.

"Sooo… how was Vegas?" When Crazzee spoke the words usually got bored somewhere between the point where they were created by her vocal chords and the top of her throat. By the time they reached her mouth they'd already lost the ambition to go out into the world and make something of themselves.

"It was fun."

"I hope you didn't have too much fun." Crazzee gave him a look of mock scorn. "I wish I could've come with, you know how much I love Vegas."

"It was a boys-only weekend, something I explained to you a million times. I promise I'll take you next time."

"You better. I just need to get a couple things here and then we can go." Crazzee and Cam walked off in opposite directions, Crazzee to the DVD aisles and Cam to the magazines. It was where Crazzee found him at the completion of her shopping. He was sitting on one of the antique-looking benches perusing a tattoo magazine. Both her hands were full. In her left was a yellow plastic shopping bag overflowing with DVDs and other accessories, in the right… well, it wasn't exactly what you would call full. Years ago she lost the full use of her right arm from a condition she contracted as a teenager. Over time it caused the arm to turn into a phone and purse rack. The hand had lost the ability to release the phone from its grip and the arm had been bent into a V shape by an extra-large short-handled designer purse which was connected to the crook of the elbow. With her head she motioned to the heavy shopping bag, her good arm was beginning to strain from the weight. Cam stood up, threw the magazine down onto the bench where it made a sharp slap, and relieved Crazzee of her purchased burden.

One of the Station's employees heard the slap. The employee was what some people would label as 'alternative', but since everything that used to be alternative had become mainstream and everything that used to be mainstream had become alternative, labeling her wasn't so straightforward anymore. Her long blondish-pink hair had thick braids of blue and green dispersed throughout it. The nose and lips were pierced and the earlobes were stretched and filled with pentagram ear plugs, but their circumference wasn't so large, yet. Anime and other types of female comic characters were tattooed on her arms and on what could be seen of her back. Her clothing style could be characterized as cyber/goth/punk, if it had to be labeled as something. On her feet were thigh-high vinyl platform boots. Around her neck hung her name tag and in big red letters it read: SYN.

Syn approached Cam. "I didn't know your mom lived in a record store."

Cam looked around and was taken aback when he realized Syn was actually speaking to him. "What?!"

"You obviously think your mom lives here and is going to come and clean up after you."

Cam looked down at the magazine lying on the bench and in a childish voice replied, "I'm sorry, OK Mom."

Syn picked up the magazine. "OK. Just put it back next time, alright kiddo?"

Crazzee grabbed her boyfriend's hand and led him away. "I like this place, but why do they have to have so many freaks working here?"

Cam shrugged in response and glanced back at Syn as he and Crazzee left.

Ever the gentleman, Cam opened the door of his apartment and let Crazzee enter first.

"Do you want a drink or something?" Cam continued his gentlemanly ways.

Crazzee was engrossed in whatever drama was going on in her phone. "Huh? Yeah, whatever."

Dishes, glasses, utensils, pots, and pans were only washed as needed; it left the cupboards and drawers barren and kept the sink and dishwasher full. The dishwasher never contained clean dishes since no one ever remembered to buy dishwasher detergent; it was only a storage area for dirty dishes. Cam searched in vain for a couple clean glasses. He found two which were only slightly smudged and removed the stack of dirty pots and dishes from the sink so he could rinse them out. The sink looked odd empty, so Cam replaced the stack of dirty pots and dishes. By pouring generous helpings of vodka and energy drink onto the ice in the recently rinsed glasses, Cam made his favorite cocktail. Of course Crazzee's had a little extra vodka and after she took her first sip she monotonously exclaimed, "Damn! You know I have to work tomorrow and I already had like three drinks at the restaurant."

Cam took a large sip of his beverage. "Me too. So what? Let's go sit down."

As Crazzee entered the living room she saw T asleep on the couch. Next to him on the coffee table was a three-foot glass bong. "Crap! I didn't know he was here. I would've been a little quieter. I didn't want to like wake him up," shouted Crazzee in a loud whisper.

"Don't worry about it." Cam grabbed a small cushion off the couch. "HEY T." He threw the cushion at his face. It didn't faze the sleeping T; his only reaction was a little sigh and a slight adjustment of his body.

"Once he's out, nothing can wake him up, especially after spending some quality time with his girlfriend." Cam gestured to the bong. "Let's go to my room instead. I don't want to hang out with that sleeping, stinky lump. Plus I have something I want to show you."

"Is it something I've seen before?" Crazzee raised her eyebrows.

"Not yet."

Crazzee sat on the edge of the bed sipping her drink while Cam stood before her and began a striptease. He peeled off his shirt and proceeded to flex the muscles in his arms and chest. Then he turned around and leisurely unbuttoned his pants, letting them fall to the ground.

"You got a tattoo!" Crazzee squealed.

Cam turned his head to her in surprise. "How did you know?"

"It's like right there on the back of your arm. What is it?"

Cam twisted his arm around to try to get a look at the tattoo.

"The other arm, silly."

He twisted the other arm around, but could only see pieces of black circles. With his pants still around his ankles, he penguin-walked into the bathroom and stood in front of the mirror where he got his first good look at the new addition to his body. "What the fuck?!" It came out as a whisper, but Cam's internal reaction wasn't as muted.

Crazzee called from the bedroom. "Don't you know what it is?"

Transfixed by the tattoo, Cam didn't hear her. He searched his memory for a time when he could've had the tattoo done. He knew he'd gotten shit-faced in Vegas, but shit-faced enough to get a second tattoo? It was the only possible explanation he could come up with.

"Baby?"

He had to tell Crazzee something. Telling her he got drunk and forgot getting a tattoo wasn't going to fly. Luckily Cam had developed the ability to weave believable stories from the barest of threads. It was a skill he'd learned during his younger days of juggling multiple women, sometimes on the same day. "Sorry, I was just looking at the order of the symbols. Since I can't really see them, I forgot how they go." Waddling back into the bedroom, he sat down next to Crazzee. "They represent the six continents. I got them because I want to travel to all of them someday." Cam was almost convincing himself—the secret of a good lie.

"I always thought there were like seven continents." Crazzee was kind of an expert in geography. One of her ex-boyfriends had a large map of the world above his bed.

Cam realized he forgot a whole continent, but it was too late to change his story. His mind had to weave like the wind. "I guess if you include Antarctica there are, but why would I want to waste my time going that far to freeze my ass off and look at a bunch of snow?"

"Are you gonna take me to any of these places or will they be more boys-only trips?"

"Of course I'll take you, baby." Cam didn't come close to convincing himself with this whopper.

Crazzee bought it though and with overwhelming gratitude grabbed Cam by the back of the head and shoved her tongue in his mouth. His mind was still too distracted by the recent discovery on his arm to take things to the next level, so he let his johnson take control. It didn't have any interest in how and when the tattoo was put onto Cam's arm. Its primary concern was to get Cam to do what Crazzee expected him to do, her. Cam was reminded he couldn't accomplish this task if she was fully clothed, so he undressed her. When his johnson got a peek of her thin, orange-tinted naked body, it knew it was time to get to work and sprang into action. Cam's shoes, pants, and underwear came off with one fluid motion. She noticed he was still wearing his socks. (Cam's johnson had the forethought to keep the original ankle tattoo covered. It didn't want Cam to have to explain a second tattoo and risk getting Crazzee out of the mood.) "Aren't you going to take those off?"

"My feet are cold."

"Whatever." Crazzee hopped onto Cam, getting herself in one of her many favorite positions. "Let's see if we can wake up T."

The noises which emanated from Crazzee came straight out of a pornographic film, which wasn't a coincidence since she was purposely mimicking the sounds from pornographic films. She thought these were the kinds of grunts, moans, and screams men expect to hear during sex. Cam's johnson knew she was overacting and didn't care. It thoroughly appreciated her over-the-top performance and became filled with so much inspiration that it had Cam flip her around so it could get into one of its many favorite positions. The noisier Crazzee got, the harder and faster Cam's johnson worked away. A combined grunt/moan/scream signaled she had reached her big finale. Cam's johnson enjoyed it so much, it felt an overpowering urge to shower her with applause. The curtains closed and Cam's johnson withdrew, but would stay vigilant until it was called up for the next performance.

Crazzee didn't succeed in her goal to wake up T; he continued to sleep soundly on the couch. In fact her exuberant exertions to reach this goal (along with a night full of cocktail consumption) had caused her to collapse into a deep slumber herself. Her body spooned into Cam. He put his arm around her in such a way that he was able to get a decent look at the new tattoo. He stared at the six circular symbols until he fell asleep.

Waiting impatiently, Cam stood at T's desk. T was listening to his deskmate Chuy tell his daily marijuana-fueled adventure-mishap story. It involved his neighbor's dog, a Frisbee, and his friend's little brother Calaca's baggy pants. Suffice to say, Calaca ended up running home in his *chonies* to the unending amusement of Chuy and his buddies. T turned around after the story's obvious ending and gave Cam some attention. "What's up? You were still in your room when I left this morning, were you late or what?"

Cam's impatience was visible. "Yeah, a little. I need to show you something."

T leaned back in his chair. "OK, go for it."

"Not here, let's go to the bathroom real quick."

Chuy glanced over and gave Cam an odd look which T noticed and didn't like. "You know this kind of shit looks pretty gay, but since we're friends I'm willing to take that risk, this time."

Cam and T stood in the handicap stall facing each other. T made sure no one saw them enter the stall together, but he was still very nervous someone would recognize his pair of feet. He knew his shoes were quite recognizable. Familiar with Cam's history of women, T assumed the worst. "Dude, I told you to always wear a condom, even with your chick. You never know."

"My dick's fine. I want you to take a look at this." Cam

rolled up his sleeve as far as it would go and showed T the tattoo.

"First of all, thank God your dick is fine. I didn't want to have to look at your junk. I'm not homophobic or anything, but the less cock I see in my life the better. Second, when did you get that tat?"

"I have no fucking idea. Did we go back to that tattoo shop?"

"I don't think so, but a lot of that weekend was a bit of a blur dude. You could've gone back while I was passed out in the hotel and not even remembered. It could be like that time I got drunk and won that poker tournament. I don't even remember sitting down at the table." It was one of T's fondest memories he couldn't remember.

"I never believed that story, but… maybe something like that could've happened to me. Why would I get *this* tattoo though? I have no clue what it's supposed to be or even what it means and now I'm stuck with it forever."

"It means you made a mistake and now you'll always be reminded of it, dumbass! Let's hurry up and get back before that prick Chuy starts spreading rumors about us."

"I got to take a piss first."

"Well, I'm not staying for that." T looked under the stall door to make sure no one else was in the bathroom and left.

After T had gone and he was alone in the bathroom, Cam approached the mirror. Sleeve still pulled up, he took another look at the six symbols. He thought if he stared at them long enough, the memory of their origin would return. It didn't. What did return was the question of what possessed him to permanently get these things put on his arm. If he was really that trashed why wouldn't he just get a naked lady, a dragon, or a stupid cartoon character tattoo (he already got a tribal) like a normal drunk person on vacation would? The answer had to be somewhere in his brain. He replayed the weekend over and over again and none of the muddled memories included getting a second tattoo. The sound of someone opening the door abruptly brought him back to the present moment of standing in front of the mirror in the Reboot Financial men's room being watched by the Cam behind the glass.

CAM FACED THE familiar view of a repeating quadratic pattern. It appeared to be hand-carved into the door he was standing in front of. In actuality the door was mass-produced to look as if it was a one-of-a-kind creation; small imperfections were even incorporated into the design to give it a feeling of authenticity. Almost every house in the neighborhood had the same door with the same imperfections. Out of all those identical doors it was this door Cam had had no other choice but to open during his childhood and adolescence. Rarely had he ever been in a rush to face whatever was in store for him on the other side. Still, he felt a nagging obligation to once again turn the cold metallic knob and push.

"MA! Are you here?!"

Instead of being welcomed in by his loving mother, a big black and white pit bull charged towards him. Cam was caught off guard and wasn't able to react in time to avoid the onslaught of licks the dog attacked him with.

"HYDROX, NO!" Cam's mother jogged down the stairs, grabbed the animal's collar, and gently dragged him to his chewed-up dog bed, saving her son from further saliva saturation. "Sorry, I'm watching my co-worker's mother's dog while she's in the hospital. They don't allow pets in her apartment, so... ." She gave her son a hug and a kiss on the dry part of his face. "Hi honey, I'm so glad to see you."

"You too. I knew it was your day off so I thought I'd come over for a free lunch."

Cam's mother gave his cheek a pinch. "Such a thoughtful boy." They made their way into the spacious open plan kitchen/diner. "How's work going?"

Cam grabbed the materials he needed to create his lunchtime specialty, a peanut butter and jelly sandwich. "Now that the quarter-end is over, it's not as hectic. The job itself is OK, I can't complain. It pays the bills."

"Like I always tell you, as long as you're happy, I'm happy for you. Let's have some tea. Could you use those long arms of yours and grab the kettle for me?"

Cam turned around and reached up to get the kettle. During his reach, the back of his shirt raised up enough to expose black Asiatic symbols tattooed on the lower right part of his back. Seeing it, his mother lifted the shirt a little higher to get a better look. "What's this?"

"That's my butt. Are you checking me out Ma?"

"It *is* a nice behind, but I was actually looking at this tattoo here. When did you get this?"

Cam wrenched his head around in an attempt to see

the tattoo. He was only able to get a glimpse of it due to its position on his back, but the glimpse was enough to cause a sudden heat to rise up from deep in his core to his face, turning it red. A few beads of sweat appeared on his forehead.

"Oh, I got that when I was in Vegas," Cam replied as nonchalantly as his voice box would allow. "I'll be right back." He rushed to the bathroom and removed his shirt and tried to get a good look at the tattoo. Reflected in the mirror, he saw it clearly, a vertical grouping of black Asian-looking symbols. On the towel rack he noticed a washcloth. He grabbed it, applied soap and water, and tried to scrub the tattoo away. Seeing the black wasn't fading, he scrubbed harder, trying to remove the skin itself. He had tried the same procedure with the previous tattoo, but this time it had to work. The ink was embedded deep in the skin. It wasn't going anywhere.

"Goddamnit!" He loudly whispered as he threw the washcloth onto the floor. He turned back around and looked at himself in the mirror. "What the hell is going on?!" The Cam behind the glass didn't answer.

Cam heard his mother call to him from the other side of the door. "You OK in there?" She must have heard the unbathroomly sounds he was making.

"Yeah, I'm fine." Cam made himself presentable and joined his mother at the table where a cup of tea and a PB&J were waiting for him.

"So… it looked like you got yourself a tattoo there. Can I see it again?"

Cam hesitantly stood up, turned around, pulled his shirt up, and exposed the unsuccessfully removed tattoo.

"Why is it all red like that?"

"Oh, I had to clean so it doesn't get infected. Sometimes I forget I have the damn thing."

"What does it mean?"

"It's Tibetan for peace. Well at least that's what the guy told me. For all I know it means chumpy white dude." As neither Cam nor his mother knew how written Tibetan was supposed to look, the symbols seemed Tibetan enough.

Cam's mother forced a smile. "Well I think that's nice, but try not to make a habit out of it, OK? I like your body just the way it is."

"Join the club." The words left his mouth before he could stop them.

Cam's mother wanted to change the disconcerting subject of body art, so she did. "I heard from your brother the other day. He and the expectant mother are doing well. They're very nervous and excited about the baby. I'm really looking forward to my trip out there to see my new grandchild, I can't wait! It's too bad you can't come. Your brother would love to see you. He said he hasn't heard from you for a while, you should try to write to him more often. Sometimes I get the feeling he's homesick and a little bit lonely."

Cam's attention wasn't in the present moment but in all the possible past scenarios where a tattoo could've been placed on his back. "What? Yeah, I'll try to shoot him an email sometime."

"Also, your father called me yesterday. He, the wife and the kids are getting settled into their new place." His mother took a scrap of paper from the counter and handed it to Cam. "Here's his new address and phone number. He said he can't remember the last time he's spoken to you. Maybe you could give him a call."

Cam glanced over at the clock. "I've got to get back to work." After giving his mother a quick hug he headed to the door.

Cam's mother called after him. "OK, it was nice seeing you honey. I love you."

"You too, bye." Cam slammed the door shut, leaving his mother with his untouched sandwich and tea.

"Fuck, fuck, fuck!" Cam repeatedly slammed his fists onto his steering wheel. "Just breathe dude, relax… relax. If I can just relax and think back this will all make sense." Cam noticed the time. "Oh shit, now I'm gonna be late!" He started his car and sped off. When he unclenched the fist of his left hand to grab the steering wheel he found a piece of crumpled paper. "What the fuck is this?" Seeing the word 'Dad' written across the top jogged his memory. "Oh yeah."

He let go of the paper and out of the corner of his eye watched as the wind sucked it out of the partially open driver's side window into the passing traffic. It floated over the roofs of a few cars before it finally landed on the sidewalk near the feet of a man with long black hair, wearing a long black coat. Cam turned his head and tried to get a look at the man and nearly succeeded in crashing into the car in front of him. After regaining control of his vehicle he looked back and saw nothing but empty sidewalk.

"…we're on our way to this party in the canyon when the five-o lights us up for a suspected DWM, you know, driving while Mexican. Chico's driving, you know Chico, so of course we have a shit-ton of weed on us and he ain't stoppin'. I guess he's been watching too much of that *Fast and the Furious* shit because he just fuckin' floors it. I'm like 'Chico, what're you doing?' Then he goes 'I know this canyon man, I'm gonna lose 'em.' So I say 'just because you got a shaved head doesn't make you Vin Diesel or something.' He just keeps going faster and faster around all these insane corners, almost running off the road at every turn. The *hynas* in the back seat are screaming and the cops are yelling for us to stop through their speaker. Chico's driving like he's in some kind of *Tokyo Drift* car, but we're in his mom's fuckin' Taurus and he flips it on the next corner. Next thing I remember I'm crawling out of this upside-down car with Chico and the two girlies. Then we look back and the thing bursts into flames, and the funny part was…"

Cam's patience for Chuy to finish his story of misadventure had itself finished. "Hey T, could you come with me real quick?" Chuy gave T a disappointed shake of the head as he got up to join Cam.

Together again in the handicap stall, T reinforced his displeasure with Cam's request. "Seriously Cam, Chuy is really gonna start thinking you and I are doing a little sword-fighting in here. What the hell is going on?"

"Screw that prick, this is important. Look." Cam lifted his shirt and revealed the symbols on his back.

"Damn, another tattoo. When did you get that one?"

Cam responded with an exaggerated shrug.

"What the fuck? Are you saying you don't remember getting this one either?"

"Yes, that's what I'm saying. When could this've possibly happened?"

"Dude, how should I know? I have no idea where you are or who you're with most of the time, even though most people treat me like your goddamn personal secretary. Whenever they can't find you they're always like 'hey, where's Cam?' or 'what's Cam doing tonight?'"

"What the hell are you talking about? I'm always around."

Cam received an 'are you serious?' look from T after his absurd remark. "Do you know that we call you Cam Copperfield behind your back? We'll all be hangin' out somewhere and before we know it, you've vanished into thin air."

"Come on, I don't do that."

T's 'are you serious?' look returned with a vengeance. "Dude… for example, the other night at our quarter-end boozefest. After a few hours of partying I turned around and you were gone. No one even saw you leave."

"I remember saying 'later' to everyone. You guys were so drunk you probably just forgot."

"I don't know about everyone else, but it was obvious *you* were feeling no pain. Maybe you stumbled off somewhere and got that tat."

"I would remember something like that, I know I would."

"You didn't remember getting that one on your arm. Maybe you should lay off the sauce for a while." T patted Cam on the back. "I've got to get back to my desk. I know that prick Chuy is telling everyone I'm in here planting tulips." After checking the bathroom was empty, T rushed back to his desk leaving Cam alone.

Before he returned to his own desk, Cam stopped at the mirror and took a good look. As usual, the other Cam stood there behind the glass. He had the same perfectly plucked eyebrows, the same well-moisturized skin, and the same awesome hairstyle, but the Cam in front of the glass wasn't a hundred percent positive he was the same person.

"Do you think I drink too much?" Cam asked Crazzee as he took a sip of his vodka/energy drink cocktail. He'd carved out a small space to sit on the edge of her bed, giving himself the bare minimum amount of comfort while he watched a movie with her. Her bedroom had no other seating options. The chair and loveseat were both piled high with clothing, shrapnel from the time her closet exploded. The door hadn't been able to take the pressure anymore; it still couldn't be closed properly. Overflow from the chair and loveseat found its way into shopping bags that encircled her bed and what couldn't be stuffed into the shopping bags was temporarily set on the bed itself. It was a miracle Cam was able see the entire TV screen; DVD cases were stacked to their tipping points all along the edge of the TV stand and on the floor surrounding it.

"Well, whenever I see you you're usually drinking something, but how should I know what you do when you're not with me? For all I know you're at some bar getting drunk with a bunch of dirty skanks. That might be your plan right after you leave here." Crazzee glared at him from her nest of clothing further up the bed.

"Whoa! I always tell you where I'm going and what I'm doing. Usually I'm at the gym or playing ball, so my phone is turned off and that's why you can't reach me."

"Convenient excuse."

"Goddamn, I was just asking you a simple question and you have to get into all this again. What do you want me to do? My gym doesn't allow cell phones on the floor and I can't ask the ref to call a time-out every time my phone rings. If you're going to be like this, then I'm going." Cam stood up, finished his drink, and tried to find a spot to set his glass down.

"Yeah, whatever, go! Go and bang those big-tittied whores you hang out with. I know that's what you like anyway." Crazzee hugged her chest and began to sob.

The sight of her crying gave Cam no choice but to stay and try to console her. He joined her in her clothing nest and put his arms around her trembling body. "What the hell are you talking about? Big-tittied whores? Where the hell did that idea come from? You know you're the only one I want." Crazzee was still resisting his hug, so Cam reluctantly played the card he knew she was waiting for. "I love you, you know that right?" She nodded slowly, turned the spigot off, and returned his embrace.

Crazzee's tear-stained face caused a stirring in Cam's pants. He had always been partial to women in emotionally vulnerable states. Cam started with the requisite kissing and fondling—he wanted to get it out of the way so he could get to the good part as soon as possible. The flurry of activity awoke Crazzee's little dachshund, Banana Jamma, who had been sleeping in the cavern of shoes under the bed. He proceeded to make repeated unsuccessful attempts to jump up onto the bed and join the action.

"Could you get that dog out of here?" Cam didn't like distractions.

"Don't worry, he won't bother us. He's just curious."

"That dog's a goddamn Peeping Tom and I told you I can't do it if he's watching."

Crazzee got up and scooped the dog into her arms. "Come on BJ, Cam's being mean again. You'll have to wait outside." Banana Jamma didn't appreciate being separated from his woman and his outrage could be heard behind the closed door.

With the interference removed, Cam had the concentration he needed to begin the process of inserting himself into Crazzee in a variety of positions at varying speeds. Crazzee responded to the insertions with another boisterous performance, but with the volume turned way down as her parents and her little brother were down the hall in the living room watching TV.

Following the physical expression of their lust, Crazzee watched Cam dress. He had a nice body and she knew he knew she knew he did and she also knew he never missed an opportunity to show it off. During his dress-tease she saw the tattoo on his lower back. "Hey, when did you get that?"

Cam automatically launched into his prefabricated story. "A few days ago. I always heard tattoos were addictive, I guess it's true. What do think of it?"

"It's cool, but why did you get it in such a lame spot? It looks like it was just like randomly placed on your back."

"It's an ancient peace symbol from Tibet and I was told that's the traditional spot on the body where it's supposed to be placed."

"Oh OK. I didn't know you were into all that mystical kung-fu stuff."

"Yeah, I'm trying to be a more peaceful person, but it isn't easy when you're always breaking my balls."

"I'm sorry. I'll try to be more Tibetenese from now on."

"Good. I'll see you later." Cam was grateful she hadn't noticed the fact he left his socks on during the insertions. He hadn't yet thought of a story for the tattoo on his ankle and he didn't feel like spending any more time in Crazzee's cluttered cosmos improvising one.

"Bye baby." Crazzee was sad to see him go, but his absence was filled by the outraged little dachshund who had been waiting impatiently at the door.

"Goodbye and thank you." The call ended with one more customer satisfied with the fantasy of shrunken debt. Cam was glad none of the people who called him understood basic mathematics. Suddenly a masculine blend of mint, lavender, and harassment filled his nostrils. He turned his chair around and found his super-supervisor standing behind him.

"I don't know how many times I've told you. You have to end every call with 'thank you for choosing Reboot Financial'."

"I know, but I assume by the time the call ends the customer still remembers who he called."

"When you assume you make an A. S. S. out of you and me. Just remember to end each call properly. Thanks." Cam's super-supervisor floated off to pester some more of his underlings.

Cam needed a break. "Do you want coffee or something?"

"Hmm?" Cam's deskmate was occupied with rearranging her ever-growing collection of little toys from fast food restaurant children's meals.

Cam stood up. "Do you want a coffee?"

She held up her seemingly bottomless can of diet soda. "No I'm fine, thanks."

Unbeknownst to Cam, his path to the break room was under constant surveillance. The Coug's desk was positioned in a way so she could monitor all of his comings and goings. Their random meetings were never random. As Cam made himself a cup of coffee, she walked up behind him and invaded his personal space. "Morning cutie."

"Hi." Cam then made a rookie mistake. It was an off-hand comment he made under his breath, but he stupidly said it loud enough for the Coug to hear. "Man I wish I had a time machine and could skip this week and go directly to the weekend."

The Coug pounced. "It's funny you mentioned time machines because I just watched *Back to the Future*. Did you know that Robert Zemeckis, the writer and director of the movie, got the idea to use a DeLorean as the time machine from me? I was in a meeting with Bob and some of the cast and crew of *Romancing the Stone*—I was going to be Kathleen Turner's stand-in. We were the same size then, not so much anymore, she's gotten a bit bulky. So, towards the end of this meeting Bob started talking about the next movie he wanted to make, *Back to the Future*. He told us the plot and how he wanted to use an old refrigerator or something boring like that as the time machine. After the meeting we were walking out to our cars and he saw me open the door of the DeLorean I was borrowing from my boyfriend at the time. 'Nice car,' he said. 'Thanks,' I told him, 'you should use something classy like this as your time machine and not some old piece of junk.' And of course he did just that."

Cam went against his better judgment, but he had to know. "Were you there when they filmed the scene where the Mexican guy gets his hand bitten off by the alligator?"

"No, I had a problem with my visa, too many outstanding warrants, so I couldn't go on location and be in the movie."

"Oh. Well I have to get back to work now, see ya." Cam maneuvered past the Coug as carefully as possible to avoid any bodily contact.

"Not if I see you first."

On his way back to his desk Cam passed Chuy. "Hey, do you want to go to the bathroom with me? You show me yours and I'll show you mine."

"I doubt I'd see much." Cam continued on his way. "Fucking prick."

He wasn't in any hurry to get back to his desk and drown in the inevitable flood of calls, so he made a detour to the window where he'd sometimes go and enjoy the view. The sliver of sky above the building next door was overcast, just a gray blank, which only left the view of the building itself. From his vantage point Cam could see into its sixth-floor office. They had the same modern cubicle-less office plan, the same desk setup, the same wireless headsets, and the same office monkeys attached to their computers. He watched them pretend to listen to their calls, doodle on the backs of old invoices, nervously swivel in their chairs, and mimic the actions of hardworking, satisfied employees whenever someone important walked by. Questions floated through Cam's head. Was their supervisor as super? Did they also have a Coug on the loose? Did they get paid more? Were they hiring?

There was no question as to who was the star of the local basketball league and that was Cam himself. The stats, which he reviewed and regularly updated, didn't lie; he led the league in shooting percentage and in overall points. It didn't matter to him that membership in the league wasn't based on athletic skill, but on the willingness to pay the fees and show up. What did matter was that he was the best. Cam's team was a combination of old school friends and friends of those friends. Tonight they were playing in the gym of a nearby community college and as usual he was the last to arrive. He found his teammates on the court warming up. His team's roster had five other players:

RC—small forward—had a scruffy Brad Pitt look with the confidence and charm to match. Irresistible to the ladies.

Lambda—power forward—a tall thin black guy who'd grown out his afro to a ridiculous size because he was the only black guy around and didn't want anybody to forget it.

Boinkman—point guard—had known Cam since kindergarten and thanks to his Japanese heritage hadn't grown much since. His speed and toughness made up for his lack of height.

Lurch—center—if you've seen any incarnation of the Addams Family, his name says it all.

Old Bob—shooting guard—probably in his mid-forties, but elderly to the rest of the guys. He took every game deadly serious and was never without his prescription sport goggles, sweat bands on his head and wrists, knee braces on both knees, and the best basketball shoes money could buy.

"Hey guys." Cam greeted each of his teammates with personalized combinations of handshakes, high fives, hugs, and/or fist bumps. "Who we playing tonight, I forget."

"Do you ever even look at the schedule dude? I'm surprised you know where to show up each week. We're playing the Fire Ants." R. C. was usually annoyed with Cam's feigned lack of interest; it was supposed to be his specialty, but Cam always somehow out-feigned him.

"What are they? A bunch of little gay dudes or something?" Cam began to remove his outer shell of street clothes.

"No, I think most of the guys on the team are exterminators." Boinkman had already scoped out the competition and wasn't impressed.

Lurch chimed in. "I remember those guys, I hated defending them. They smelled all chemically."

Lambda couldn't let his remark go without a response. "Don't fret it Lurch, you hardly ever play any D anyway. You just hang out under the net with your big-ass body until the ball ends up in your hands."

"Yeah like you're some kind of great defender. It's just your hair's so big nobody can see around it." Lurch was impressed with his own quick yet weak comeback.

Cam stepped out of the crossfire of somewhat entertaining insults to concentrate on getting his body ready for the game. While he was bending over to stretch his legs and back he heard R. C. yell, "Boinkman! Dude, what are you doing? Are you staring at Cam's ass?"

Cam stood up and turned around to find Boinkman right behind him. "Boinker, I know I have a great ass, but be a little more subtle when you feel the need to gaze upon one of God's greatest creations."

"Fuck you guys. I was trying to figure what the hell that tattoo on the back of his leg is supposed to be." Boinkman's voice always went up a couple of octaves when he yelled.

A familiar heat rose from the pit of Cam's gut and spread throughout his body. He had to sit down. Once on the ground he had no choice but to continue stretching to camouflage his internal volcano of shock and anger from the guys.

"Why'd you sit down? I wanna see this tattoo." R. C. forgot to pretend not to care.

"I think you just want an excuse to look at my ass too. Maybe *this* is the team of gay dudes."

"Come on, we just want to see it." Boinkman of course meant the tattoo and not Cam's ass.

Cam stretched out the leg behind him and turned at the waist to get a look at the back of his thigh. He saw a squarish black block almost the size of his palm. The inside contained six interlocking circles, and squiggly shapes rimmed the edges. He looked up at the guys and hocked a credible loogie of bullshit. "Look. Happy now? It's a Native American wind symbol. It's supposed to help me stay quick."

Boinkman laughed. "You don't need any extra help in the wind department dude. Just drink a carton of chocolate milk and you'll be blasting away in no time. I remember that time we drove up to Santa Barbara together, you produced so much wind I nearly passed out."

They all turned when they heard Lambda yell, "R. C., BOINKMAN, KIRK! Come on guys, let's go."

R. C. and Boinkman jogged away, leaving Cam alone on the ground. He gave himself a few stinging slaps to the face to get his mind back to the place where it needed to be so he could actually play a basketball game. He jumped up, grunted loudly, and ran over to join his team on the court. "Lambda, did you just call me Kirk?"

"Yeah, like Kirk CAMeron, you know, Mike Seaver on *Growing Pains*."

"I heard he's all Jesusey now."

"Yup, he's out there spreading the word man."

On the court waiting for the game to start, Cam spotted a man in a long black coat with long black hair exit through the doors at the far end of the gym. He readied himself to pursue, but before he could the referee blew the whistle indicating the start of the game. The ball was tipped into his hands and his basketball brain instinctually took over.

Cam rushed home after the easy win over the Fire Ants,

skipping the post-game get-together. He was intent on grilling T about the origin of the thing on the back of his leg. If T didn't know how it got there, then what? No, he had to know. Unfortunately T was asleep in his usual spot on the couch with his glass girlfriend parked beside him. Cam knew it was useless to try to wake him, so he'd have to wait until tomorrow to ask about the tattoo. Instead he went into the kitchen, found the least-filthy glass in the dishwasher, rinsed it out, and filled it with alcohol. On the way to his room he could've sworn he saw one of T's eyes open and watch him, but when he turned to look, T was sound asleep.

The alcohol wasn't doing what it was supposed to do. Cam was still completely freaked out about the fact another tattoo appeared on his body. He had no idea how long it'd been there as he wasn't in the habit of checking the back of his legs. Now there were three, three tattoos he had no memory of getting. It was plausible he got the other two during drunken stupors, but not the third. The whole idea was too absurd to think about. He'd already spent hours scrutinizing the symbol that was now forever stuck to his leg. His brain needed a break from the tight grip of tattoo obsession or else it was going to burst a blood vessel. He thought maybe a journey into the cold, anonymous depths of cyberspace would get his mind off his terrestrial problems, but liftoff was delayed by a message from his brother, keeping him temporarily earthbound –

Hey Cam,

I haven't heard from you for a while, how are things going out there? The novelty of this pregnancy is wearing off and the reality of it is taking its place. I'm really going to be a father, I still can't believe it. I just hope I'll do a better job than Dad did. As for my career, a shitty job is a shitty job wherever you are, but the bills have to be paid. Paris is a cool place to live, but it'd be a lot better it there weren't so many damn Frenchies everywhere. Talk to you later.

Blocko

Cam decided he'd write back right away instead of taking the usual two to three months to respond. At least it'd keep his mind distracted for a little while.

Hey Blocks,

If you can just stick around you'll be a ten times better father than Dad was. Not much new going on out here, same shit, different day.

Every morning Cam woke up expecting that the whole mysteriously appearing tattoo thing was only a bad dream. He'd walk into the bathroom, look in the mirror, and see a body free of black markings. It never happened; in fact Cam had to add an extra step to his morning routine, a complete body tattoo check. He even bought a large hand mirror to assist him with it. He would stand naked in front of the mirror and look over his entire body, which was now lightly speckled with tattoos. A few were what seemed to be forms of writing, some were symbols, and others were crude figures of people and/or animals. The majority of the tattoos were located on the back of his body and could only be seen with the hand mirror.

Thoughts of calling the police or seeing a doctor occasionally crossed his mind, but his improbable story would probably get him sent to a psychiatrist who would either pump him full of drugs or put him in an institution and then pump him full of stronger drugs. The last thing he wanted was to be labeled 'fucked in the head', so he set up a camera to record himself as he slept to see if he could find out for himself where the tattoos were coming from. In the morning there was never anything on the recordings. As with all the other tattoos, he had no clue how he acquired the latest addition to his family of ink—the most worrying so far. It was groupings of small triangles with straight lines extending from their tips. They began on the back of his right shoulder and climbed halfway up his neck. All of the previous tattoos could be easily hidden under his clothing, but not anymore. He didn't know how he was going to cover this one up. Wearing a scarf was out of the question. This was Southern California; the only people who wore scarves were old women, effeminate men, and European tourists. High-collared shirts would make him look like a complete idiot and probably wouldn't cover the entire tattoo anyway. A turtleneck sweater was the only viable option, but it would be a damn hard look to pull off.

His morning trips to the mirror were becoming more frightening by the day and trying to avoid them was impossible. He was never able to look away from the tattooed man staring at him from behind the glass.

Like you said, work is work wherever you are, but my

job is alright and I like the people I work with (at least they're not French), so I can't complain.

Wearing his headset and one of the stylish turtleneck sweaters from his growing collection, Cam sat at his desk nodding in response to whatever inane thing the client was rambling on about. He stared blankly at his computer screen while his right hand unconsciously doodled triangles of all shapes and sizes. The doodling was so furious that the pen was tearing apart the paper. After the phone call came to its merciful conclusion, he threw the headset onto the desk. "I need a cup of coffee, you want anything?"

His deskmate smiled and shook her head as she took a big sip of her diet cola.

The Coug struck before Cam was even able to get the coffee into the cup. "Hey you."

He turned around and saw that she just happened to be in the break room at the same time as him. "Hi, I'm almost done."

"No need to rush. Could you please hand me a mug?"

Grabbing a mug off the high shelf caused the back of Cam's turtleneck sweater to rise and expose a portion of the Asiatic tattoo on his back.

"I didn't know you were inked. Let me see." The Coug took hold of the back of Cam's turtleneck sweater and attempted to lift it to get a better look at the tattoo. Cam sharply pulled away and dropped the mug. It shattered when it hit the floor. "Goddamn it!" He knelt down to pick up the pieces.

"You don't have to be ashamed of having tattoos. I

think they're really sexy. I remember the days when I was a regular at the Whiskey and the Roxy. I was kind of a groupie for the Crüe. Nikki Sixx and I had a lot of good times together. Even back then he had quite a few tats. Not a lot of people had tattoos back then, not like today, mainly just rockers, bikers, and sailors. Nikki would sometimes take me to the parlor with him when he got inked. He always asked me if I wanted any work done and I always refused. I'm really afraid of needles or else I'd probably be covered in tattoos by now. I guess that's a good thing though, it would've ruined my modeling career."

Cam threw away the pieces of the shattered mug. "Why is it that every time I come in here for a cup of coffee I have to listen to one of your *rad* stories of the eighties? I just want a cup of coffee. I don't want to hear about your unofficial membership in the Brat Pack, or about your time as Belinda Carlisle's personal coke assistant, or how your childhood was the inspiration for Punky Brewster. Seriously, where did all that get you? You have a lousy dead-end office job and hit on guys almost half your age. From now on could you please just let me get my coffee in peace so I can hurry up and get back to my desk and listen to more moronic sob stories?" He left the break room without a cup of coffee.

"Sorry," the Coug told Cam's back.

Cam of course ran into Chuy on the way back to his desk. "Hey, nice turtleneck. Trying to hide that big hickey your new boyfriend gave you?"

"Actually your mom gave it to me. When she takes those teeth out she can really get some strong suction going. You should see my cock, she destroyed that shit."

"Fucking prick," said Chuy as Cam walked away.

I hit the gym a few times a week and play ball whenever I can. I have to keep myself ready for when the NBA finally gets off its ass and decides to draft me.

The Cam behind the gym's wall of mirrors watched the Cam in front of the glass attempt to complete his final rep with weights too heavy for him. Every single vein in each of his arms tried to escape the skin as the Cam in front of the glass curled the dumbbells up towards his chest. His face turned red and sweat gushed from his pores. He was going to complete the rep even if it tore his arms apart. It was *his* body and he wasn't going to let a plague of tattoos take it from him. This thought repeated itself over and over in his head giving him the strength needed to get the dumbbells to his chest and complete the rep. His soaked shirt clung to his skin, leaving him no choice but to remove it. The Cam in front of the mirror looked past the ugly black marks all over his body and admired his freshly pumped physique. Maybe if he worked out hard enough his muscles would grow so big they'd tear the tattoos from his skin.

More and more Cam looked forward to his basketball league games where he could spend a couple hours of refuge in his basketball mind. The remarks and taunts from his teammates about his growing body-art collection bounced right off him. His mind contained a singular thought, win at any cost. It brought him mixed results—the team's record did improve somewhat, but his new style of play wasn't making him many friends.

"Come on! Give me the ball!" Cam shouted to RC. Since he was obviously the best player on the team, Cam was rarely open. The opposition always made sure he was well guarded, usually by two of their best guys. It left his teammates open more often, but that didn't necessarily mean they got the ball more often. While trying to weigh his options, R. C. hesitated with his pass. His hesitation didn't sit well with Cam. He shook off his two defenders, ran towards RC, and practically took the ball out of his hands. Cam now had three defenders after him. Passing the ball to his wide-open teammates wasn't a thought that crossed his mind. All he could see was the basket in front of him. He used a tricky spin move he'd been working on in practice and lost one defender. The other two he attempted to split as he aggressively charged the hoop. One gave way but the other stood his ground, which caused a violent collision and knocked the final defender to the floor. The ref blew his whistle, calling Cam for the foul.

"What?! There's no way that was on me, his feet weren't set. It was totally a blocking foul."

"I saw you intentionally charge into him, it's on you." The referee wasn't a big man and was a bit intimidated by Cam's muscular frame, but he put that aside; he had a job to do.

"Then maybe you should get your fucking eyes checked because that foul wasn't on me."

"I've already warned you about talking to me like that. Now you're outta here." The ref blew his whistle again and motioned for Cam to leave the court. Fear nearly cracked his professional veneer when Cam didn't leave and instead came barreling towards him. Luckily his teammates intervened and escorted Cam from the game.

"Dude, you gotta chill out. Why you takin' this shit so seriously? We're not in the NBA, you don't got any million-dollar endorsements. It's only a league game man," said Lambda as he led Cam away.

Cam didn't hear a word he said. His mind was still in its basketball refuge planning the next win.

After that I like chillaxing with a nice beverage, you know how it is.

Work and various combinations of gym, basketball, and girlfriend filled most of each day, but it still left the alone time in bed while waiting to fall asleep; the time when the mind becomes active with thoughts of its own creation, ultimate destruction and everything in between. Cam's tattoo problem was something his mind desperately wanted to understand, but couldn't and caused it to obsess, going over every aspect of it in a continuous loop. Alcohol was the best solution to (temporarily) close this loop and transform tattoo-problem-obsessed mind back into happy-go-lucky fun-lovin' Cam mind. T was more than willing to assist with the transformation.

"Here take this." T handed Cam a shot.

"What is it?" asked Cam.

"Drink it, you'll like it."

"But what is it?"

"Stop being such a pussy and drink it."

Cam downed the shot, which in turn twisted his face into a mask of revulsion. "Not bad." The words struggled to leave his throat.

Laughter poured out of T. "Damn, I can't believe that didn't knock you off your stool. That was some strong shit."

Cam stood up tall. "I can handle whatever." He staggered and sat back down. Then a flash of panic shot through him. "Why is my neck all hot?! It feels like something is squeezing it. What did they put in that shot?"

T's laughter increased. "You're mister turtleneck now, remember?"

Cam grabbed the neck part of his turtleneck sweater and yanked on it, trying to stretch it out. "I hate this fucking thing. I look like a goddamn Ivy League douchebag." Cam did his best drunken imitation of how he thought an Ivy League douchebag would speak. "Jeeves, would you come in here and wipe my bottom? It's a bit of a mess back there. I must have eaten a bad batch of caviar. Make haste please, the stench is offending my delicate sensibilities." He returned to his normal drunken voice. "I don't even know why I'm wearing this thing."

T had to suppress his laughter to speak. "I'm pretty sure it's to hide that neck tattoo of yours. You said only prisoners, gangbangers, and scumbags have neck tattoos."

"Oh yeah, thanks for reminding me, dick. It was a rhetoracial... ratoricycle... . It was a fucking question I didn't need the answer for." Suddenly Cam received another answer he didn't want. The question concerned how much alcohol his body could stomach. "I need to get to the bathroom, I think I'm gonna yak."

"Try not to fall asleep with your head on the toilet. I

don't feel like dragging your boozed-up ass home again." T grabbed his bag and followed Cam as he stumbled towards the bathroom.

I'm still hanging out with Crazzee, I can't seem to get rid of her. No, it's cool. We have a good time together.

The sudden appearance of tattoos all over Cam's body didn't cause any drama or raise much concern with Crazzee. After his third or fourth one, she stopped asking about them. To Crazzee, tattoos were accessories and since tattoos were 'in', fashionable accessories. Having a boyfriend with tattoos made her look better, cooler, and trendier. She had no reason to question why he was constantly having ink imbedded in his skin. Which was great, because as good as Cam was at inventing explanations for each new tattoo, even he couldn't continue making his stories sound believable.

Crazzee *did* have a problem with the increasing amount of time Cam was spending away from her. He gave her the reasons why—he was doing a more intense fitness regime, he had to work overtime more often, he was attending a lot of basketball practices, he was tired and needed to sleep because of all of all the above—but she didn't care. She told him he had to cut back on these extra-curricular activities and spend more quality time with her.

Their increased quality time began with a stop at one of Crazzee's favorite clothing stores. She needed to take a quick look at a couple of things. The large purse lodged in the crook of her elbow hindered the process of trying on outfits, so it was detached and handed to Cam. "Would you be a dear and keep an eye on this for me? I promise I'll only be like five minutes. Thanks baby."

Cam knew her concept of five minutes was actually closer to thirty. "No problem babe, take your time." He took the purse, found a small bench near the glass wall at the front of the shop, and sat down. When he turned to take a look outside he found his view blocked by the transparent reflection of himself in the glass. It was his day off, so he wasn't stuffed into one of his trademark turtlenecks, but dressed in a well-fitted t-shirt decorated with the emblem of his favorite superhero. Wearing a t-shirt made quite a few of the tattoos visible, so the first glimpse of his reflection caught him off guard. He always tried to see past the tattoos, but as they continued to multiply, it became more difficult.

He rationalized that lots of guys had tattoos these days and it wasn't such a big deal, but the fact was most of these guys had more conventional designs, usually symmetrically placed and, unlike Cam, their tattoos were there by choice. Cam's tattoos consisted of strange writing, odd symbols and figures, all placed without any discernible pattern. Every one of them was black, some looked professionally done and some were very amateurish. From a distance his bare skin looked dirty or like he had a disgusting skin disease and this was what caused the occasional subtle stares from strangers. Some of these strangers looked through the glass at him as they passed by outside. He studied their reactions and interpreted them all as 'why would such a good-looking guy do that to himself?' For him that was the worst part of it—if he were ugly, fat, or even bland, it wouldn't have mattered as much, but he was handsome and all those people thought he was purposely sabotaging his looks.

One particular stranger off in the distance caught his eye. It was a man with long black hair, wearing a long black coat. Cam got up and looked around for Crazzee so he could return the purse to her and leave, but he couldn't see her. She was probably in one of the dressing rooms, so he grabbed the purse and ran outside. Cam stood in the middle of the passing crowds looking in every direction for the man, but he was gone. The stream of shoppers continued to flow, doing their best to avoid the tattooed obstruction with the giant purse.

There really isn't much more to say. I'll write back when something interesting is actually going on. Good luck with the whole father thing.

Later

Uncle Cam

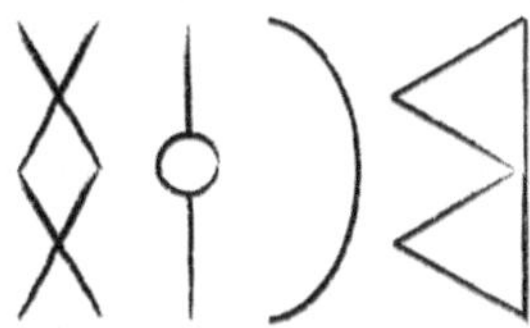

AN INKED OBSTACLE brought Cam's morning routine to an abrupt halt before it could even begin. The moment he saw his face in the mirror he knew his life couldn't ever be the same. On his right temple running from his hairline to his eyebrow were four small geometric symbols. It was what he'd been most dreading since the tattoos started appearing. Holding himself back from punching the mirror and smashing it into a thousand pieces took tremendous self-control. Figuring out how he was going to hide this one became the morning routine's only step.

He could start wearing a hat, but it probably wouldn't be able to be pulled down low enough to cover the entire tattoo. A beanie might work, but in Southern California only skaters or hipsters wore them. Since he wasn't a balding eighties rocker, a bandana was out of the question.

Cam grabbed his little bottle of makeup. He applied it generously over the tattoo, but the result was terrible. It was obvious he was trying to hide a big facial imperfection with a bad cover-up job. Having people know he wore makeup was worse than having a facial tattoo. Maybe he could comb his hair over it. He tried, but his hair was too short and besides, it would've looked stupid. Serious consideration was given to calling in sick and finding a professional makeup artist to help him. It was ruled out because of the probable expense and likely embarrassment. There was one thing he could do, he knew it was temporary, but it was better than nothing. He got a large Band-Aid and stuck it over the tattoo. He'd tell everyone he was elbowed during a basketball game.

Cam stared into the black nothingness of his computer screen while it reassembled the countless bits of data it needed to aggravate him for the rest of the day. He didn't go and get a coffee during the prolonged process, but sat patiently and waited. After his last run-in with the Coug he didn't go to the break room anymore.

His deskmate shuffled in with her diet soda in one hand and a large bag of goodies in the other. "Happy Friday! Only six more days until the next one."

"Are you serious when you say shit like that? Does it actually make you happy knowing you work the majority of your life away at a meaningless job and all you have to look forward to are those precious two days a week when you're truly free from this place? And I bet all that free time away from staring at your screen here is spent staring at your TV and computer screens at home. What kind of life is that? What's the point of it?" Cam turned back to his screen and resumed staring into the black nothingness.

"I need a cup of coffee." His deskmate scuttled off in the direction of the break room.

Cam heard the long, low beep in his headset. "Reboot Financial, how can I help you to reboot your credit?"

"So you're saying you've dug yourself in a deep hole and you want me to give you a magic shovel so you can dig yourself out. Ma'am, I hope you realize magic shovels aren't cheap. It's going to cost you, a lot."

The long, low beep sounded again. "Reboot Financial, how can I help you to reboot your credit?"

"Yes, you will have lower monthly payments and yes, you can spend all that extra money on not paying your debt. In fact you can use the extra money for a down-payment on a replacement jet ski for the one that was repossessed."

The long, low beep tolled for the final time. "Reboot Financial, how can I help you to reboot your credit?"

"If I understand you correctly, the collection agencies are ruining your life by constantly asking for the money you owe them. You probably live in a nice house, have a new car or two in the driveway, a giant ultra HD TV with surround sound in the living room, digital cable with eight hundred channels, a top-of-the line computer with high-speed wireless Internet, all the latest devices, a gym membership you've used twice, and I bet you eat out most every night of the week and drink the weekends away. Now the time comes to pay and you're outraged? Your life is built on a borrowed foundation and the owners want it back. If you had any understanding of the concept of gravity you'd know you can't stand on thin air. I can sell you a very expensive parachute, but it's only going to slow your descent into the thing called reality."

"Why are you getting angry with me sir? It's the past you that thought credit was free money and got you into this mess. He's the person you should be angry with, not me. Sir, are you there? Sir?"

Cam swiveled his chair around and saw his super-supervisor standing right behind him. "Umm, we need to talk. Could you please come with me?"

Carrying a box full of little toys and basketball paraphernalia he'd collected over time and had been decorating his desk with, Cam exited the office accompanied by one of the building's security guards. "I'm not going to jack anything on my way out. You don't have to walk me to the door like a damn criminal."

"I have to, company policy." The building's security guard always hoped the fired employee he escorted out would try to start some shit or cause a scene so he could use some of the techniques he learned watching ultimate fighting clips on the Internet, but it never happened. The fired employee would usually just walk out in silence or in tears. Once the fired employee was outside and off the building's premises, the security guard's job was done and he could return to his post and watch more ultimate fighting clips.

Box of stuff in hand, Cam looked back at the building he was just escorted from. It was the place where he'd spent the majority of his waking life for the past three and a half years, the place he rushed to every weekday morning (sometimes even on the weekends), the place his whole life had been built around, and in an instant it had as much importance as any other of the faceless heaps of glass and stone surrounding him. He turned around, threw the box against a palm tree, and continued on to his car.

Cam was already on his third cocktail when T found him at their usual 'let's start the weekend off right' bar. He sat down next to him and skipped the foreplay. "What the fuck happened today?! Why would you blow this job? You were making good money, man. The job market sucks right now and the chances of finding something with even close to the same salary are pretty damn slim. The worst part is now everyone at the office is asking me what the hell is wrong with you."

He'd been asking himself the same questions, but Cam hadn't given himself any straight answers. "I really don't know what happened today. Honestly I barely remember saying what I did to those customers or why. You know how a lot of times in dreams you're yourself, but at the same time you're not yourself; you're not really in complete control of what you're doing and saying in the dream. Kind of like an actor in a movie following a script, but in the dream you never get to see the script you're following. That's the only way I can describe what happened. Next thing I know I'm being told to go home because it's my last day."

"I don't dream, so I have no idea what the hell you're talking about, but it sounds like a pretty bullshit reason for losing your job. I hope you have some savings bro, because I'm not covering your half of the bills. And since you were fired for being a dumbass actor following some mysterious script, you're not going to get any unemployment money. *I* still have a job and it's Friday, so I want to drink." T called to the bartender. "Shots, you know what we like." He gave the bartender a wink and the bartender gave him an understanding nod in return.

Cam pounded the shot and before he knew it, a fresh one was in his hand. T looked at him and made a sort of toast. "Drink up and forget about all that shit. Nothing you can do about it now anyway, so let's have a good time tonight."

"Yeah, fuck it." Cam downed his shot and began the process of trying to remove the memory of doing the things he didn't really remember doing.

Without a job to construct his life around, Cam's days collapsed. The seventeen or eighteen hours of consciousness per day he was used to having shrunk considerably. Nothing screamed at him anymore telling him when to wake up, so he got up when he was tired of sleeping. Daytime TV and video games killed hours in a matter of minutes and before he knew it, T was already home and they were tag-teaming his glass girlfriend.

Hunting for a new job wasn't one of the activities that helped shorten his day. He knew discrimination was technically illegal, but no reputable company was going to hire him looking the way he did. Cam may have been out of work, but whomever or whatever was tattooing him wasn't. The tattoos kept on showing up. The latest had materialized just above his left jawline—a scribbled hump with a long wavy line extending from its bottom right and finishing in a tiny loop.

"What am I going to do? Look at me! No one is ever going to hire a person looking like this and these things aren't ever coming off. I looked into tattoo removal. You know what they do? They slowly burn them off over time with lasers. The treatments are expensive and usually take years, and sometimes even leave behind scars. I might as well go and join the freak show over at the Station." Crazzee had stopped by and was sitting with Cam on his bed. His lack of prospects for future employment opportunities had gotten the better of him and he needed to vent his frustration.

Crazzee asked the obvious question. "Then why do you keep getting more and more tattoos if they're like causing so many problems?"

Cam's first instinct was to launch into a story of ink addiction, explain how he had no control and couldn't stop. Then beg for her support while he went through rehab. Instead he decided on the truth. He knew the truth would make him sound insane, but he had to tell her, even though the addiction story would've been a lot easier for her to swallow. "Listen, I know this doesn't make any sense, but I haven't been going to tattoo shops to get inked. The tattoos are just appearing and I have no idea where they're coming from."

"Wait, just wait a minute. You're saying the tattoos just like appear on your body. What about all those times you told me what the tattoos meant and why you got them?" For the first time ever Crazzee heard her boyfriend admit he lied to her and she didn't know whether to be angry at him for lying or happy that he finally trusted her enough to be completely truthful with her. The fact that he had no idea how his tattoos got onto his skin was beside the point.

"I had to tell you something, I couldn't tell you what was really happening. You'd think *I* was crazy." Cam felt good telling the truth, though he knew this truth sounded way less believable than any of the rookie lies he came up with in his youth.

"I don't understand. Are you saying someone like comes into your room at night and tattoos you? You'd have to be really drunk or roofied or something to not feel it. And why would someone do that? I don't get it."

"I don't either, but maybe that's what's happening, I don't know. It could be a government experiment in psychological warfare. They want to see how far they can push a person before he loses his shit." Cam's diet of daytime TV included large portions of conspiracy-theory-flavored documentaries.

"I hope you're not going to tell me that you think T is like some kind of secret agent sent to mess with you."

Cam's eyes momentarily lit up at her suggestion, but returned to normal after he thought about the absurdity of a lazyass pothead being involved in something so complex and clandestine. If it weren't a social taboo to urinate in the living room, T would've had a bedpan under the couch so he could eliminate the monumental effort it took to walk to the bathroom and back. "No… but something's going on and I don't know what to do."

Complex conspiracies were beyond Crazzee's scope of knowledge, but issues with body acceptance were something she knew all about. Cam needed someone who understood what he was going through. "I know it sucks not having control over how your body looks and believe me, I completely understand how you're feeling. I want to confess something too. You know my mom, she has like really big boobs, right? So all through the time I was growing up I thought I'd have big boobs like her when I got older. When I started going through puberty I waited every day for my boobs to get big, but they never did. After years of waiting I went to my mom and was like 'Mom, when am I going to get big boobs like yours?' Then she admitted to me her boobs were fake and that her real boobs were small and mine probably would be too. I was totally crushed. I had to live with the embarrassment of going through high school with these little things." Crazzee grabbed her breasts. "When I can afford it, I'm going to get implants, but until then I have to go through life with small boobs. I have to live one day at a time and go out there and face the world every day no matter how freakish I look." A few tears escaped from her eyes. "I've never told anyone that story before."

Crazzee had been threatening to get implants since Cam first started going out with her. He always talked her out of it because she had nice tits and he thought she'd go cartoonishly big like her mother and ruin them. Cam gave Crazzee a big hug to show her that he loved her despite her terrible affliction.

She hugged him back and felt better having gotten that heavy burden off her chest. Suddenly she pulled away and looked Cam in the eye. "I have a great idea. Let's go to the beach tomorrow. We'll be out in the open in our swimsuits with like no place to hide and have each other for support while we face the world. Plus I really need to work on my tan."

"Isn't this nice?" Crazzee had just finished applying suntan lotion on Cam's black polka-dotted back and while it felt good having lotion rubbed over his body, he didn't think it was nice having so much of himself exposed in public. Passers-by were giving him short curious looks and making quick attempts to decipher his encrypted skin. They all continued on their way disappointed. Cam had never been ashamed of his body, but today the desire to cover it up was overwhelming.

After putting in the work to prevent the sun from ruining her boyfriend's skin, Crazzee stood up and stretched. Every male head on the beach within viewing range turned towards her young, toned, well-proportioned teenie-bikinied body. "See? Everyone is staring at us, but who cares? Look at that guy over there." She pointed out a seriously overweight man casually walking on the water's edge in a speedo a couple sizes too small. "Would you rather look like you do now or like him, disgustingly fat? Gross. *He* doesn't care what people think or he wouldn't be like strolling around in front of everybody with his giant belly hanging out."

Being compared to an obese exhibitionist did little to ease Cam's unease. He knew if he stayed on his towel he'd continue to be nothing but a sideshow attraction for the ever-growing number of families arriving for a day at the beach, so he decided to get in the ocean where at least some of him would be covered. "I'm going for a swim, be back in a little while."

He jogged down to the shoreline and as soon as the water was knee-deep, he stopped to gaze at the vast ocean that lay before him. Small waves rhythmically crashed against his legs, carrying with them countless spheres of sand. Each one of the tiny individual grains was powerless against the force of the tide. It swept them up from their seemingly established positions into a mass of swirling brown fog that passed over Cam's feet and with every pass it left a little more of the once-established sand, slowly burying him. He closed his eyes and imagined the sand getting to point where it covered his entire body. The thought of being completely covered by sand was comforting.

The comfortable thought changed into an uncomfortable feeling when he became aware of a slimy something aggressively exploring the inside of his mouth. His brain told his hands to get the intruder out, but they were already occupied. Each hand had a tight grip on a damp cotton-covered roll of flesh. Cam opened his eyes to find out what was going on and at first could only see an unfocused face which apparently was attached to his own. As he detached himself he felt a sharp something jabbing into his back. He turned around to find a French-tipped finger pointing at whatever was behind him.

"Who the fuck is that?!" Crazzee's anger launched the words from her vocal chords and out through her mouth long before they had the chance to become bored.

Cam turned back around to see a full-figured gal in a long wet black Minnie Mouse t-shirt. It clung to her body and accentuated her generous curves. He also wanted to know who the fuck she was. "I have no idea who she is. I've never seen her before."

"You've never seen her before? You were just like making out with that beached whale like five seconds ago. How do you explain that?"

The full-figured gal spoke up. "What'd you call me?" She moved Cam out of the way and stepped up to Crazzee.

"This has nothing to do with you, so why don't you get back in the ocean where you belong." Crazzee's rage blinded her to the foolishness of insulting a woman almost twice her size.

"You're lucky my kids are here or I'd kick your narrow ass up and down this M F-ing beach." She grabbed the hands of a couple plump children in wet t-shirts who had been standing and staring at the painted man. "Let's go." As she walked away she had one final comment. "You'd better learn to keep your *boyfriend* on a tighter leash, honey."

Cam was still in a state of shock at the situation. "I swear I have no idea what happened. I was about to go for a swim and the next thing I remember is that woman all over me."

"I've put up with your flimsy bullshit excuses for way

too long, but this is it. Today was like totally the final straw. I'm done. I can't believe I was sympathetic about your so-called tattoo problem. It's way obvious you have some like secret life or something you've been hiding from me all this time. I'm sick of being played."

"But… baby, I'm telling the truth, you have to believe me. I…" Cam's plea of innocence was shot down before it had any chance to make impact.

"Enough! We're done." Crazzee turned her back on him and walked away.

Cam was left standing alone amongst a small group of spectators who had been watching the scene play out. As these people obviously found his distressing situation so entertaining, he thought he might as well take a bow. He received a smattering of applause in return.

With dry crusted sand still clinging to him, Cam dropped his beach gear on the floor near the front door. He went straight into the kitchen and fixed himself a stiff drink. T was in the living room playing his favorite driving video game, taking hits off his glass girlfriend between races. Cam joined him on the couch. "Well, Crazzee and I are done."

"So. Go and get with one of your other chicks then." T didn't take his eyes from the screen; a slight miscalculation in his steering could've caused him to become involved in a horrific crash.

"What other chicks?"

"Come on. Don't tell me Crazzee was the only chick you were banging. Do you have any idea the number of the times she called or texted or came by looking for you? I always had to tell her that I didn't know where you were."

"Dude, are you serious? I told you that whenever I wasn't out with Crazzee I was probably at the gym or playing ball."

"Damn, your web of bullshit is so thick that even you can't keep track of where you're supposed to be. I bet you don't remember the difference between where you actually were last night and where you told everybody you were."

"I was with Crazzee last night. We made plans to go to the beach. Which was a great idea by the way, I'm so glad we went." Cam's sarcasm went unnoticed, but the statement of his whereabouts didn't.

"Crazzee called last night looking for you. She said you guys had plans to go to the beach yesterday and you didn't call her back."

"Stop fucking with me OK? I had a rough day and I'm not in the mood for your shit." Crazzee did give him a hard time this morning, but he assumed it was because he overslept and was late picking her up.

"I'm not fucking with you. Man, you're really messed up if you can't even remember where you were last night."

Cam suddenly stood up, tore his shirt off, and flung it at T. He rubbed his hands over his inked body. "Why are you doing this to me?!"

The distraction caused T to spin out of control and smash into a wall. "What the hell?" He picked up the shirt and threw it back at Cam.

"There's no other logical explanation for it, you're the one doing this to me. What is all this weird stuff tattooed all over my body? Are they coded messages they give you designed to drive me crazy and make me do stuff? They must be paying you really well because I know how much you make at Reboot and it isn't enough to afford all those shoes and clothes you buy and that giant truck you drive. So how do you do it? Do you drug me and bring in a tattooist or do you do the tattoos yourself? No, I know, you drug me and then the man in black comes in and does the tattooing. Right?! Is that why I'm having trouble remembering things, because of all the drugs you're giving me?"

"Holy shit Cam. First, sit the fuck down and relax. It looks like you're going to have a heart attack. Second, who are *they* and why would anyone pay me to drug and tattoo you? Seriously think about it. A man in black? Come on dude, this isn't the *X-Files*. By the way, about my so-called expensive wardrobe, they have these things called credit cards. Maybe you heard about them during all those years you worked at Reboot. And like most people in the world I took out a loan for my truck. I'll be paying that shit off for a long time."

Cam struggled to catch his breath. "I don't know who *they* are, probably government scientists doing some kind of research on how to cause psychosis and then use it to make people do things."

"I doubt the government is employing someone who smokes as much bud as I do to do anything. All those government jobs require drug testing and there's so much weed in my system that I practically piss green."

"OK then, give me an explanation of what *is* happening to me that makes sense," Cam demanded of the suspected covert agent.

"Maybe you have something like that guy in *Memento*

had, a kind of amnesia. The tattoos could be messages to yourself."

"Why would I tattoo messages on myself that I don't understand? Wouldn't a bunch of Post-It notes stuck around my room have been a lot easier?"

"I guess the messages are so important that they need to be with you permanently and the reason you don't understand them is because your amnesia made you forget what they mean."

"What?! If for some reason I wanted permanent messages on myself, I would've had them written in fuckin' English."

"Well for *some reason* you didn't and if you want to find out what they mean, you'll have to get them deciphered, idiot. You'll need to find a Robert Langdon to help you."

"Who the fuck is Robert Langdon?"

"If you were into American literature like I am then you would know that Robert Langdon is a symbologist and the main character in those *Da Vinci Code* books."

"You're telling me to go and get help from some made-up person."

"I know you're not this dumb, but just in case you are I'll say this very slowly. The character is based on what real people do. You need to go to one of the colleges around here and find someone like him to help you."

Cam thought T's theory about amnesia and encoded tattooed messages to himself was nonsense and was probably just a weak attempt at a cover story to throw him off his trail, but the idea of finding someone who might be able to translate the crap tattooed all over his body *was* a good idea. Cam was surprised he didn't think of it himself.

"OK, I'll check that out, but what am I supposed to do with myself now? Look at me. I can't keep going on living like this. Always trying to hide these goddamned tattoos. Never knowing when or where the next one will appear. Trying to live a normal life while someone or something is conspiring against me."

"You have to stop fighting it and just own it. Like it or not you're stuck with those things, so just accept them. It's like when I was told I needed glasses. I can't wear contacts and I don't trust those lasers they shoot in your eyes, so I had no choice but to wear them and believe me, I was pissed. I didn't want to spend the rest of my life looking like some fucking nerd, so I decided to just own the situation. I buy designer frames and make them an accessory to whatever outfit I'm wearing. They make me look like an intellectual and chicks dig smart."

"What happens when they find out you're actually a complete moron?"

"How about you let me get back to my game? I was kicking ass until you came in here and started screaming like a little bitch." T got back in the driver's seat and resumed racing his virtual opponents. "I hope you're going to clean up all this sand that fell out of your vagina—it's everywhere."

"Maybe I will, if I can remember. I'll tattoo myself a reminder so I don't forget." Cam gave T one last suspicious look and made a mental note to put a lock on his door. He then went into his room to change into something more comfortable.

CAM EMERGED FROM the Station's back room and onto its sales floor the owner of a new look, a look he decided was more appropriate for a guy covered in tattoos. After hours of intense Internet research and some careful deliberation he chose to be a punk. He began by dying his hair jet black and shaving it into a mohawk. Next, he cut off the sleeves of all his old t-shirts and bought faded black jeans a size too small. At an upscale thrift store he found a pair of pre-scuffed ten-hole Doc Martin boots and a well-used leather biker jacket covered with old punk band patches, studs, and spikes. He imagined its previous owner was now middle aged with a wife, kids, and a mortgage - his calls for anarchy replaced by calls to his investment broker regarding his 401k. Finishing off the look was the official Station nametag which hung around his neck and read 'Cam'.

Accompanying Cam on his debut was the Station's

owner, Burn. An older man either in his fifties or sixties, nobody knew for sure. He wore his thinning blond hair long in the back and short everywhere else. His denim vest and ragged t-shirt emblazoned with the logo of a long forgotten 1970s psychedelic rock band did nothing to hide his sizeable potbelly. He had on jeans that matched the age and color of the vest and their cut accentuated the thinness of his legs. When they reached the first aisle of DVDs they stopped.

"Hey, thanks again for giving me a chance, I really appreciate it." Earlier in the afternoon Cam had handed Burn his application and after a short conversation was hired on the spot.

"Yeah, OK. I know you don't have much retail experience, but we needed to fill the tattooed-dude-with-mohawk position. The last one grew his hair out and went back to school to waste his time studying business or something. You said you liked movies, so this will be your section." Burn motioned to both sides of the DVD aisle in front of them. "Keep it organized and stocked. Yeah, um… basically help out the customers if they need it and um… just be cool with everyone, OK. I'll be doing my thing in the back if you have any questions."

"OK, cool." Cam was left to begin his new job. He wasn't at all sure of what to do with himself; it was also his first day out in public as a punk and there was so much he didn't know. How were punks supposed to act? How did they talk? Did they work hard or rebel against the system they were hired to maintain? Cam was going to have to hurry up and learn to become the mask he was hiding behind and make sure he wasn't exposed as the tattooed imposter he truly was.

As a distraction from the awkward fit of his disguise, he threw himself into his work. He thought he'd begin by making sure all the DVDs were in alphabetical order. It was a mindless task, but it was a lot better than being chained to a desk waiting for the dreaded long low beep. Tons of DVDs had been misplaced, it was going to be a big project, but he would enjoy creating order from the chaos.

Before he was able to alphabetize the first DVD, he saw a man with long black hair wearing a long black coat a few aisles over. He wasn't going to let him escape this time. Cam moved as fast as he could without actually running—he didn't want to scare the man away. Cam arrived in the aisle and faced him. The man looked back at Cam. His face was partially covered by a full black beard which reached down to the base of his neck, but the face behind it wasn't old, it looked nearer to Cam's age. His black trench coat was of a different era, but its silver buttons still shone. Underneath he wore a collarless black button-up shirt and a nametag hung from his neck. The usual black cord had been replaced by a thick silver chain and the nametag read 'Ras'. He offered his hand to Cam. It was automatically taken and given a firm shake.

"You must be our new mohicaned colleague. I am called Ras, as you may have discerned from the designation inscribed on my name plate." The voice didn't match the body. It had the high tone of an adolescent whose testicles were on the verge of descending into manhood.

"Hey, what's up. I'm Cam." His voice dropped an octave in a subconscious effort to assert his superiority.

"It is a pleasure to make your acquaintance."

An uncomfortable silence followed, during which they looked each other over. Ras seemed to be studying Cam's tattoos while Cam looked for any familiarity in Ras. He doubted this was the same man in black who was perhaps assisting with T's suspected government research, but nothing was beyond the realm of possibility anymore.

"So… is this a cool place to work or what?" Cam had to say something; Ras's scrutiny was becoming unsettling.

"I would say labor conditions in this establishment are satisfactory and since the retail market for hard copies of recorded auditory and visual entertainment is in a steep decline, we are not regularly assaulted by a great number of patrons. My only complaint is the paltry sum which is our wage."

"Well, I guess people like us can't complain too much about that, can we? I doubt many other companies would give us the time of day. I could have all the education and experience in the world, but because I look different I would never even get a chance. In my opinion, that's discrimination." Cam thought he might as well begin entrenching himself among these outcasts sooner than later.

"Spot on and well said! We must be valued by the strength of our character and the weight of our intellect and not by such trivial matters such as mode of dress or preferred grooming choices." Ras gave Cam a hearty pat on the back. "Here you will surely find asylum from the uncouth appraisal of the hoi polloi. Now I must return to the task at hand, my friend. Burn is a lenient overseer, but we still must earn our keep."

Cam had succeeded in fooling the first round of freaks

that he was one of them and was relieved, but it wasn't a cause for celebration. He was now officially an outsider. A member of a group he spent his whole life avoiding and ridiculing out of fear of somehow slipping down to their ranks. Dual emotions of anger and sadness washed over him. He had to fight the urge to run out of the store, shave off the mohawk, put back on his normal clothes, and find a way to hide the tattoos so he could return to his real life. Special movie makeup had to exist that would cover the tattoos. It was probably expensive and time-consuming to apply, but it was better than living as a freak. No, it'd only make him a different kind of freak. Covering himself in thick layers of makeup would turn him into a living wax-work figure of the pre-tattooed Cam. A too-perfect replica of what he used to be would greet him from behind every reflective surface, constantly reminding him he was living his life in an unconvincing disguise of a person who had already been permanently disguised as a freak. There was no going back, he was going to have to stick it out as an outsider; maybe it wouldn't be that bad.

"Hey new guy! Come check this out." Cam followed the voice and found Syn sitting on a table in the back room holding a magazine. He remembered her; she was the kooky chick who gave the maternal speech to his previous self. In the meantime her hair had turned bright red with purple streaks and platinum tips and her clothing seemed more dystopian. Sitting next to her were two other female employees. One was a heavyset Asian-American dressed

Goth-lite, either too afraid or too lazy to take the plunge into the full Goth regalia. The other was a skinny blonde with a short, probably self-inflicted haircut. Her tattered t-shirt was too small and her jeans were very low cut, exposing sharp hip bones slicing through the waist band. Cam had been rummaging through one of many carts full of DVDs parked in the back room looking for movies to restock his section when he heard Syn call for him. She wanted to show him a couple of pictures in the magazine she was so lovingly holding. "Look! That's me and that's me." Cam wouldn't have recognized her if she hadn't said it was her. In the photos her makeup, hair, and outfit were so elaborate it made the Syn holding the magazine look casual in comparison.

"Wow, cool pictures." Cam's reaction was as nonchalant as he thought a punk's reaction would be.

"Yeah, I know. I was at the second annual Gothtek Lifestyle Festival and a photographer from Cyber Noir took some pics and put them in their 'zine." Syn turned back to the girls. "Stellar is gonna be so jealous they didn't use any of her pics. I've got to show this to Burn." Syn and her posse got up and left. Halfway down the hall she turned back and yelled to Cam, "See ya, wouldn't want to be ya!"

"Who would?" Cam asked the universe. He stood alone in the back room and looked around at all the posters hung up everywhere; he didn't recognize any of the people looking back at him. Band stickers wallpapered portions of the room and not even one of these musical groups was known to Cam. This was the place where he was meant to fit in and he never felt so out of place in his entire life.

Cam was slumped on the couch mindlessly watching the emotional reactions owners were having after seeing the results of their pets' extreme makeovers when T came barreling through the front door of the apartment dressed in his work clothes. He threw his jacket on a chair and sat down next to his drastically changed roommate. "I still can't get over what a psycho you look like now, Travis Bickle."

"You said to own it bro… wait, did you just call me by your name? Isn't your last name, uh… *is* it Bickle?"

"Wow. Did you shave some brain off too? Travis Bickle is the taxi driver in that movie *Taxi Driver* who goes nuts and cuts his hair into a mohawk. I know for a fact you've seen it, I watched it with you. Jesus Christ! And you know my last name isn't even close to Bickle, dick."

"Did you say you have something close to a pickle dick? No wonder you have such a hard time finding girls to go out with you." Cam's sidesplitting humor caused him to come down with a case of the giggles.

"It's pretty obvious you've been molesting my girlfriend. I hope she isn't covered in your slobber." T grabbed his big glass bong from her supplication at Cam's feet and packed the bowl. Before taking a hit, he thoroughly sanitized the rim with his sleeve.

"Hey. I took your advice and spent the afternoon online looking for symbologists at the colleges around here. Know what I found, nothing. There's no such thing as a symbologist, that *Da Vinci Code* dude made it up. The closest thing I could find was a linguist. One of the universities in L.A. has a bigass department for that kind of shit, so I sent 'em an email. I told 'em I was a tattoo artist working on a book deciphering the meaning of tribal skin art, pretty good huh?"

T's attention had already shifted. He was focused on inhaling as much THC into his lungs as possible. "Yeah, let me know how that goes." Once his girlfriend had serviced his needs, he was able to refocus his attention on more important matters. "So, any hot chicks at your new job?"

"Not really. There is this one chick though, she's got a nice body and an OK face, but she's all tatted up and dresses like a post-apocalyptic Rainbow Brite."

"Sounds like she's right up your alley. I hate to say it, but I think your days of dating normal girls are over, dude. Maybe she's into some kinky shit. This could really broaden your horizons, if you know what I mean."

"Yeah, I know what you mean and I don't want to end up locked in a cage with a tube up my ass. I like trying new things, but not in my butt." Cam took his turn with his roommate's girlfriend.

"Why does your idea of kinky always involve things stuck up your ass? Remember the time we met those two dominatrix-looking chicks at that club in Hollywood? You were afraid to go back to their place because you thought the blonde one was going to ram a kielbasa sausage up your ass."

"I didn't say that. I said I was afraid she was going to ram *her* kielbasa sausage up my ass. I'm pretty sure those chicks weren't chicks. It's cool with me if you're curious about that world and I won't judge you if you want to start sailing the seven seas as a butt pirate."

"Shut the fuck up." T removed his girlfriend from

Cam's embrace. "Trust me, they were chicks, alright. You're just scared of stepping out of your comfort zone."

"Look at me. I was fucking deported from my comfort zone and had my citizenship revoked for life. I can't ever go back."

"Exactly. You were too scared to leave it, so maybe that's why you were forced out."

"Yeah and someday I'm going to find out by who and that person's going to wish they were never born. My life was perfect before all this shit started happening and now I have to live as this guy." Cam gestured to the tattooed punk sitting on the couch. "Give me that." He roughly grabbed T's girlfriend from him and inhaled until his lungs were filled beyond their capacity. His exhale released a cloud of smoke so massive it temporarily encased him in a white euphoric bubble. Inside it Cam was bodyless—without clothes, hair or skin to inhabit, and free from the judgment having an outward appearance always brings. The moment of freedom evaporated with the smoke surrounding him and Cam was once again the guy on the couch T barley recognized as his roommate.

Wheeled carts overflowing with CDs and DVDs sat parked near the back wall of the Station, waiting for someone to put them away. Unofficially it was the new guys' job to make sure every one of those CDs and DVDs were placed in their correct location in the store. Veteran Station employees loathed doing it and usually walked around carrying small stacks of CDs, giving them the illusion of working while they socialized with each other and did their best to avoid customers.

Cam was the newest guy, so the bulk of the work was left to him. Assisting him was Rodge, the other man in black, but he didn't wear a long black coat or have long black hair. His unnaturally black hair was at an in-between stage, too short to tie back into a ponytail and too long to stay put in any kind of style. He held his hair in place by tucking it behind his ears, but it never stayed there. It escaped every chance it got and had to be continually returned to its hated home. His black t-shirt was from a Cure concert, which according to its cracked and disintegrating white lettering, had taken place many, many years ago.

"Do you like The Cure?" All of Rodge's conversations with new people began the same way.

"They're alright I guess. I like that song where he's talking about hanging out on the beach with a gun in his hand." Cam referenced the only Cure song he could think of at the moment.

"That song is called 'Killing an Arab'. It was inspired by the Camus novel *The Stranger*. The song isn't about racism or genocide or anything like that. You might think that because of the title, but it's actually a meditation on the meaninglessness of existence."

"Heavy stuff. I'll have to listen to it again sometime." Cam noticed a customer was standing behind Rodge patiently waiting for him to finish his conversation. Cam motioned to the patient customer with a slight nod of his head and a raise of the eyebrows. Rodge got the message and reluctantly let the customer lead him away.

Syn appeared in his place holding a small stack of CDs she was pretending to put away. "I see you were given an introduction to the philosophy of The Cure 101. Rodge has a PhD on the subject. I once spent forty-five minutes listening to his dissertation on why Robert Smith wears smeared lipstick."

"Why?" Cam assumed Robert Smith was the guy with the wild hair in the faded picture on Rodge's shirt.

"It was a slow day and we were stuck behind the counter together."

"No, why does he wear smeared lipstick?"

"Oh, I don't remember much of what the fuck he was yammering on about. It had something to do with the rejection of gender roles in society. The more interesting question is you." Syn looked directly into Cam's eyes.

Cam felt if she stared into his eyes long enough she would be able to see behind the punk façade and expose him as an imposter, so he looked away. "So… what's the question?"

"What's your deal? What're you in to, blah blah blah."

"I don't have a deal. I woke up one morning, looked in the mirror, and this is what I saw." Cam motioned to his still-intact punk façade.

"Deep. So, what kind of music are you into?"

Cam then realized how poorly he'd prepared himself for the role he'd taken on. The last time he'd listened to punk music was in his teens when one of his buddy's girlfriends brought a punk rock compilation for their drive to Magic Mountain and played it over and over again. He wasn't even sure what kind of punk music a guy with his look would listen to, so it was lucky Cam found himself standing near the store's 'Underground Punk' section. He hoped this was the kind of punk music a guy with his look would be listening to. "I'm into mostly underground punk. You know, bands like Bloody Diaper, Chode Stain, The Crusty Socks, and Mexican Afterbirth." Afraid she might ask him follow-up questions about these bands he'd never heard of, Cam took the attention from himself and put it on Syn, just where she wanted it. "What kind of shit do you like?"

"I like all kinds of music. I'm into Victorian anarchtronic music like The Nun's Hood, Midnight Fang Kiss, and Stigmata Splinters. I also listen to Swedish dark ice trash, bands like Dryck Fläder and Talanglösa Rövhål. Lately I've been checking out a lot of bossa no wave, The New Death Frogs, Three Point Maneuver, and Van Gogh's Crotch Locket are pretty cool. When I want to mellow out I listen to electro-ambient folk, Jam Hoarder is great. My favorite band right now though is Lipgloss Holocaust. They're an all-girl neo-post alternative apocalyptiko band. They're fucking amazing. They're actually playing in L.A. pretty soon, I can't wait. You should come and check 'em out."

"Yeah that sounds cool, I might do that." Cam made a mental note to fill his music library with all his favorite bands and listen to them for the first time.

"Well, I gotta put the rest of these away." Syn gently bounced the stack of CDs she was holding. "See ya."

"Alright." Cam watched her walk away. He always had a lot of success with the ladies, but his confidence in that area had taken a huge blow lately, for obvious reasons. He didn't know if the new Cam would have the same kind of success. Syn would be the first test.

Cam exited the back door of the Station carrying large plastic bags full of the store's garbage, another one of the unofficial jobs the new guy had to perform. After throwing them into the dumpster he noticed Ras standing against a wall smoking a cigarette.

"Do you indulge in this vice as well?" Ras still wore his long black coat despite the temperature's insistence there was no need for it.

Cam joined him at the wall. "What?"

"Would you care for a cigarette?" Ras pulled a silver Edwardian cigarette case from one of the many pockets of his long black coat, opened it, and offered it to Cam.

The old Cam only smoked marijuana, but he thought the new one would probably rebel against his health and smoke cigarettes too. "Sure, why not. Thanks." Cam put the cigarette in his mouth and then realized it wasn't going to spontaneously light.

Ras pulled a silver Zippo from another pocket and lit the cigarette. "Are you finding fulfillment in your new-found profession?"

"Yeah, when I was a kid I dreamed of emptying trash cans for minimum wage. No, so far this seems like a pretty chill place to work." Cam knew his mother would be angry if she found out he was smoking; her father died of lung cancer brought on by a lifetime of the bad habit. The cigarette would probably be the last thing she'd notice about the new Cam though. He hadn't seen her for some time; he couldn't face her looking like he did.

"I wish to inquire about your name. Is it perhaps the

shortened form of Camford, Camworth, or Cammerson?" Ras's cigarette was nearly finished which meant his smoke break was nearly finished, but he wanted to find out more about the new fellow, so he lit another one.

"No and it's not short for Cameron either. My real name is Marcus, but only my mom ever calls me that anymore." Cam was exhausted from improvising stories about himself and thought revealing his given name wouldn't compromise his disguise.

"How is the moniker Cam possibly derived from Marcus?"

"You probably can't tell by looking at me, but I'm really into basketball." Something about Ras made Cam let go and really talk. He seemed to truly listen and was actually interested in what was being said. He didn't spend the conversation thinking of what to say next and waiting for the chance to say it. "There was this one NBA player named Marcus Camby and one day on the court somebody started calling me Cam Baby and it stuck. Then after a while it became Cambrodia or Cambro for short. Now it's just Cam. It's a helluva lot better than what they called me back in the day."

"Would it be agreeable for me to entreat you to disclose this?"

"Yes, it would be agreeable. Jesus, you must kick ass at Scrabble. They called me Funky B." Cam knew he was giving away more information than he should. The new him probably shouldn't be so open, but it was just spilling out.

"Were you a hip-hop artist or a member of a street gang?"

"Yeah I was in the Vista del Mar Gringos. We were the

hardest group of white boys in Southern Orange County. No, the name, as you would say, was derived from the group Marky Mark and the Funky Bunch. Marcus/Marky, Funky Bunch/Funky B, get it?" Cam hoped Ras didn't notice the embarrassing shade of red his face turned while he was divulging the origins of his prepubescent nickname.

"As you may or may not have surmised, my appellation comes from my physical resemblance to the Russian mystic and monk Grigori Rasputin. If only I had his powers of influence over the fairer sex, if you understand my meaning." Ras forced a laugh and gave Cam a pat on the back. "I dare say the women of Orange County are not as sophisticated as those in the court of Tsar Nicholas II."

"No, I guess they're not." Cam didn't want to look like he was ignorant of Russian history, so he pretended he understood what Ras was talking about.

"No matter my friend, there exists a wide world beyond this diminutive county. I have yet tasted its riches, but shall."

"Yeah, it would be nice to get the hell out of here someday." Cam took a long last drag on his cigarette and blew the smoke straight up into the sky. He watched with envy as the smoke dissipated and became indistinguishable from its surroundings.

The shower door opened and Cam stepped out from behind a wall of steam and approached the mirror. He wiped away the condensation and took a close look at himself. For the old Cam, this step always came before the shower, but the new Cam didn't follow his predecessor's rules. The first thing he noticed was the hair around his mohawk was beginning to grow back. He grabbed the razor and began to scrap the hair from his head. The front done, he took his hand mirror to do the back. Before he started, he saw a black mark on the right side of the base of his skull, just behind his ear. With closer inspection he saw it was a rough approximation of a fingerprint. Without thinking, he attempted to rub it off, but of course he knew it was never coming off. He shrugged and finished shaving.

Head and face shaved, mohawk spiked, and his punk uniform carefully put together, Cam came out of his bedroom and found T sitting in his usual spot on the couch playing video games with his loyal girlfriend right next to him. One eye glanced up at Cam. "Whatcha doin' tonight? Do you want to go out and get a few drinks?"

"Nah, I'm going to a concert with that chick from work I told you about."

"That Rainbow Brite Beyond Thunderdome chick? Really? Who're you going to see?"

"I don't know. Some band she likes."

"Where at?"

Cam pulled a crumpled Station receipt from his pocket and read the back. "It's somewhere in L.A., at a club called Squalid. You're the one who told me I can't get normal chicks anymore, so I'm gonna see how this goes. What're you doin' tonight?"

"I don't know yet. I'll probably just hang out here for a little while with the ol' ball and chain and see what happens." T caressed the cool glass of his bong.

"Well, you two have fun together. Later."

"This can't be the right street, there isn't anything here except a bunch of closed factories and warehouses." Cam glanced down at the directions on his GPS and then out the windows of his car. He was in an industrial part of the city. Streetlights were few and far between, making signs and addresses almost impossible to read. "I swear to God if this GPS took me to the wrong place I'm going to smash the shit out of it." He slowed his car down to a crawl and stuck his head out the window in an attempt to get a better look at the numbers on the buildings. A number on one of the buildings matched the number in the address on the back of the receipt. "Well… according to this thing, I'm on the right street and that's the right address, so I guess this is the place."

Big-rig trucks and delivery vans lined the street in both directions, forcing him to park a few blocks away. Walking back to the alleged location of the concert, Cam continued his conversation with himself. "I hope that chick wasn't fucking with me and sent me to some sketchy area in the middle of nowhere to get my ass kicked by a group of her cyber friends. Maybe this is some sort of initiation prank she pulls on all the new guys at the Station. I should just go back to the car and go home."

He stopped in front of the building which had the same address Syn had given him and double and triple checked it was correct. It was a vast nondescript structure protected by a chain-link fence wrapped in green material. A section of the fence was on wheels and had been partially slid open. The thick chain which presumably kept it locked dangled from its opened edge. It was difficult to tell whether it had been simply unlocked or broken into. Cam took a tentative step through the gap and found himself in a giant paved area. Loading docks lined the building in front of him. The only way forward was a small road that disappeared around the corner of the far end of the building. He followed it and found himself in a narrow alley that stretched before him in complete darkness.

"Why am I doing this? No chick in the world is worth being mutilated and murdered in some psycho's torture dungeon." Cam's conversation with himself had lowered to a whisper.

He turned his phone on, giving himself a fragment of light to walk by. Gravel crunched beneath his slow steps. A gust of wind rattled the chain-link fence to his right, scaring the crap out of him and causing his heart beat to increase even more. Dark shapes lurked on the edges of the feeble light his phone produced, so he picked up his pace in case they decided to follow.

After traveling seemingly miles and miles, Cam reached the end of the road. He turned and saw a faint light coming from around another corner. The top of his head took a tentative peek around this final corner to discover the source of the light. It was coming from a metal-grill-covered lamp above a doorway. Below it sat a large bald man on a stool smoking a cigarette. The light reflected off his shiny skull, creating a halo.

A light also came on above Cam's head, illuminating some pressing questions. Was this how it was going to end? Was the tattoo experiment finished? They did successfully turn him from a normal guy into a mentally unstable freak, so this could be the place where he'd be taken to the next level or maybe just gotten rid of to destroy the evidence. Was everyone at the Station in on it or were some of them also victims? He had to find out even if it meant it was the end for him. They'd get him sooner or later anyway.

With as much courage as he could muster he approached the man on the stool. The number of tattoos the man had on his bare arms and neck made Cam's skin almost bare in comparison. He could also be an unknowing victim or maybe he'd already been turned into one of them. The tattooed man on the stool looked Cam over. "Twenty bucks."

Cam supposed they had to keep up the charade of the concert so he'd go in willingly. He paid the stool man and was let through the door. Once inside he found himself in a fog-filled void with creepy music attacking him from all sides. He wished the sadistic bastards doing this to him would just get it over with and do what they were going to do instead of putting him through all these cheap horror-movie theatrics. He continued forward and when some of the fog cleared the first thing he encountered was a floating white expressionless face with dead black eyes. Cam had enough, he was going to find the source of all this and confront it.

The source turned out to be a DJ. He was wearing a black PVC body suit and the black lights above him made his white mask glow and appear to float. On either side of his speakers were powerful fog machines pumping out mysterious atmosphere into an otherwise boring warehouse, where a makeshift bar and stage had been set up and a few old couches and chairs had been scattered about. Cam found out from one of the 'bartenders' that even though he'd gotten there at the advertised starting time for the event, nobody ever showed up at that time. No attendee wanted to be among the first to arrive and have their grand entrance missed, so the vast majority came two to three hours late. Fortunately for Cam no one was there to see him commit the faux pas of being on time.

A couple hours and many beers later, people started to trickle in, most of them dressed for a nuclear winter ball. Another hour and some more beer later Cam thought he saw a familiar face in the fog. The familiarity was confirmed when the face in question came running over; actually it really couldn't be called a run. It was more of a quick stomping shuffle, the closest thing possible to a run Syn could pull off in the towering platform boots she was wearing. When she eventually reached Cam, she gave him an excited hug. He looked her over; her extravagant makeup and outfit had transformed her into a caricature of herself.

"I'm glad ya made it." Syn dragged Cam into the crowd.

"Yeah, I thought I'd stop by and check it out." Cam was wildly out of his element among these amassed celebrants of Armageddon, yet at the same time it was strangely comforting being a freak in a room full of freaks.

Syn ended their short trip through the fog next to a girl with an outfit as elaborate as hers. Her purple dreadlocks were held back by a pair of purple-tinted goggles and a gas mask studded with steel spikes hung from her neck. "This is my friend Stellar." Stellar glanced at Cam and turned away.

"Hey." Cam said to Stellar's cold shoulder.

"So… how do I look?" Syn spun around.

"You look great, but I feel a bit underdressed. I knew I should've worn my biohazard suit."

Syn pushed him. "Shut up. What do you think of this place?"

Being there alone for hours made him an expert on the place, but Cam looked around as if he'd just arrived. "It seems alright, not the most convenient location in the world though. I have to admit, I had a little trouble finding it."

"It's not always here dummy, it changes every time. Part of the fun is finding the venue. The last one was in an old container ship docked at the port in Long Beach. That was amazing."

"So, when does this band you like start playing?"

"Who knows? Whenever they're ready I guess. Why don't you go and buy us some drinks like a good little boy."

"OK Mom." Cam saw Syn give him a double-take as he vanished into the mist on his way to the bar.

Cam found it difficult to find the girls again. The fog had thickened and the amount of similarly attired women had increased. He nearly gave the drinks to the wrong pair of girls; one of them did have purple dreadlocks, so it was an understandable mistake. After Cam delivered the alcohol to the correct set of purple dreadlocks, Stellar placed her two first fingers over her lips. Cam wasn't sure if this was her way of thanking him or her way of telling him not to speak to her. He looked to Syn for help in translating her gesture.

"She wants to know if you have a cigarette." Syn turned to Stellar. "Stel, I thought you quit."

"No, I'm hoping for an early death." Stellar was still looking expectantly at Cam.

He patted his pockets and shrugged. "Sorry, don't have any."

"Maybe someone else here can help me to feel the soil falling over my head." Stellar walked off in search of a smoke.

Before he had the chance to interpret her enigmatic response, Cam felt Syn pulling him forward. "Hey, it looks like the band's almost ready. Let's get closer to the stage."

The music stopped and the stage lights came on, turning the collected fog and cigarette smoke blue. From out of the blue appeared a petite woman with a completely shaved head dressed in a female officer's uniform from a war fought long ago. Her intense glare was enhanced by the heavy and intricate makeup around her eyes. When she stepped up to the microphone her small platoon of female soldiers began to produce deep dark tones from their electronic instruments, building up the sound gradually until the song burst open and their commanding officer let her voice be heard.

Here I stand before you all

Clothed in this disguise

Your dressed-up doll

Feeling every set of eyes

Looking right into me

Searching for any imperfection

Wanting me to be

The impossible perfection

You won't see, won't be shown
Because…
I hide behind this microphone
Alone, alone, ALONE
I cry and moan behind this microphone, alone

This makeup, a veil, a mask
My voice, the song, a distraction
All of it, part of the task
My natural reaction
To keep the real me from you
It's all done with a purpose
As I'm scared you'd view
The underneath as worthless

You won't see, won't be shown
Because…
I hide behind this microphone
Alone, alone, ALONE
I cry and moan behind this microphone, alone

Cam felt the singer's intense stare and words pierce

through him. He thought she'd somehow discovered his status as a fraud and was publicly exposing him through song. When he took an apprehensive look back at the crowd, he was relieved to see no one was paying him any attention. They were rhythmically swaying to the music, entranced by the performance. Cam joined in and conformed with the sway. He glanced over at Syn and she smiled back at him, also unaware of his status as an imposter. A realization then struck him—would it even be possible to spot an imposter in a building full of people hidden beneath thick coatings of costume? He supposed everyone around him was an imposter in their own unique way. The thought eased his anxiety enough to allow him to do what he came here to do: Syn. Behind that get-up she was still just a girl and imposter or not, Cam was still a man. He had what girls wanted and he knew how to use it. With an almost imperceptible forward movement, he danced closer and closer until they were face to face, their bodies nearly touching. Cam kept eye contact with her while his crotch gyrated within an inch of hers. The move usually worked with the normal girls in the normal clubs he used to go to. He didn't see any reason why it wouldn't work here. In fact it worked perfect. Unable to bear not having her magnet complete its pull, Syn yanked his body against hers and violently kissed him.

The long night of kissing and groping continued in front of Syn's car. It took a blast from her car horn to stop them. Stellar popped her head out the passenger's side window.

"So, am I supposed to just stretch out and wait until your mentality catches up with your biology?"

Syn still held Cam around the neck. "I better get going."

Cam let go of her waist. "Yeah me too. I'm glad I stopped by tonight."

Syn looked down at his jeans. "I know."

Cam covertly adjusted himself while Syn walked over to the driver's side door. Before she got in, she dramatically blew him a kiss. Cam walked to the passenger's side window and looked in. He knew it was important to also get on the good side of a girl's friends. "It was nice to meet ya Stellar, I hope you had a good time tonight."

Without looking at him Stellar mumbled, "I was bored before it even began."

Over Stellar's slumped body, Cam gave Syn one last goodbye. "See you at work."

"Yes you will." Her car peeled out, eager to remove itself from the source of its driver's lust.

Getting into his own car, Cam noticed a man with long black hair wearing a long black coat walking alone in the shadows across the street. He started to get back out of the car to investigate, but decided delving into the darkness would only taint the good mood he was in. "Fuck it." He got back into the car and left, leaving the shadows behind. Whatever they contained would have to join the ever-growing list of his life's unsolved mysteries.

CAM JOURNEYED THROUGH the Station collecting every bit of its unwanted recent past for disposal. It had to be done on a daily basis or everyone inside would ultimately suffocate under the surplus of their history. He threw it all in the dumpsters behind the building where it would be picked up and buried deep below the ground, hopefully to never resurface.

Before going back inside, Cam followed the smell of smoke and found Ras doing his duty of keeping the back wall from falling over.

"Hey, can I bum a smoke off you?" Cam had learned that smokers were refunded the years of life they lost to the habit by their employers in small increments during all the extra breaks they took.

Ras produced his silver cigarette case and opened it. "Certainly you may, my friend."

Cam took a cigarette and put it in his mouth. It hung there unlit until Ras generated a flame. "Thanks." He then joined his colleague in buttressing the unstable wall. "Have you heard of a club called Squalid?"

"Give me a moment to ponder." Ras took an extra-long drag and released it. "No, I cannot say I have. Is there a reason you have put this particular query to me?"

"I was there on Saturday and I could've sworn I saw you."

Ras chuckled in the manner of a Victorian stage actor or how he assumed an actor of that era would chuckle. "Absurd, quite absurd. You see, I rarely frequent discotheques. My social skills for gatherings of that sort are lacking. My evenings are usually spent in the company of long-dead scribes."

"So… you're telling me you get off on hanging out in graveyards. Hey, whatever tickles your pickle man."

"Heavens no! I meant I enjoy perusing the classics."

Cam gave Ras a pat on the back. "I know. I was just fucking with you. You need to chill dude. Maybe get out of the house once in a while and find some live female companionship, if you know what I mean."

"I comprehend what you are suggesting and I do have contact with women through electronic networking, but I find these are speculative propositions at best."

"OK, so you talk to girls online, that's cool. Have you ever met any of these chicks in real life?"

Ras pulled out another cigarette. "A rendezvous was attempted."

"What happened?"

"We converged at an appropriate location, a fine family eatery. With me was a single red rose I had purchased for the occasion. I presented the lady with my offering, which she gladly accepted. We adjourned to the table, I on one side of the booth and her on the other. As we began to converse, it became apparent she was put off by my manner. I must admit I too was struggling not to judge the proverbial book by its cover."

"Why, what'd she look like?"

"The dimensions of this book's cover were of such a mass that opening it would have taken a Herculean effort."

"Well, you did agree to go on a date with a fat chick, didn't you?"

"The likeness I received before we were personally acquainted was of a woman of considerably less girth."

"Yeah, that's the problem with meeting people online. On the Internet you can be whoever you want. We should go out to a bar sometime, so you can meet some non-virtual girls." Moments after Cam made the suggestion, he realized he had no idea if a bar existed in Orange County (or anywhere else in Southern California) that would have women who'd be interested in a guy like Ras.

"Yes, I would enjoy joining you on a social outing."

Cam flicked his cigarette, the way he had seen it done in countless movies. "Cool. I'm already late getting back in, see ya." He turned around and headed inside.

"I see your nape is in receipt of a further addition to your already impressive assortment of inked etchings."

Cam felt a familiar burning rise in his face and touched the back of his neck where a bird constructed from an assemblage of triangles now sat engraved in black ink. "I guess it is."

He locked himself in the Station's employee bathroom; he wanted to see what the hell was tattooed on the back of his neck. In the small mirror above the sink he tried to get a look at the tattoo he'd missed this morning. Sleep didn't come easily anymore (unless it was assisted by large amounts of alcohol and/or marijuana), so getting out of bed was becoming harder and harder. He got out of bed so late today that he only had time for an abbreviated version of his morning routine which didn't include the tattoo check. By taking T's advice and owning the tattoos, Cam thought it would make them stop or at least slow them down. Nope, they kept coming, sometimes even two or three at a time. The continuing loss of control over his body was maddening. His only consolation was that in his current environment, no one ever questioned his constantly changing appearance.

There was no way he was going to be able to see the back of his neck in the small mirror above the sink, so he took a photo of it with his phone. He then found an unoccupied part of the back room to go sit and take a look at his new tattoo. After viewing the geometric bird, he noticed he'd a missed call. One of Burn's few rules was that all phones had to be turned off while working. A few phone addicts had been fired for too many violations of the rule and Cam couldn't afford to be one of them. The missed call was from a number he didn't recognize, but the caller had left a message. The voice in the message spoke with exaggerated professionalism.

"Hello, this is Alexander Cole, department coordinator for linguistics here at the university. I received your email regarding your research project. Of the members of our faculty, Professor Sergei Valeska would be the most qualified to assist you. His areas of study include historical linguistics and semiotics. He has open office hours on Thursdays between five PM and six PM. As it is the last week before his annual sabbatical, this Thursday is his last available until the beginning of the next semester. His office is located at Eight-Thirteen Hanton Hall. Have a good day."

The message gave Cam a small glimmer of hope that he might be able to unravel the fabric of riddles covering his body and uncover the source of the ink. Before he had a chance to pull the phone from his ear, he felt a tap on the back. He turned around and found Syn standing behind him. "Hey stranger."

"Hey you."

Syn sat down next to him. "You know what? I actually had fun with you the other night. We have to do it again sometime soon."

"Sure, why not."

"Well… I was checking the schedule and we both have this Thursday off. I know a cool restaurant you can take me to. It's called Saka Dagamis. They do some awesome Indian fusion. Then after dinner we can get a couple cocktails and see where the night takes us."

Cam began to fidget with his phone. "Umm… this Thursday?"

Syn's smile fell off her face. "If you don't want to, just tell me. I'm a big girl."

He spun the phone around in his palm a few times. "Of course I want to."

"Good. You can pick me up out front at six." Syn licked his cheek and skipped away.

Cam looked down at his phone, turned it off, and returned it to the darkness of his pocket.

Hidden beneath the cover of a sweatsuit and its hood, Cam entered the gym and began to search for his teammates. He found them practicing on a court on the opposite side of the building. None of them recognized the approaching hooded stranger. "Hey guys! Sorry I'm late." They did recognize the voice coming from the shadowed mouth.

"We didn't think you were coming. We were sure you'd flake on us this season." R. C. launched the ball towards the hoop.

"What the fuck you talking about, of course I'm gonna be here. I want to make it to the finals. We got so damn close last time." Cam started to do a little light stretching.

Boinkman grabbed the rebound of R. C.'s missed shot and passed it to Lurch. "Maybe if Lurch can learn to shoot something besides layups, we might have a chance."

Hearing the criticism of his shooting abilities, Lurch halted his drive to the basket and attempted a jump shot. It went in, after a couple lucky bounces off the rim. "What the fuck? I carried this team last season."

Lambda grabbed the ball. "No Lurch, you're

thinking of the ball. You have to bounce it sometimes, it's called dribbling."

Old Bob finished the last of his sprints across the court and was breathing and sweating heavily. "Cam, you should get warmed up. We start playing in fifteen minutes."

"Yeah OK." Cam had been dreading this moment for some time, but he wanted to just get it over with, so he disrobed and revealed to his teammates the black-ink infection covering his body and the radical new haircut. They all stopped what they were doing and stared, speechless. Cam knew he had to say something to acknowledge the elaborately embellished elephant in the room or it would be one hell of an uncomfortable game. "I know, I know. I look a little different than the last time you guys saw me, but I can ball just the same and that's all that matters here. Let's just leave it at that, alright?" He grabbed a ball and began to dribble towards the basket.

R. C. picked up the other ball and took a shot. "Mr. T is right, we're here to play and not to judge. We have to show no pity and go out there and kick those fools' asses."

The team chuckled; even Cam cracked a smile. At least he was only making fun of the haircut, one of the only things on his body he still had control of. The team warm-up resumed and when Boinkman had a chance he approached Cam, reached up, and put his hand on his shoulder. "What happened man? Why did you do this to yourself?"

"I didn't do anything Boinker. This is who I am now."

Lambda ran up to them. "Come on guys, the game's about to start."

The game was a very one-sided affair. The opposing team, a bunch of IT guys calling themselves the Mega Bytes, never had a chance. Cam was playing basketball on an entirely new level. He didn't see the other team as a group of men who just wanted to get out and have a little fun and who were more suited to playing basketball sitting on a couch plugged in to a game console. He saw them only as obstacles in his way to a victory achieved by controlling the skill, strength, and stamina of his body. By the second half the outcome was already a given, but Cam continued to play as if it were the final minutes of a championship game—he never let up. Towards the end, his own teammates were exhausted trying to keep up with him. They also felt bad for the other team, who had lost the heart to finish the game.

R. C. thought he saw tears in the eyes of some of the IT guys as they left the gym. "That wasn't even fair. It's nice to win, but making nerds cry wasn't as fun as I remember it back in junior high. Damn Cam, you really came to play didn't you? That new hairstyle must give you some crazyass aerodynamics. I've never seen you move so fast."

"Those geeks had some really rancid B.O., I was just trying to keep away from the stench. I guess deodorant technology isn't on their radar. Maybe they'll invent an app for that." Cam downplayed his performance, but he was proud of it. Proud of the way he took control of his body and used it to achieve an overwhelming victory.

"Great game, Cam. Keep it up." Stripped of all his basketball gear, Old Bob was the epitome of ordinary. He could have easily blended into any crowd in the country.

Cam's elation at winning became overshadowed by his envy for the ordinariness Old Bob effortlessly possessed. Ordinary was an adjective he would've taken offense to if anyone had used it to describe him in his pre-tattooed life. Being just another face in the crowd was something he now fantasized about.

On their first official date, Cam sat across from Syn at a small table in the center of the Indian fusion restaurant Saka Dagamis. Cam would've preferred a table in a dimly lit corner, but Syn specifically requested to be seated somewhere in the center of the dining room. Many of the diners stole glances in their direction as they were seated and continued to do so as they waited for their food. Cam was getting used to the covert glimpses and secret stares he got whenever he was out in public, but being the literal center of attention in a large room full of people was making him uncomfortable.

Syn noticed the stealth spectators were causing Cam to squirm in his seat and to rearrange his silverware over and over again. "Ignore those lame losers, they're just jealous. They wish they had the balls to express themselves like we do. The world is full of boring people with big dreams. Instead of being who they truly are, they all conform to what they think other people want them to be. And these other people are conforming to what the conformists think they should be. So in the end we have nothing but a herd of sheep following each other around in a giant circle."

Cam stopped messing with the silverware. "I guess

you're right. I'm just sick of being judged by people who don't know who I am and where I'm coming from."

Syn raised her voice slightly. "You know what? Fuck 'em, fuck 'em all. You know who *you* are, that's all that matters."

Cam picked up his wine glass. "I'll drink to that." They clinked their glasses together and took big sips of the house wine.

The Indian fusion food arrived right away. Cam had eaten de-fused Indian food many times and wasn't able to see any difference in the food which was brought to them. He didn't want to seem ignorant, so he didn't ask Syn about the food. Instead he brought up the subject that most girls in his experience liked to talk about, themselves. "You've been working at the Station since it opened, haven't you?"

She finished chewing as she answered. "Yeah… almost two years now, I think."

"Was it busier back then? I know I've only worked there for a little while now, but it seems like we don't get a whole lotta business. Most people don't really buy CDs and DVDs anymore, so how does Burn afford to stay open?"

"Here's the thing about Burn… and before I tell you, remember that this is kind of inside shit so don't go spreading it around." Syn took a large gulp of her wine. "OK, so Burn started working in record shops when he was a teenager. Back when record shops just sold records. I guess he got caught up in the lifestyle of being surrounded by music and always getting to hang around with cool people like us, because he ended up spending his whole life working for a certain record store chain. You know the one—that masterpiece of American cinema *Empire Records* was supposed to be based on it. As you know, that chain and most every other chain that sold music went out of business, leaving Burn with nowhere to go. Luckily for him, one of his relatives died, I think it was his aunt or something, and left him an assload of money. He used that money on the one thing he knew and loved and opened the Station in the same exact building he used to work in. On opening day he told all of us that as long as he's around, the Station will be around. Now all of us have somewhere to go and we all lived happily ever after, the end."

Cam had finished more than half of his meal and still couldn't figure out what the Indians fused his food with. He thought he tasted raisins in his curry, but he didn't know if that was normal or not. "What's with the train station theme?"

"I don't know, I never asked. Maybe Burn is one of those guys who gets off playing with trains in his basement. Anyway, don't you think it's a beautiful story? He was able to resurrect his one true love from the dead."

"Yup, and we get to work in the corpse of his zombie wife."

Cam's response didn't go over well with Syn. "Why are you such a dick?"

"You know you love it." Cam knew she knew he knew she liked bad boys. Good boys were boring.

"All you boys are the same. Sometimes I don't know why I even bother." She had a hard time keeping the pissed-off look on her face.

"All the same huh? Look at me, I couldn't be more different."

"Under the hair and all that ink, you're still just a boy."

Her façade cracked and a smile appeared. "But I guess I am a sucker for you *different* boys." She grabbed his forearm and began to trace one of the symbols on his skin. "I've been meaning to ask you about your tats. I've never really seen a collection of work like yours. What does all this stuff mean?"

Cam had been expecting the question for a while now. He was surprised it took her so long to ask. Maybe it was taboo in her world to ask about someone's tattoos before you got to know them. A little on-the-spot improvisation wasn't going to cut it with the amount of tattoos he had these days. After reading a couple articles on the Internet he came up with a plausible and somewhat charming story to explain why his skin was covered in strange writing and symbols.

"It's kind of a long story, but I'll do my best to explain it." Cam finished the last of his wine. "I always assumed everyone around the world had the same definition of love as we do here in this country, but while I was researching one of my first tattoos, the Chinese character for love, I discovered that the Chinese see love a little different than us. It's such a serious and sacred thing to them that the word is never used lightly, only when they truly mean it. On the other hand, in this country we love on tons of different levels. We say we love our car, a song we heard on the radio, or a cheeseburger we had for lunch. I had a co-worker who would always tell me how much she loved her pink pen. She would also always tell me how much she loved her husband. From an outsider's point of view it sounds like this lady has as much feeling for a cheap piece of plastic as she does for the most important person in her life. This got me obsessed with finding out how other cultures around the world define love. I learned some see it as a sense of connection, some see it as an unbreakable bond, and others as friendship. Instead of getting tats of the common words and symbols for these ideas of love, I wanted to find the most obscure ones I could. Some of the words and symbols I have on me are ancient and some are still used by native tribes throughout the world. I do all this with the help of a friend of a friend, Professor Valeska. He's a linguist and has become almost as addicted to this project as I have. Whenever he discovers a new word or symbol representing love, he emails it to me. Then when I have the money and time, I get inked. In Professor Valeska's last email he told me about this recently discovered little tribe in the rainforests of Brazil who see the bird as a symbol of loyalty and loyalty to this tribe is their idea of love. Their bird symbol on the back of my neck is my newest addition. So in a way, by getting all these tattoos, I'm transforming myself into a being of pure love."

The story worked exactly the way it was supposed to—Syn melted. "That is one of the sweetest things I've ever heard. I guess you really are different than other boys." She leaned over the table, pulled Cam toward her by his shirt, and kissed him hard. She then whispered in his ear, "Maybe we could skip the cocktails tonight and go back to my place. You can show me some more of your love."

When Cam returned home he expected to see T comatose in his usual spot on the couch next to his girlfriend.

It surprised him to see T still conscious. "Shouldn't you be passed out by now?"

"No, I'm all into this show about psychic warfare during the Cold War. Those fucking Russians tried all kinds of crazy shit. So, how did it go with that cybertronic Strawberry Shortcake chick? Did she let you install your hardware?"

Cam half smiled and raised his eyebrows. "Maybe."

T began loading his girlfriend. "Nice. Did she strap you to a leather cross and beat you with cold spaghetti?"

"What the hell? I think you need to chill out watching all that kinky shit online and watch some normal porn once in a while. I didn't need to do any weird stuff with her. Underneath all that crap she wears, she's just a chick and a good old-fashioned drilling works every time. And a long night of that can really tire a guy out, so I'm going to bed. See ya."

A large cloud of smoke containing the words 'good night' was released from T's mouth.

Cam got in bed and began to go over the night in his head. Despite what he said to T, he was actually disappointed Syn didn't have any strange sexual habits and once she was out of all her PVC and leather, her body didn't impress him much either. Her tight outfit had hugged her in all the right places, but without it her tits were a bit droopy, her waist's circumference increased, and her ass flattened. Cam then imagined her without the piercings, tattoos, makeup, and outrageous hairstyle and realized Syn was completely average. Their night of sex confirmed this. Cam would never complain about getting laid and the sex wasn't bad, but it wasn't anything special either, it was just average. She preferred missionary and liked it gentle and slow. She said, "Animals do it from behind fast and hard. I'm not an animal." After a relatively short time her orgasm arrived with a few soft moans. She then waited patiently until Cam finished. He hoped the next time would be better.

He checked his phone to see if she called or messaged him. He wanted to know her opinion of their night together. No calls or messages from her, but there was a message from his brother:

Hey Cam,

What the hell is going on out there? Mom hasn't heard from you for months and then I see your new profile pic. At first I thought I was looking at the wrong person's profile page, but with a closer look it was a barely recognizable you in the photo. I know it's your life and body to do with what you want, but why go to that extreme? Did you hate your old self so much? I can completely understand wanting to get away from yourself. Hell, I spent most of my adult life trying that, living in all those different states and different countries. I know it's a cliché, but no matter how far you go you can't run away from who you are. Trust me. I'm learning to accept who I am and now that this baby is coming, the running has to stop. I refuse to do what Dad did to us. Please, you have to let me know what's happening. Also give Mom a call, she's very worried about you.

Blocko

Cam covered his eyes; he didn't want to see the screen anymore. It was still there, glowing after he uncovered them. He reread the message and slammed his fist onto the bed. "Fuck 'em."

He immediately wrote his response:

Hey,

You were right about one thing, it's my life to do with what I want. I'm not running from anything. I'm into some new stuff these days and the way I look now is just part of my new lifestyle. I'm having a great time, so just because you feel trapped, don't piss on my parade. And by the way, you did do what Dad did. You took off the first chance you got. You left me alone here with Mom and that boytoy piece of shit second husband of hers. You say I haven't seen her for months and she's worried. You haven't seen her for years. How do you think that makes her feel? I got to go. Later.

Cam

He knew something like this would happen after changing his profile picture, but he had no choice, he had to change it. Syn would eventually ask him for a friend request and when she did, he couldn't have a pre-tattooed picture of himself on his page. It wouldn't match up with the stories he created about himself, but the new picture didn't match up with anything from the life of the guy in the previous picture. All the friends and family of the guy in the previous picture were going to want to know what happened to him. Cam wished he knew the answer.

It was the dreaded moment all perpetrators and victims of bad break-ups hope will never happen, a surprise encounter with the ex. In Cam's case it was doubly worse—he had an unexplained drastically different appearance and he was standing behind the counter of a record store ringing up customers, a huge step backward from his former career in finance. Crazzee happened to be the next customer in line. Cam didn't see her until she put her purchases on the counter. All the blood rushed to his head at the shock of seeing her standing in front of him. He tried to keep it casual. "Hey, how's it going? I didn't expect to see you here."

Crazzee was having a difficult time keeping her emotions in check. "You know I shop here sometimes."

Cam began to scan her purchases. "So you just came in to do some shopping and not to see me."

A piece of anger escaped Crazzee's tight hold. "OK, so I saw your new profile pic and I had to come and see if you really looked like that in person. My god Cam, did I ever know the real you? You used to like always talk shit about people who look like you do now."

Cam grabbed a bag and put her purchases inside. "What can I say, people change. That'll be thirty-one sixty-two."

She handed him her credit card. "People don't change that fast. Who was I in love with all that time?"

He swiped the card and set it on the counter. "I don't know."

Crazzee grabbed the card and her bag of purchases. "Me either." She rushed out of the store.

Cam hadn't noticed Syn watching the encounter with Crazzee. She was standing too far away to hear what was said, but she could see Cam obviously had some history with the girl. She rushed over to him and interrupted the transaction taking place between him and the current customer at the counter. "Who was that boring-looking girl?!"

Cam tried to keep his attention on the customer. "Nobody."

Syn didn't like being ignored. She took the CD he was scanning and slammed it down on the counter. It surprised both Cam and his customer. "She sure seemed like she knew you, so who is she?"

"Just somebody I knew a long time ago." Cam was now looking at Syn. The customer eyed the CD on the counter, unsure whether to wait for Cam to finish the transaction or leave and try to buy it another day.

"I hope so. If you want to be with me, then you're with me. I don't want you flirting with every skanky girl that comes into the store. OK?!"

"Yeah OK." Cam was flattered by her jealousy and at the same time it scared him that it had reared its ugly head so soon.

"Good." She grabbed his crotch. "Just remember to keep it in your pants bucko. Now get back to work." She let go of his jewels and flicked the CD across the counter to the customer, freeing him from limbo. He quickly paid and scampered away with his prize, leaving Cam alone with his thoughts.

Ras, who had also apparently been watching the exchange, approached the counter. "Female problems?"

Cam looked up. "No Ras, I'm not having my period. It's not that time of the month yet, but thanks for asking."

"I was alluding to the altercation with Syn over the flaxen-haired beauty with whom you were previously conversing."

"Yeah I know. Jesus, I should know by now that chicks are chicks no matter what they look like, what they're into, or where they're from. I could really use a cold refreshing beverage right about now. Do you want to stop somewhere after work and get a drink?"

It couldn't be seen behind all the hair, but Ras's face lit up. "A post-work libation sounds most pleasing."

"Getting shitfaced does sound pleasing, doesn't it?"

Ras was brought to one of Cam's old hangouts, a hip bar not too far from the offices of Reboot Financial. Cam wanted to go somewhere familiar to quench his thirst and was annoyed when they walked in and turned every head. They were both clearly out of place in a place where adhering to the latest trends was the unofficial dress code. Thirst overrode his irritation and they both sat down. Cam had mainly chosen the place on the strength of their drinks and his Caucasian didn't disappoint. For Ras any bar would've been fine as he only ever drank straight vodka. Midway through his third, his discomfort eased slightly and after a couple strong Caucasians, Cam also had mellowed somewhat, but just below the surface his anger was bubbling.

He hated always being reminded of his new status in the world as a self-made freak.

Their conversation of course steered towards women, a subject on which Ras had strong opinions, but little real-world experience. "I must confess something to you, Cam. The appeal of the true occupation of my namesake, of monk, has been growing substantially the older I become. I feel in our modern age, the biological imperative of pairing off and engaging in coitus is a poor return on investment. Yes, yes, I know it is necessary to propagate our species, but according to current population figures we have had a plethora of success in this enterprise, so it is obvious men the world over are not concerned with operating at a loss. If you calculate the time, labor, and funds men invest in procuring opportunities to attract and interact with the opposite sex, I speculate the totals would be of a far greater proportion than all of their other pursuits combined."

Even if Cam didn't always fully understand what Ras was saying, he could usually get the gist. "You're right Ras. Guys spend most all of their time and energy trying to get laid and once we do, then what? Does it make us happy? Yeah, maybe for a little while until we get tired of the person we're with and want someone else. It's a vicious circle man. If we spent all that wasted energy on something productive, imagine what we could do. Shit, when I look back on my life, most everything I've ever done was to get girls. Even playing basketball, the thing I love doing the most, well the second most, I started doing just to impress a certain chick in one of my classes."

"Was the ploy successful?"

Cam took a large sip of his beverage. "You know what?

Once I joined the team I realized I could pull way hotter chicks than her and I did. But look where all that pussy has gotten me, nowhere. I'm making minimum wage while all those dorks in my class who never got laid are probably doing great things and making bank."

"Most likely you would have perceived me as one of these purported dorks. Today you and I find ourselves in the same position."

Cam gave him a pat on the back. "You're probably just a late bloomer. With that big brain of yours, you'll be a multi-millionaire bigshot someday and I'll be the old weirdo cleaning the toilets of your luxury offices."

Ras was embarrassed by the compliment. "The future is an enigma filled with unforeseen mutations. Speculation is futile."

"You're telling me." Cam raised his glass. "Let's drink to the mysteries of the future." Their glasses slammed into each other and produced a sound loud enough to cause some of the nearby patrons to look over. The glances lingered long enough to become stares. Cam's anger rose to the surface. "What're looking at?! You enjoying the show?!" The patrons quickly looked away.

Ras put his arm around him and his surprisingly strong grip kept Cam from getting up. "Calm yourself, my friend."

Cam took a few deep breathes and a large inhale of alcohol. "OK, OK… sorry about that. I'm just so sick of being stared at like I'm a friggin' sideshow attraction."

"Forgive me for enquiring, but why then have you manipulated your appearance to such an extreme degree? You must have been aware the artistic engineering of your epidermis would result in continual observation and scrutiny by the excess of simple-minded peons this tavern and the world overflow with."

His head in his hands, Cam mumbled, "I didn't do this to myself."

Ras moved a little closer. "I feel I didn't hear you correctly. Are you attempting to convey you didn't construct the outward aspect which the world beholds?"

"Never mind, forget it. I'm just a little buzzed." Cam picked up his glass and tried to take another refreshing drink, but all he received was a puddle of melted ice.

"No, pray continue. I desire to hear how this crowded canvas of skin came into being."

"I honestly don't know. I woke up like this." His glass was empty, but Cam instinctively took a drink from it anyway.

Ras created his own interpretation of Cam's answer. "You awoke from the slumber of mediocrity, shed the skin of conformity, and emerged transformed into the being which had always dwelled inside of you."

"No, I literally woke up this way. I get up most every morning and find new tattoos on my body. I don't know where they come from or what they mean. It doesn't make any sense. The few people I've told don't believe me and I wouldn't believe it either if it weren't happening to me. I keep hoping this is all a bad dream and I'll wake up my normal self again." Cam spun his glass on the table in the off chance the motion would somehow replenish the alcohol it now lacked.

"Very intriguing indeed." Ras finished the last of his vodka.

Cam saw the wheels spinning in Ras's head; he

imagined them as the dusty inner workings of an ancient clock. "And no I'm not a drug addict and I don't have multiple personalities or anything like that."

"Those explanations came to mind, but I have a more unconventional theory."

"Oh yeah? I got to hear this, as long as it doesn't involve aliens. I don't want you telling me that my body is some kind of intergalactic message board."

Ras looked Cam in the eyes. "I believe a curse may have been placed upon you."

Cam, expecting a different kind of answer altogether, almost laughed out loud at hearing Ras's theory. "Seriously? So all I need to do is kidnap a beautiful young girl, lock her up in my apartment until she gets Stockholm syndrome—which causes her to see beyond my hideous appearance and fall in love with me. Then this true love will magically change me back into a handsome prince. C'mon dude, stop fucking with me. We both know there's no such thing as true love."

Ras didn't even crack a smile. "I have made extensive studies in the subject of cultural anthropology, with an emphasis on shamanism. Through this I have found abundant evidence of the practice of using spells to do harm or bring misfortune. The methods differ as widely as the cultures which employ them. I likewise know of cultures which procure tattoos as protection against evil or to obtain luck or magical power. Therefore, I believe it is highly plausible that these two practices could be combined. The curse itself could be embedded in the skin."

This time a few chuckles did escape Cam's gaping mouth. "Man Ras, I think you've had a little too much to drink. You're talking some pretty wild shit. If that were true, why would anyone go through the trouble of putting a curse on me? I've never insulted any old gypsy women or disturbed ancient burial grounds. I'm just a regular guy who never did anything to hurt anyone. I'm a good person, this shouldn't be happening to me."

"Brief me on the tattoos' inception and together we can attempt to disentangle this conundrum." Ras almost looked excited.

"During a drunken night in Vegas me and my buddy got tattoos, that's it. After that first one, more started appearing until I looked like this."

"May I please view the original tattoo?"

A boot thudded down on the edge of Ras's seat. Cam unlaced it, took it off, and pulled down his sock, exposing his first tattoo. Ras produced a silver-handled magnifying glass from one of his many coat pockets and closely examined the design.

"Well?"

"An intricate and lovely design. How did you come about selecting this specific motif to place on your body?"

Cam returned his foot to the boot. "I guess I picked it out from one of the books they had on the counter there. I told you I was drunk, I don't remember everything that happened that night."

Ras leaned back in his chair. "I advise returning to this establishment to discover the origin of the design and the identity of the artist. The most expedient process of curse reversal is to locate the originator and have them remove it. You may not have been purposely cursed. You may have merely chosen an ill-fated tattoo."

"I guess it can't hurt to go back and check it out."

A late-model silver Toyota Camry hurtled through a featureless desert, trying its hardest to get through the huge waste of time and space between Orange County and Las Vegas as fast as possible. It sped by big-rig trucks piloted by zombie drivers caught perpetually between the world of the conscious and unconscious, minivans full of families attempting to bond by traveling to a far-off location and forcing themselves into small hotel rooms, and cars full of paycheck slaves anxious to lose their money and memory.

Cam and T fell into the last group; at least it was what Cam wanted T to think. "Man, I really needed to get out of town for a little while."

"I know, you told me like eight times already." T took a hit off the joint he was holding and passed it over to Cam. "Can you even afford this trip with the shit money you're making at that record store? Remember you still have to pay your part of the rent. I'm not going to cover your ass because you don't want to get a real job."

Cam exhaled and passed the joint back to T. "Don't worry, I still have some savings left and you never know, maybe I'll hit another jackpot."

"That'd be cool, but the odds of that happening are pretty fucking slim." T took another large hit, but didn't pass it. "Oh! I forgot to tell you, a certain someone at the office was asking about you."

Cam looked over in expectation of receiving the joint,

but it didn't come. "Could it have been a certain annoying older female?"

"Wow, how'd you guess? She saw your profile pic and thought you looked sexier than ever. She was asking me how you were doing and where you were working now." T took another large hit and finally passed it over.

"I pray to Jesus you didn't tell her where I'm working. That's just what I need, a goddamn stalker." Cam momentarily freed a hand from the wheel to take a deep and deserved hit. He passed what was left of the joint back to T. "I knew I should've canceled that account. Everybody and their mother's been up my ass since I posted that fucking picture. I only did it so that chick Syn would think I always looked like this."

T took one last hit and threw the roach out the window. It bounced off the windshield of a car behind them which brought its driver out of his highway hypnotic state and was alerted to the fact he forgot to change the station and had been actually listening to country music for the last thirty miles. He was lucky he turned it off when he did; another twenty miles or so and his ears could've been permanently traumatized. "Don't worry, I told the Coug you were working as a janitor at some high school. She's not allowed within a hundred feet of any high school in the county, so she can't check out the story. And by the way, I don't think posting a picture of yourself is going to convince that chick you always looked like this. I doubt she thinks you came out of your mom's vajayjay with a bad haircut and covered in lame tattoos. Speaking of your mother, has she seen the famous pic yet?"

"I doubt it. She doesn't have time for all that

social-networking nonsense. I'll go see her eventually. I'm just waiting for the right moment."

T began to roll a fresh joint. "What, until you dye your mohawk green and cover your face in piercings?"

"I was thinking I'd go see her after Blocko's kid was born. She'll be in a good mood then." Cam looked over impatiently at the joint in progress.

"No matter how good a mood she's in, she's still going to shit a brick when she sees how fucked-up her son looks."

"Yeah whatever. I don't want to talk about it now, OK? This is supposed to be a trip to get away from that crap." Cam rolled down his window, leaned his body out as far as it would go, and shouted, "VEGAS BABY!"

Wind from the rolled-down window upset the flakes of marijuana of T's joint in progress, forcing him to start over. "God I hate you."

"Where in the hell are we going?" T didn't recognize the part of Vegas Cam's Camry was heading into. It was an area northeast of the Strip, an area without any flashy hotel/casinos, a no man's land. The guys had arrived during the late afternoon and caught the city before it applied its makeup of darkness and dazzling lights. Without it Las Vegas was quite unattractive, especially here. The blinding sunshine exposed cracks in the streets' poorly laid asphalt, cigarette butts blown against the curbs waited in piles for rain to wash them into the sewers, and people sizzled while waiting at bus stops adorned with ads for prostitution and legal advice. T watched as they passed strip malls and fast food restaurants and then passed more strip malls and fast food restaurants. "You can't be lost dude. Our hotel has the tallest tower in the city. I can fucking see it. Look, it's right over there."

Driving at a senior citizen speed, Cam intently scanned the surroundings. "I want to see something."

"Well if you want to see a wide selection of nail salons and liquor stores, you're in luck."

"I'm looking for that tattoo shop where we got inked," Cam confessed.

"I think you have more than enough tattoos. Or are you such an ink junkie that you need a fix right now?"

"No, I need to find the place where all this shit started. Maybe then I can figure out what the hell's going on."

T's arms flew into the air. "Jesus Christ dude! You dragged me all the way to Vegas for some goddamn wild goose chase? How do you expect to find that place? We were both trashed that night and taken there in a taxi. Hell, you told me you barely even remember getting the tattoo."

"I do remember that when we left the shop I saw a giant pizza sign in the parking lot. It made me hungry for pizza, but of course the place was closed. Then I saw a Del Taco across the street and got me some Macho Nachos instead."

"Yeah, I remember your drunk ass tried to walk through the drive-thru, but they wouldn't serve you on foot so we had to call a taxi to drive us through. Those were some expensive nachos and I don't think the driver appreciated the fact you gave him a chicken soft taco as a tip."

Cam continued his search. "I just need to find that giant pizza sign and a Del Taco. C'mon, help me out, you were there too. The faster we get this shit done, the faster we can hit the casinos."

T took a quick glance around. "Try turning right at the next light."

A few blocks after the right turn a giant pizza came into view. Cam looked on the other side of the road. "Look, there's a Del Taco right across the street. Nice call man."

T shrugged. "I just want to get this over with."

Sandwiched between the heat of the sun coming down on them from above and the heat coming up from the asphalt of the parking lot, they walked towards the strip mall where the tattoo shop was supposed to be. Cam noticed something. "Hey that pet store is ringing some bells. I thought it was strange that a tattoo shop would be next to a pet store and I think I said something like, 'Do the dogs get discounts on their tattoos?'"

"Yeah that was hilarious. I remember my side literally splitting open and my guts gushing out onto the ground."

Instead of finding the tattoo shop he thought would have the answer to all his problems, he found an empty shell. Cam approached one of the windows for a closer look. All he could see inside was a bare concrete floor covered in dust. "No no no. It was here, it had to be. FUCK!" He turned to T who just shrugged again. Cam assumed someone had to know what'd happened to the tattoo parlor.

He tried the pet store, but he only managed to scare the young girl behind the counter. "I've only been here like a few months or something. That place next door has like always been empty." Cam slammed his hands down on the counter, which caused a chain reaction of frightened barking and increased the young girl's fear. To show her he wasn't just there to terrorize random pet shop girls he needed to buy something, so he grabbed some dog hairstyling gel.

"Have a purrific day sir." The girl's voice was still a bit shaky as she gave Cam the farewell statement she was required to give all departing customers.

On the other side of the empty shell was a nail salon. Cam walked in hoping someone would know something about the missing tattoo parlor. He was immediately engulfed in an overwhelming cloud of noxious fumes, which surprisingly seemed to have no effect on the Vietnamese women working inside or the customers receiving manis and pedis. He had to carefully ration his breath to prevent himself from passing out. "Excuse me! Does anyone know what happened to the tattoo shop that used to be next door?"

The woman nearest the entrance answered, "No tattoo here, only nails."

Cam didn't know how much longer he could survive in the toxic atmosphere. "No, I said do you know what happened to the tattoo shop that used to be next door?"

Another woman answered this time. "No tattoo here, you have tattoo enough. Go way, you scare customers."

Cam rushed back outside and took a big refreshing breath of stifling-hot polluted air. T was standing there waiting. "Now what Sherlock?"

"I need a drink." At the other end of the strip mall Cam saw a blacked-out glass door. Above it read 'The Dungeon Bar and Lounge'. "Let's go to that bar over there."

"Can't we wait until we get to the casino? That place looks like a shithole." T was already starting to sweat after wasting eleven minutes of his life in a sweltering parking lot waiting for Cam to find the elusive tattoo shop.

"I don't care. I need a drink now." He started walking away before he finished the second sentence.

T had no choice but to follow. "Shit, I knew I shouldn't've let you drive."

The Dungeon Bar and Lounge lived up to its name, at least the Dungeon and Bar parts. Cam opened the door and what they entered into was near complete darkness. After their eyes adjusted, they found themselves in a narrow space with a long bar on the left and nothing else. The lounge must have been sold to pay for the large collection of skulls and swords that lined the walls and shelves behind and above the bar. Two burly men with oil-stained t-shirts and outdated moustaches were the only other patrons. The heavy metal coming out of the jukebox shoved in the corner was from the same era as their moustaches.

Before they sat down at the far end of the bar, T whispered to Cam, "If you order a Caucasian I'll punch you in the face."

Cam ordered a couple of beers plus a question. "Do you know what happened to the tattoo shop that used to be between the nail salon and the pet store?"

The bartender set the beers down. "No idea, this is my first week here."

T heard a long sigh escape from Cam's mouth. "What the hell were you expecting to find?"

"I don't know. Something. Some kind of answer." Cam took a swig of his quality American beer.

"Dude, all the answers are in here." T tapped Cam's skull a few times. "You know that. You got to get rid of this idea that there's this ginormous conspiracy against you. Let's finish these beers and get the hell out of here. I came here to have a good time, not to go on a magical tattoo mystery tour."

While T worked on getting his beer into his belly as fast as possible, Cam only stared at the contents remaining in his glass. He wasn't thirsty anymore; he was already full of nagging suspicion. His eyes turned towards T and became transfixed on his right shoulder. There was something they needed to see, but a thin layer of cotton stood in their way. Before he knew it, his left hand grabbed T's collar and yanked it down, exposing the upper right part of his back. It was bare. T instinctively knocked Cam's hand away. "What the fuck are you doing?! Do you know how much this shirt cost, asshole?"

"Where is it?"

"Where's what?" T tried to return his shirt to its original state, but he couldn't. The collar was all stretched out.

"You know what. The stupid dollar sign tattoo you got that night."

T continued his efforts to unstretch his collar. "I didn't get a tattoo that night."

The combination of shock and anger caused by T's response rendered Cam speechless. All he could do was mutely stare at T, but his glare wasn't reciprocated. T was more interested in his damaged shirt. The two burlies at the other end of the bar found Cam and T's tussle an entertaining diversion from their usual view of medieval dungeon memorabilia and had been watching them intently. Cam noticed this out of the corner of his eye and regained the power of speech. "Whatta you fags looking at?"

The opening riff of Intoxicated Infant's "Tainted Titties" repeated itself four times and stopped. It did this over and over again until it awoke Cam. His eyes opened to near darkness. A faint yellow glow came from the edges of closed curtains. It was just enough light for Cam to see he was lying fully dressed on a bed in a tastefully decorated hotel room. He looked around for the source of the music. Not finding it, he switched on the lamp next to the bed. For some reason the action caused a dull pain in his hand. He soon discovered why—his hand was swollen and the knuckles skinned. "What the hell?"

The repeating riff started again, it was coming from somewhere near the TV. Cam found the source in the top drawer of the desk. The display on his phone said it was T calling. "Hello." Cam's voice was still groggy.

"You piece of shit. Come pick me up right now." T didn't sound very happy.

"Where are you?"

"I'm in the fucking hospital."

"Why? What happened to you?" The grogginess in his voice had been replaced by genuine concern.

"You know why asshole." T had nothing but anger in his voice.

"No, I have no idea. In fact I'm not even sure where I am right now." While he spoke he searched for and found some hotel stationary. It was the hotel where they had made reservations.

Cam's answer seemed to infuriate T even more. "Your

pussy ass ran out and left me to get my ass kicked by those rednecks. Now come and fucking get me!"

"Oh my God." Cam was shocked by T's appearance. He watched as T carefully and painfully got into the passenger seat of the Camry. His nose was bandaged and he had dark rings under his eyes. Cuts and bruises peppered the rest of his face.

T was having a difficult time getting comfortable and winced as he pulled the seatbelt across his chest. "Yeah, my nose is broken. Plus I got a couple cracked ribs. Thanks a lot fucker. If I could, I'd beat the shit out of you, but I'm so doped up on painkillers right now I can barely see straight. All I want to do is go home."

"I'm so sorry man. I swear I don't remember anything. We were in the bar and the next thing I know I'm waking up in a hotel room."

"Whatever. Your amnesia stories are getting real old. When we get back I want you out of the apartment as soon as possible."

"But I didn't do anything."

"You're right, you didn't. You punched one of those hillbillies in the face and bolted out the door as fast as you could and left me to be beaten to a pulp." T looked ahead as he spoke. It hurt to turn his head towards Cam.

"I promise you…" T didn't let him finish.

"Stop talking. I'm going to take some more of these pills they gave me and I want to be home by the time I regain consciousness. Oh, by the way, you never let me finish what I was saying to you in the bar. I was trying to say I didn't get a *real* tattoo that night, but a temporary one. I wasn't drunk enough to permanently disfigure my body with some lame tattoo." T threw a couple pills in his mouth and closed his eyes. Cam started the car and began the long drive to what used to be his home.

INK PERMANENTLY STAMPED the exact moment Cam arrived to work onto his timecard. Syn sat ignoring and waiting for him at the other end of the hall. He tried to kiss her, but she turned her head away. "How was your little jaunt to Sin City?"

Cam had to be satisfied with a peck on her cheek. "I don't really want to talk about it right now." It was obviously the wrong answer.

"What? Too hungover? Have too much to drink in the champagne room? Or did you get a concussion from being hit in the head with one of those giant plastic tits?"

Cam thought an attempt at humor might diffuse the situation. "Come on, I work *here*. Do you think I could afford to even peek inside the champagne room? If they had a Pabst Blue Ribbon room, then I might've been able to check that out."

It didn't work. "Fuck you, just tell me how many strippers you fingered."

Cam made a zero sign with his damaged hand.

"What happened to your hand? Too much violent bishop-whacking while fantasizing about all those skeezy pole grinders?"

"Actually my roommate and I were in a pretty nasty barfight. He ended up in the hospital." Cam gave the correct answer this time.

"Seriously?"

"Yeah, my roommate's nose was broken and he got a couple of his ribs cracked. I was lucky to get away with only a messed-up hand."

Syn's interest was piqued. "And the other guys?"

"I have no idea. We didn't hang around long enough to find out. The last thing I need is to get my ass thrown in jail."

Syn began to gently caress his hand. "Are you sure nothing's broken?"

"I think it's only bruised. The guy had a hard face." Cam smiled.

"So how did all this shit start?"

"We were in a bar just having a couple beers and minding our own business when these fucking rednecks started giving me a hard time about how I looked, so I snapped. It sucks my buddy got caught up in the whole brouhaha. I feel really shitty about that." Cam's answer had gone from right to perfect.

"That really pisses me off. I'm not a violent person, but I'm proud of you for standing up for yourself." She got up and gave him a hug. "My hero." Her lips became available and she used them to give him a hard kiss.

"Aw, it was nothing." Cam flexed a bicep. "For Cam Man."

Syn finally cracked a smile. "Don't push it." On her way back out onto the sales floor she turned around. "Why don't you use that super strength of yours to take out the trash?"

Collecting and throwing trash bags was difficult without the full use of his right hand, but Cam managed. After he finished, he saw Ras smoking a cigarette in his usual spot against the wall and joined him. Without saying a word, a fresh cigarette was given to Cam and lit. "Thanks." He unconsciously used his swollen right hand to hold the cigarette and the effort caused the hand to tremble.

Ras couldn't help but see this. "I see you have been wounded. May I inquire as to the cause of your injury?"

Cam switched the cigarette to his left hand and reexamined his right hand as he spoke and smoked. "My roommate and I got into a little scuffle with a couple of what you would call ill-educated peasants. I guess they weren't digging my look."

"It is a pity when confrontations turn violent."

"Yeah it sucks and the worst part is my roommate is so pissed off at me for getting him involved that he's kicking me out of the apartment. With the shit money I make here it's gonna be hard finding a new place to live." Smoking with the left hand felt very awkward and without consciously realizing it, Cam found the cigarette back in his right hand.

Ras took a long ponderous drag off his cigarette and exhaled an idea. "If I could, I would like to propose a provisional solution to your quandary. My current residence contains a modicum of extraneous space, which you are welcome to inhabit. The only fee you would incur is your portion of the utilities."

Cam's face lightened as a burden fell off his shoulders. "That would be awesome. But are you sure about this? I'm not leading the most stable life at the moment."

"Trouble burdens us all at one time or another. Giving my assistance to shoulder this weight is my duty as a fellow castaway drifting on the seas of oblivion."

"This is really cool of you, thanks man." Cam dropped his cigarette and stamped it out. "Oh, I took your advice and went back to check out the place where I got the first tattoo."

Ras flicked his cigarette butt towards the dumpster. "Did you unearth any truths?"

"No, because the place wasn't there. All I found was an empty building. It was like it never existed."

"Intriguing." Ras did the obvious and stroked his beard.

The beard stroke gave Cam the impression some sagely advice would soon follow. "So now what do I do?"

"Little more *can* be done. You must abide by the outcome the fates have chosen for you." Ras gave him a consolatory pat on the back.

"Well that sucks."

A black backpack decorated with shiny metal spikes and covered in obscure band patches sat at Cam's feet. It was left in his care while Syn tried on some new outfits. She didn't seem to be in any kind of hurry. By Cam's calculations he'd been waiting too long. Browsing the store's selection of retro-toys, ironic action figures, and clothing covered in images taken from the cartoons and video games of his childhood only managed to kill about fifteen minutes. Sitting on a tiny black pleather stool playing with his phone became boring after another fifteen minutes. His back was starting to get sore from sitting so long hunched over on the tiny seat, so he stood up and stretched. Syn's dressing room door was still closed and looking down he could see her feet pirouetting in tiny circles. He turned and peered through the glass wall of the store, which faced out onto a busy outdoor mall. Crowds of shoppers walked slowly in both directions laden with heavy bags of clothing that would soon find their way to the backs of closets never to be seen again and electronics that were obsolete minutes after their purchase.

Among this throng of consumers, Cam saw a man in black with long black hair. He recognized him as Ras. Ras stopped in front of the ice cream shop across the way and began conversing with another man. The other man looked familiar, but it was difficult to see his face as his ballcap was low and he was wearing sunglasses. Something about his cocky stance and the forced casualness of his brand-new sporty attire, which would never be used for any sort of athletic purpose, was ringing a bell in Cam's head. He took a closer look and for a brief moment the familiar man turned his head and the unmistakable beat-up face of T came into view. "What the fuck?"

Cam immediately headed for the door, leaving Syn's bag behind. No one would want to steal a bag that looked like it contained all the worldly possessions of a homeless teenager. Before he reached the door, Syn emerged from the dressing room wearing a latex body suit that transformed her body into a shape only intensive exercise and/or plastic surgery could achieve. "What do you think?" She put her arms up and turned around.

Cam wasn't going anywhere now. "Very fuckin' sexy."

Syn admired herself in the full-length mirror on the wall. "It is, isn't it?"

Cam turned back to the glass wall and looked outside, but Ras and T were gone. His eyes readjusted and he saw a vaguely familiar reflection in the glass staring back at him.

Syn noticed Cam wasn't looking in the correct location. "Hey! Who're you looking at? Keep your eyes on the prize buster, me!"

"Yeah OK. I just thought I saw someone I knew."

When he opened the door of what would soon be his former home, Cam was met by the usual spicy skunk scent his brain associated with a temporary detachment from reality. On the couch under a haze of smoke, he saw T watching TV. T's eyes didn't leave the screen. "You find a new place to live yet?"

Cam's hope of T's forgiveness or at least some

marijuana-induced forgetfulness had completely dissipated. "I think so."

"Good. I need to start looking for someone to rent that room. I can't afford this place on my own for long." T grabbed the nearly empty plastic bag of bright green foliage off the table in front of him. "I'm gonna need this month's rent before you leave." He put a large pinch of greenery into the glass bowl of his tubular girlfriend.

"How about you just keep all my furniture and shit instead, then you can charge more for a furnished room."

"Who's going to pay extra rent to sleep on a used bed with a stained discount mattress in a room filled with cheap IKEA garbage? I want all your crap out of here along with you. I'm tired of your face." T took a long deep hit from his bong.

The exhale of smoke drifted into Cam's nose and he knew this was now the closest he'd ever get to sharing T's girlfriend.

T must've noticed the longing in his eyes. "Stop looking at my girlfriend. She's off limits; not like that's ever stopped that dirty dick of yours before."

"What're you talking about?" Cam knew what he was talking about.

"You know what I'm talking about." T knew he knew.

"C'mon dude, I don't think going on like three dates with a chick makes her your girlfriend."

"Relationships move a lot faster in Asian culture."

"Mia was from Pasadena. And for your information, she's the one who got up on my jock at Young Lewis's Halloween party. It's not my fault she found my Lion-O costume irresistible. Why are you bringing up shit that happened years ago?"

"To remind you of how long I've put up with your prickishness. Leaving me to get my ass kicked was the straw that cracked the camel's ass."

"I did you a favor with Mia. Would you want a girlfriend who after a couple shots of tequila jumps on the first Thundercat cock she sees? I don't think so."

"Do me another favor, give me the rent money and get the fuck out of here."

"Alright, simmer down. I'll get it as soon as I can, OK?" A cold beer wasn't as refreshing as a hit of good bud, but Cam grabbed one anyway. "By the way, were you over at Market Plaza today? I thought I saw you talking to a guy I work with."

T looked directly at Cam. "What business is it of yours what I do?"

The defensiveness was surprising. "I didn't know you knew him, that's all."

"Me and the man in black were taking care of a little b'ness, *OK*?"

Cam knew the difference between business and b'ness. "I thought you always got your shit from the Don."

"Thanks to you I needed some pharmaceutical-strength stuff and the Don said the man in black could hook me up." T dug a plastic sack of blue pills out of his pocket and put one in his mouth. "Give me a sip of that beer. It hurts me just to breathe and these things really help." The sip became a large swig. He then returned the depleted beer. "Why don't you stop bugging me and go start packing? You already made me miss like half of the show. Now I have no idea how that chick got her truck through the blizzard."

A relic from the 1960s, barely clinging to life, leisurely passed large and ornate homes, offending them with its mere presence. Ras's VW Bug sputtered along the quiet tree-lined street while Cam followed closely behind in his own car. Every so often a cloud of black smoke would shoot out of the VW's rusted exhaust pipe and temporarily obscure Cam's view. When the smoke cleared after one such incident, Cam saw the Bug had stopped in front of one of the many affronted stately homes and Ras was exiting his vehicle. Cam pulled up behind him and did the same. "What's up? Did your car break down?"

"No. We have in fact arrived at our destination." Ras made his way up the house's long driveway.

Cam didn't follow. "*This* is your place?"

"It is in actuality the domicile of my parents." Ras continued up the driveway until he reached the wrought-iron gate protecting the rear garden.

Cam hesitantly followed. "So your parents are cool with me staying here?"

Ras unlocked the gate. "My residence is not located within the confines of my parents' home, but behind their abode."

Cam caught a glimpse of a sizeable yard beyond the gate. "Please don't tell me you live in a tent in the backyard."

"It's not as Spartan as that. Come along." Ras led him down a path running along the side of the house. Through the windows, Cam caught glances of the inside of a residence he would classify as a mansion. Just one of the chairs at the formal dining room table was most likely worth more than the resale value of his car and he would've needed to take out a mortgage to afford the table itself. He imagined interior design magazines doing full-length features about the arrangement of the throw pillows on the settee, which was what he assumed they called their couch. At the last window Cam had to stop and take a better look. The room behind the glass had walls covered by books, row upon row of books. He thought only old English barons had personal libraries. Cam didn't understand the point of owning so many books these days when everything was online; they just took up space. Within these walls of books was what appeared to be a miniature museum. Cam was clueless as to the origin of the objects displayed on tables and in glass cases throughout the room, but they looked to be from all over the world. There were wooden masks and dolls, stone figurines, jewelry—some rudimentary and some exquisite—weapons of all sorts, and things which Cam couldn't even begin to put into categories. Things coated with black feathers, things covered in intricately carved designs, and oddly familiar things that instilled a primal fear at their very sight.

Ras noticed Cam's interest in the library. "I have spent many a happy hour perusing the volumes in my father's extensive collection. He is an eminent anthropologist who has published a plethora of works on the subject, a great deal of which are employed as textbooks at universities throughout the world. His opinion of regarding tribal cultures not as primitive, but as cultures on separate paths than our worldwide, so-called modern, mono-culture has become the standard philosophy."

As usual, Cam only got a general idea of what Ras was saying, but he did pick up on the fact that his father was a bigshot famous anthropologist. "Hey, maybe your dad could take a look at my tattoos sometime and tell me what he thinks."

"My father is rarely found here in his home. Most of his work is in the field. I believe he is currently entrenched with the surviving members of a remote tribe of indigenous Australians. He is developing a new interpretation of their idea of Dreamtime."

"OK, and your mom, what does she do? Because dude, this place is pretty high didge." Cam had a hard time imagining a crusty old scientist who hung out in jungles with guys in loincloths making the kind of money needed for the wealth on display here.

"She is in the medical profession." Ras led Cam around the backside of the four-car garage. "Now allow me to present my modest dwelling." A whole new area of the yard came into view. It contained an immense immaculate rectangular swimming pool with attached Jacuzzi and at the far end of the still blue chlorinated water stood a miniature version of the main house. Ras unlocked the cut glass French patio doors and ushered Cam into the poolhouse. Cam was surprised how spacious it was inside. On his left was a decent-sized kitchen with breakfast bar and on the right was a living room with all new furnishings. Ras walked over to the couch. "The settee transforms into a quite comfortable sleeping surface."

Cam had hit another jackpot. "Wow, we've got a whole

Fresh Prince of Bel Air thing going on here. I'm the cool kid from the hood and you're just like Carlton. Except you're white and always wear black, and have a gnarly beard. OK, never mind. Then I guess we're like our own sitcom, *The Monk and the Mohawk*. Will Cam's tattoos ever stop and when will that lovable Ras finally get laid? Stay tuned to find out."

A faint smiled appeared on Ras's face. "I too foresee boisterous happenings in our new living arrangement. The lavatorial facilities are located in the rear and the upper floor contains my bed chamber." He led Cam up a narrow set of stairs into the loft. "Simple, yet efficient."

Ras's version of a monk's cell was a bit more luxurious. He did only have a dresser, bed, and desk in the room, but the dresser was an antique, the double bed obviously wasn't cheap, and on the desk sat a computer which also wasn't cheap, not a by a long shot. The monitor was almost as big as Cam's TV and the equipment attached seemed to be from ten years in the future. Cam felt he was pretty technologically savvy, but the purpose of the six chrome-encased blinking black boxes lining the floor was a mystery. Above the bed hung a large framed reproduction of a political cartoon satirizing Rasputin's power over the Russian royal court.

Back downstairs Cam made himself comfortable on the couch/his new bed. "Thanks again for letting me crash here. I'll try not to cramp your style."

Ras chose one of the barstools next to the breakfast bar for his seat and sat down, his back at the same ninety-degree angle as the legs of the stool. "Do not fret about such matters. My social interactions occur mostly with online acquaintances."

"Yeah and that's kind of sad. We got to try to get you out a little more often. This place is a definite panty-wetter. Once you got a chick back here, it'd be all over with. She wouldn't have a chance." Cam looked out through the patio doors and admired the view of the pool and Jacuzzi.

"This is a fact I realize but have failed to make reality. We have previously conversed on the subject and I conveyed to you then the fact my demeanor often repels the opposite sex." Ras unconsciously stroked his beard.

"But this sweet pad changes the whole game, man. I thought you lived in some shitty studio apartment and slept on an old mattress on the floor, but no, you live here. You have to use this place to your advantage." Cam was still looking outside because he couldn't look at Ras. The sight of a person with his appearance sitting in the epitome of California luxury wasn't something his brain was able to rationalize yet.

"I'm not attracted to the sort of women easily swayed by material offerings." Ras took a good look around at his surroundings. He had the eyes of someone waking up and not remembering where they were.

"Then you're living in the wrong part of the world my friend, but hey, if you don't mind going out with desperate fat chicks, then go for it." Cam felt bad for insulting Ras's last attempt at a date, so he changed his tone. "Listen, I'm not saying you should use this place to find your soul mate, but to just use it to have a little fun once in a while or all the time, whatever."

"I shall take your advice to heart." Ras's demeanor became contemplative.

"Good. Now I'm gonna try and find my swim trunks and make use of these awesome amenities."

Cam executed a flawless post-coital roll off Syn's naked body and found himself staring at the upper part of the cocoon of obscurity which he was encased within. Not a single piece of the ceiling or walls of Syn's bedroom was visible. The fabric of her cocoon consisted of posters from films which were forgotten shortly after their premieres, LaserDisc covers of 1980s Japanese cartoons that only Japan's middle-aged population remembers watching, postcards from places no one would ever go on purpose, and reproductions of artwork from artists who died unknown and in poverty, their deaths not really changing this status.

Syn turned onto her side and looked at Cam. "Why don't we ever go to your place?"

Cam continued to look at the ceiling. "I told you, Ras has this crazy unpredictable schedule. He'll go for days without leaving the house and other times he'll be in and out at all hours of the night. It would be awkward doing it on the couch while he's by himself in his room doing whatever he does on the Internet or even worse, having him pop in on us. It would be like rubbing it in his face that he can't get laid."

"Whatever, it might inspire him to stop jerking it to Internet porn every night and find a real girl, or guy, or something in between, who knows what that dude's into.

You've seen *my* roommates. Do you think those guys ever get any action? It's never stopped me from getting it on in here." She began to trace one of the symbols on Cam's chest with her finger.

He followed her finger's progression. "Maybe you can get Burn to arrange our schedules so we're off when Ras is working. Then we'll be sure of having some uninterrupted fun in the cabana."

"Yeah, that would be real spontaneous, having scheduled sex at your place. Maybe like a bored housewife trying to spice things up in the bedroom, I could buy a copy of the Kama Sutra and plan out which positions we'll use each time."

Under his breath, Cam said something, which upon instant reflection would've been better left internalized. "It's not a bad idea since we use the same two positions every time anyway."

The words weren't far enough under his breath. "What was that? You getting bored fucking me? Then get the fuck out of here, asshole!" She jumped out of her bed, grabbed Cam's clothes off the floor, and threw them full force at him.

Her aim was better than either of them realized. Cam's belt, which was still looped through his jeans, had a large steel buckle. In the pile of clothes that flew towards him, it was this that hit him in the mouth and cut open his lip. He automatically put his hand to the fresh injury and felt the blood leaking out. "Take it easy. I didn't mean it like that."

"Then how did you mean it, huh? You called me boring. That's the worst thing you could ever possibly call me. You have no idea how much work it is to be me." Tears began their slow progression in her eyes. "All of my outfits, hair, and makeup take hours and hours to design and put together and when it's all done, I'm completely unique."

With his bloody mouth, Cam made the necessary apology to salvage the situation. "I'm sorry. It's your uniqueness that first attracted me to you. I've never met or seen anyone like you before."

A few fully formed tears finally escaped from Syn's eyes and fell onto her naked breasts. "That's because there isn't anyone like me. When you see girls with the same look as me it's because they ripped off *my* style. I wasn't one of the sheep in high school and because of it I was completely ignored. Now I can't be ignored."

Cam had to suck on his lip to prevent the blood from dripping on the sheets. "Well you're definitely not boring and it's impossible not to notice you. The thing is I'm getting sick of my own look and the problem with this look is that it's not really changeable, I'm stuck with it. I guess I was projecting the boredom I was feeling with myself onto you. Forgive me, alright?"

"Fine. But you're not boring. I wouldn't be with a boring guy." She wiped the remaining moisture from her eyes.

"OK. Now get back in bed and let's be not boring together."

Syn reluctantly accepted his request and once near his face she saw the damage she'd inflicted. Taking a closer look at his lip, she felt a kind of pride at the power she had to cause Cam's blood to flow. Some of his blood was transferred to her lips during their make-up kiss and she enjoyed its exotic flavor.

Nothing but a blurry mass was all Cam could see after he stepped out of the poolhouse's shower and looked into the mirror. He dreaded the moment when he would have to wipe the steam off the glass and see himself come into clear focus. He thought the change of location would stop or at least slow the progress of the encroaching tattoos, but they continued to appear at the same rate. Taking his time to dry himself only put off the inevitable reveal for an extra minute or two. With the towel, he removed the condensed water that had attached itself to the mirror. Behind the layer of moisture he saw a body that had been unwillingly defaced.

The daily preparation routine he'd strictly followed most of his adult life had collapsed. He still regularly showered and brushed his teeth, he didn't want to stink or his teeth to fall out, but the rest of the steps had lost their importance. Stray eyebrow hairs and pimples were the last things anyone was going to notice on the face of a freak. Preventing dry skin and wrinkles didn't really matter anymore as his skin was already ruined. But Cam did have to keep up his punk persona for Syn and his fellow Stationeers, which meant maintaining his mohawk. He just wished the nihilistic subculture he'd chosen to be a part of didn't require such a difficult hairstyle for membership. It took a lot of time, effort, and dog hairstyling gel to get his mohawk vertical.

Cam saved the worst for last, the full-body tattoo check. It had become more and more time consuming since the area of inked skin was almost greater than the area of non-inked skin. An attempt at a tattoo chart was made and then soon abandoned. A record of his transformation was too depressing. Instead he just eyed himself from bottom to top, front and back, looking for anything unfamiliar. Some days it was easy like last Wednesday when a two-inch black vertical line intersected with horizontal and diagonal lines appeared under his right eye. A day that also nearly saw a coincidental two-inch vertical bloody gash appear under his right eye. Today wasn't as easy. With his trusty hand mirror and some detailed searching, he found something new on the back of his right leg just above where the knee bent. Cam watched the news enough to recognize what appeared to be Arabic writing embedded in his leg. He licked his thumb and tried to rub it away hoping maybe just this one time it would be non-permanent ink; it never was. The inevitable discovery caused the obligatory string of swear words to spew from his mouth. All that was left to do now was to put on his punk-rock disguise and he'd be ready for the day.

Upon exiting the bathroom, he saw Ras standing near the breakfast bar counting a large wad of cash. Ras jumped at the sight of Cam and stuffed the money into one of his many pockets. "You startled me. I periodically fail to recall I am not the property's sole occupant."

Cam sat on the couch and began to lace up his boots. "Yup, I'm still here." He looked up at Ras with a conspiratorial twinkle in his eye. "It's cool, I already know about your little side business. It looks like it's making you some mad cash."

"My ancillary enterprise affords me the luxury of some

supplementary pocket money." Ras began to fidget with something in another pocket.

"Is it worth the risk though? What if you got busted? You got a pretty good thing goin' on here man, you could lose it all." Cam once again admired the poolhouse and the cleanliness of it. The maid had been in the day before.

"Trifles such as that do not concern me. The products I peddle are one-hundred-percent legal. I am merely bypassing the pharmaceutical companies' stranglehold they maintain over their market. My customers are denied access to FDA-approved products because they are unable or unwilling to be enslaved by a healthcare system whose only goal is profit. The well-being of its clients is secondary." Ras delivered his little spiel as if he had recited it countless times to countless numbers of customers uneasy with the idea of taking part in an illegal transaction.

"I doubt most of the people who buy your pills need them for medical reasons. They just like getting fucked up." The image of T's battered face suddenly popped into Cam's head.

"The reasons for use are inconsequential. Products authorized by the government for sale in a free-market economy must be available to anyone with the desire and capital to purchase them." Cam thought the postscript sounded as if it were designed to ease the minds of customers who weren't totally convinced by the convoluted logic of the original pitch. The postscript's additional heaping of convoluted logic made you feel like you were a true patriot fighting the evils of communism when you willingly took part in the commendable act of buying drugs from Ras.

"So what are you? A kind of Robin Hood dealer,

stealing from the rich and selling to the poor at marked-up prices?" Cam wasn't one to judge, but he did anyway.

"After covering my own expenses I only make a modest profit." Ras's hand reflexively went towards the pocket containing his humble bundle of bills.

"Well, whatever works for ya. I have to go to work now and make my own modest profit selling stuff to people too stupid to realize they can get it free on the Internet." Cam grabbed his wallet, phone, keys, and nametag and left the cabana. He walked past the Jacuzzi and the pool, made his way around the edge of the extensive, immaculately manicured grounds, took the path along the side of the obnoxiously sized house out into the neighborhood full of houses built to outdo each other's obnoxiousness, got into his used car, and drove off to his minimum-wage job.

It was the part of the workday Cam always dreaded—the part of the day where he was trapped behind the register and forced to ring up customers' purchases. There was nowhere to hide from the steady stream of strangers standing face to face with him, looking at him, judging him. An advantage to working the early afternoon shift was at least the customers were few and far between. The disadvantage was that these few customers were mostly composed of old women on shopping excursions from the retirement resort up the road. For them, CD technology was a recent discovery, DVDs were something the grandkids bought them for Christmas to collect dust next to the TV, and computers were scary, virus-filled boxes. One of these women set her pile of re-mastered nostalgia on the counter and looked Cam in the face. "Didn't that hurt?"

It was one of a series of questions he got on a daily basis, especially from the silverfox set. The others included 'are those real?', 'what does all that stuff mean?', and 'why would you do that to yourself?' The question would usually be accompanied by one of the long blatant stares given to car accidents on the side of the road. Cam scanned the pile of CDs into his register and sighed. "Did what hurt?"

"Getting all those tattoos. Especially those on your face." She continued to stare.

"More than you'll ever know. That'll be seventy-four ninety-one." Cam completed the transaction and was relieved by the fact that no one else was in line.

At the far end of the counter Rodge was pricing a stack of CDs. Cam approached him. "I'm getting so sick of this."

"Sick of what?" Rodge wasn't making a lot progress with his task as he kept getting interrupted by the hair falling from its place from behind his ears, which of course he had to return.

"Being treated like a sideshow exhibition. Can't these people see that I'm actually a person with feelings behind all this ink?"

"It *is* a lot of ink and most people can't or don't want to see anything beyond the surface. It's too much work." Rodge took a little break from pricing and hair-replacement.

"I don't want to deal with it anymore, I can't. These days all I want to do is move to a little cabin in the middle of nowhere Montana. Then I wouldn't have to put up with any of these assholes' stares or listen to their retarded comments. I doubt the trees and birds care whether I'm covered in tattoos or not." Cam's eyes glazed over as he imagined himself alone in the woods, not one set of judgmental eyes for miles in any direction.

"You know, I kind of felt the same way for a lot of years. I could only see myself through the eyes of all the people around me and my brain told me they didn't like what they saw. I was too fat, my skin was too zitty, I was boring, I was too dumb to make anything of myself, I would never be as good looking and successful as everybody else, I was a useless human being. Some weeks I couldn't even leave the house. As a last resort I started taking antidepressants. They worked and I was able to leave my house again. I didn't have the feelings of hopelessness or anxiety anymore. I didn't feel all those critical eyes judging me anymore. In fact I didn't feel anything anymore. I was numb, which after a while, was worse than feeling bad. By protecting myself from all that sadness, I was also protecting myself from any possible happiness, so I stopped taking the pills."

"You seem OK now. What helped you get through all that shit?" Cam didn't think Rodge's past problems with his self-image and depression had much in common with his own issues. Those things could be fixed; a body covered in unwanted tattoos couldn't be. But he was genuinely curious how Rodge beat his demons. Cam was open to taking any kind of advice he could get.

"I found the help I needed where I should've looked in the first place, in a Cure album."

Cam internally rolled his eyes and politely gave Rodge the opportunity to speak about his favorite subject. "Which one?"

It was an opportunity he never missed. "The album is

called *Bloodflowers* and the idea behind it is the moment we're living right now is all that really exists. We are all bloodflowers, we bloom for a short time and then wilt away. We have to cherish the beauty of the flower of now. It was this idea that helped me to stop wasting my life wallowing in all the garbage I created in my head and live more in the moment."

"It's a nice idea dude, but honestly, this moment right now really sucks." Cam saw an older woman approach the counter with her stack of CDs. He prepared himself for her inane questions and staring eyes and returned to his register.

TWO CONFLICTING SENSATIONS ran through him. The fragrance of fresh-cut grass filled his nose, bringing with it the happy memories of childhood games in the back yard with his brother. At the same time he was experiencing a painful pressure on the back of his neck that prevented him from moving. This lack of movement limited his view to a scene composed of nothing but fuzzy green shadow. After some intense focusing, he discovered the source of the overwhelming scent. He was face down on someone's lawn. Shifting his concentration to his neck, he analyzed what was holding him down. It was hard bone covered with a polyester blend, most likely a knee. His arms were roughly pulled behind his back and cold metal encased his wrists. The metal dug into his skin as he was pulled into a standing position. Cam spoke up. "What is this? What's going on?"

The other police officer, the one not standing behind Cam, answered. "We were contacted by the owner's home security company about a possible intruder. On our arrival we observed you exiting the premises with this backpack." The officer held up a backpack covered in punk-rock band patches, bands Cam had been pretending to be into.

"This is a huge mistake. I live here." Cam heard what can only be described as a guffaw from the officer standing behind him.

"Do you have any identification which can prove this?" the backpack-holding officer asked rhetorically in his most professional manner.

"No, I haven't had a chance to change my ID yet." Looking like he did in the kind of neighborhood where Ras lived was guilt enough. The circumstances surrounding his apprehension were only the icing. If his skin had been a few shades darker, he'd already be on the way to the station. In the meantime, the flashing lights of the police car had attracted a small group of neighbors. It was supposed to be a safe neighborhood, as all wealthy neighborhoods are supposed to be. They were there to ensure this intrusion was punished.

"OK, then you'll have to come with us." Cam was led to the awaiting car, but the short journey was interrupted by the rumble of a vehicle purposely neglected by the owner to maintain the consistency of his appearance. The sight of Ras emerging from anything but a beat-up VW Bug would've been disconcerting.

Cam turned to the officers behind him. "Wait, that's my roommate. His parents own this place."

Ras approached the skeptical officers. It wasn't the first

time he had dealings with the police in his neighborhood, obviously. The current set of officers hadn't dealt with him yet and didn't recognize the prince of the manor. "Sir, do your parents own this property?" The backpack-holding cop didn't hide the cynicism in his voice.

"Yes, Officer. May I present you with my personal identification?" His ID was removed from an upper outer front pocket of his coat and handed to the officer. From experience Ras knew the act of reaching inside his coat made the police nervous. "My mother was contacted by our home security company about a disturbance. She was unable to investigate this herself on account of the nature of her profession. She requested me to assess the situation myself."

Backpack-holding cop looked over the ID. The address was correct but it was a struggle matching the fresh face in the photo with the hair-covered mess standing before him. He handed the ID back. "This gentleman claims he lives here with you."

Ras returned the documented proof of his life before being known as 'Ras' to its place. "Yes, he resides here with me."

Hands still manacled, Cam reinstated his claim. "I told you I lived here. I probably just accidently tripped the alarm or something. I don't really remember what happened."

Ever the natural skeptic, backpack-holding cop unzipped the backpack and peeked inside. His skepticism was confirmed when he saw a pile of shiny sparkling objects. He removed pieces of antique jewelry, small tribal objects carved from precious stone, and a pair of ancient bracelets intricately fashioned from sheets of solid gold. "I suppose all this belongs to you."

The site of his parents' precious possessions coming out of Cam's grungy backpack cracked Ras's carefully constructed veneer. "That's my mom's jewelry she inherited from her grandmother. And the rest is a part of my dad's collection he's spent a lifetime acquiring. Those bracelets were a gift from Peruvian spiritual leaders in appreciation for the work he's done in helping to document and conserve their native cultural practices; they're priceless. I let you stay here with me and you rip off my parents. What the fuck Cam?! All of this stuff is irreplaceable."

The site of the parents' possessions being removed from his backpack had an even greater effect on Cam's demeanor than Ras's veneer. His shock was prominently displayed on his face and momentarily trapped his words in his throat. They eventually and ineffectually escaped. "I swear I have no memory of putting any of that stuff in there. I would never even think of doing anything like that."

Backpack-holding cop's skepticism was infectious and Ras had caught some of it. "I can't believe I was naive enough to actually fall for your tattoo dilemma. I should've known befriending me and planting the roommate idea in my head with your sob story was all a part of your con. You just wanted access to my parents' valuables so you could keep funding your goddamn ink addiction."

Cam was re-dumbfounded at Ras's leaps of logic and knew nothing he could say would change anyone's mind. The two officers had heard more than enough anyway. The cop standing behind Cam nudged him towards the still-awaiting police car. "Come on tattoo boy, get in. I hope that ink is indelible, I don't want it smeared all over my back seat." He slammed the door shut and left Cam staring at the reflection of himself in the police car's window.

A weary face looked back at Cam from the darkness of the passenger's side window of his mother's car. He continued to look into the somewhat familiar face as he broke the extended silence. "Thanks again Mom."

His mother was obviously shocked at her son's drastically altered appearance. She had a hard time keeping her attention on the road as she attempted to reconcile the fact the vandalized man sitting next to her was still her son. He looked out the window, and her eyes searched his reflection for something of the little boy she used to hold in her arms. She couldn't see him, but she knew he had to be in there somewhere and she was determined to find him.

"Of course honey, but why, why did you do this to yourself? It's such an extreme change. I barely recognized you when I first saw you in that horrible place. And the arrest for burglary? If you needed money, you could've asked me or your father, we'll always help you out. I love you, but I don't understand any of this."

"That makes two of us," Cam said to the face in the glass.

"What was that?" His mother had only heard the mumble he gave so often as a response during his teenage years.

"I said I don't understand any of this either. I think I'm losing my mind and probably need serious psychological help. I don't know what to do anymore. Mom, I'm scared."

Cam put his head down. He couldn't bear the sight of the face in the glass or of his mother.

"Why didn't you come to me earlier? Maybe we could've prevented some of this." Moms don't like being left in the dark when it comes to their children's problems and Cam had completely blinded his mother during his involuntary transformation.

"I didn't want you to see me like this. I was ashamed."

"Marcus, no matter what happens, you'll always be my son." She reached over and gently took hold of his hand.

He let his hand be taken, turned his head, and allowed his mother to look into his face. A sad smile was all he could manage to give her in return. The water she saw pooling in his eyes said everything she wanted to hear. Cam held the water in place until he turned back to the glass where he watched the liquid spill down.

Cam's unremembered last roll of the dice caused him to land on the square that sent him right back to the beginning of the game. He was lying down on the bed of his old bedroom, the place where as a child he studied maps and dreamed of seeing all those far-off lands, the place where as a prepubescent boy he dreamed of traveling the country playing professional basketball, the place where as an adolescent he dreamed of nothing but getting the hell out of this room and never coming back to it ever again. His mother had turned it into a guest room. Every remnant of him had been removed except the stickers and pieces of stickers on his old dresser his mom couldn't clean off. The

Laker's purple and gold, a few X-Men here and there, and parts of Teenage Mutant Ninja Turtles welcomed him back with their obsolete familiarity. He heard a soft knock on the door. "Come in." The door was opened before he got the words out of his mouth.

His mother sat down on the bed. "I have some good news. You might be off the hook. I was just talking with our lawyer and he said your friend dropped the charges. The family doesn't have time to deal with the hassle of going to court and since they got everything back there was really no harm done. The state may still decide to prosecute, but our lawyer thinks it's unlikely."

"That's a relief. I don't think I could've handled dealing with all that legal crap." Cam's relief wasn't very convincing. He thought some jail time might have at least stopped the tattoos from coming for a while. "Thanks again for letting me stay here. I don't have anywhere else to go."

"You know you're always welcome here. Dinner's almost ready, so why don't you come downstairs?" She gave his mohawk a loving rub and returned to the kitchen.

"OK, I'll be right down." The iota of familial warmth that began to burn inside him and gave him a glimmer of hope was instantly snuffed out when he saw himself in the mirrored doors of the closet. Any hope of escape from the disaster staring back at him was pointless.

Generous amounts of alcohol usually do the trick when you need a break from your memories. In the midst of his third beer (cocktails are too expensive when you make minimum wage) Cam still had the full retention of everything he didn't want to remember. He thought seeing Syn would make him feel better. She'd agreed to meet him in the town's lousy imitation of an Irish pub, but it was more than thirty minutes past the arranged meeting and she still hadn't arrived. He looked at his phone, nothing. She probably didn't want to see him anymore, but five minutes later his spirits rose when he heard the unmistakable clomping of her oversized boots, which always signaled her arrival. She joined him in a dark booth in the back corner of the bar.

Cam looked across the stained and pitted table at her. "I didn't think you were coming."

"I wasn't that late was I? Not more than usual." She pulled out her heavily decorated phone to check the time.

"No, it's just I'm surprised you still wanted to see me after what happened," he said into his beer glass.

It was Syn's turn to be surprised. "Why!? I'm your girlfriend right? You think I'm gonna ditch you over some bullshit like a little arrest?"

Cam had to take a large sip of beer. "It's not the arrest part I was worried about. It's that I screwed over a friend. But I really didn't mean to do it. I wasn't in my right mind when it happened. I actually can't remember trying to steal that stuff from his parents' house. I don't even know how I got in. I do know I'd been getting quite a few prescriptions filled at the Ras home pharmacy and I probably overdid it that day." A drug-fueled blackout story was much sexier than an unexplained temporary amnesia story.

"That's what I figured, so it's alright. But I am pissed that I've been sitting here almost five minutes without a drink. Why don't you use those sticky fingers of yours and snatch me a Guinness."

After licking the foam from her upper lip she continued. "Speaking of Ras, I heard he had a talk with Burn about the whole sitch. I guess you can't come back to the Station until all this shit blows over."

Cam took a drink from his fourth beer. "Yeah, I got a call from Burn the other day. He told me I was on indefinite suspension. I have no fucking clue what I'm gonna do now. It's not like I was making good money there, but at least it was a job."

"Don't worry about it. I know some people. We'll find you somethin'." She gave him a knowing wink.

"Cool." He wasn't acquainted with that particular wink and was somewhat apprehensive to meet it. Cam decided to put off the meeting and instead introduced one of his well-known subjects to the conversation. "By the way, I didn't tell you, but my basketball team made it to the finals. The championship game is next Thursday. You should come check it out."

"Ummmm, yeah, the thing is, I'm not really into sports." Syn saw the pathetic anticipation on Cam's face. "But I guess I can try and stop by."

"Could you wear a cheerleader outfit with a really short skirt and bring some pompoms? The team could use the support." Cam knew he was pushing it, but some weight needed to be removed from the heavy mood.

"Of course I will. How did you know it was my dream in high school to be a cheerleader? As soon as I get home I'll start practicing my routine. In fact I just thought up a cheer. Win, win, win or I'll decapitate you and use your head as the ball." Her delivery was the epitome of deadpan.

For the first time in days, an unforced smile crossed Cam's face. "Not really that catchy, but keep working on it." Something compelled him to lean over the table and give her a kiss, which she grudgingly accepted.

Ball after ball fell through the basket without touching the rim. Some bounced off the glass first, some came in at a high arc, and others were drilled through with so much speed, the net below didn't move. From behind the three-point line or from right underneath the basket, it didn't matter. Cam was making everything go in despite the fact a row of five hastily drawn symbols appeared on top of his shooting hand the morning of the big game. It wasn't a coincidence, he knew they were put there to distract him and spoil one of the only good things he had left in his life. They failed; it made him even more determined to win.

His shooting prowess didn't go unnoticed by the opposing team warming up on the other end of the court. After making a particularly difficult shot, Cam turned to his opposition and gave them an exaggerated wink. He then gave his teammates, who were warming up with him, some words of encouragement. "We beat these guys the last time we played them, so there's no reason why we can't do it again."

After missing an exceedingly easy layup made easier by the fact he could nearly touch the rim without jumping, Lurch threw out a question. "Who are these guys again?"

"It's those dudes who smell like ham, the Ball Hogs. I think they're butchers or something." Lambda was practicing his crossover dribbling, but the ball kept crossing over to the other side of the court instead of to his other hand.

R. C. wanted to verify the team's game plan with everyone. "So are we sticking to the same strategy we've used all season?"

"What? Getting the ball to Freakshow?" Boinkman gave Cam a light pat on the ass.

"Exactly," R. C. confirmed.

"Come on guys, my girlfriend showed up. Couldn't you lay off that Freakshow shit for one night?" Syn was sitting in the bleachers with the friends and family of both teams. There were about twenty-five people in total, more than quadruple the usual amount of spectators. Cam told Syn the game started forty-five minutes before it actually did. She had only just arrived and was already fidgeting with her phone.

"Yeah right, like you calling me Lurch all the time really helps me with the ladies." His shot attempt from directly in front of the basket bounced off the rim and back into his hands.

"Lurch, I doubt your name has anything to do with you not getting any. More likely it's your face." R.C. dodged the ball hurled at his head and ran giggling from the lumbering Lurch.

"Lurch smash." Lambda began to Frankenstein walk around the court to the laughter of his teammates.

Old Bob noticed a possible problem on the other side of the court. "Hey guys, I think we've got a ringer on our hands." A large black man was beginning to warm up with the other Ball Hogs.

"So because he's a big African American fellow, that automatically means he's good at basketball? Old Bob, you've seen Lambda play, you oughta know by now stereotypes aren't always true." Boinkman smiled at Lambda.

"Stereotypes are stereotypes because they usually have a basis in fact and in this case the facts speak for themselves." Old Bob along with his teammates watched as a stereotype slam-dunked the ball again and again without any apparent effort.

"Are there black butchers? I've never seen one. Where'd they find that dude?" Lambda's ignorant and somewhat racist thoughts were on all his teammates' minds, but he was the only one with the skin color dark enough to say them out loud.

"They probably placed an ad saying 'Can you handle balls? Can you repeatedly put it in the hole? In return we'll give you all the meat you can take.'" R. C. respectfully kept his answer free of any racist overtones.

"Bringing in a ringer means they know they suck at basketball and that they can't beat us on their own. A team of five chumps and a champ isn't going to win this game." Cam was loud enough for the entire court to hear.

"But Cam, there aren't ties in basketball." Boinkman made the obvious association.

"Let's just get out there and fucking play." Cam led his team to the center of the court.

As everyone expected, the game was basically a one-on-one match between Cam and the Ball Hogs' ringer. The rest of the players were only occasional accessories. The ringer had a definite size, skill, and speed advantage over Cam, but Cam's focus and drive were absolute. Plus whenever the ringer tried to read Cam's next move, he ended up reading what was on his body instead. He'd find himself trying to decipher a part of an arm or a piece of a back during crucial plays. With less than twenty seconds left to play in the game, the Ball Hogs led by only two. All the accessories were exhausted being accessories and the ringer was more tired than he expected to be playing against out-of-shape amateurs, but Cam still felt fresh; he could play another four quarters.

The Ball Hogs had possession of the ball and were playing cautiously, passing it back and forth trying to run down the clock. Old Bob was carefully studying their passes and correctly predicted the trajectory of the next one. He knocked the ball away and it miraculously ended up in Lurch's hands. Dribbling wasn't his strong suit so he got rid of the ball as soon as he saw two Ball Hogs charging towards him. A fast-thinking Boinkman raced by and picked up Lurch's panicked pass. Adhering to the team's game plan, Boinkman made sure the ball found its way into Cam's hands. Knowing he had only a few precious seconds left on the clock, he drove full speed to the basket in an attempt to make a layup and tie the game. Before he could get the shot off, a black muscled arm came out of nowhere down onto his arms preventing the shot. The referee blew his whistle on the unmistakable foul and awarded Cam two free throws.

As he prepared to make the first shot at the free-throw line, Cam began to hear the whispered chant of 'Freakshow, Freakshow, Freakshow' coming from the bleachers and then from his teammates. Looking in the stands, he saw Syn had put her phone down and joined in the chanting. His first shot was a little short and hit the front of the rim, but it got a lucky bounce and fell backward through the hoop. After the applause and cheers, the 'Freakshow' chant resumed even louder. Cam knew deep down this game didn't have any real meaning, there were no scouts from the professional basketball leagues in the stands, there would be no lucrative sponsorship deals, there was no cash prize or expensive rings for the winners (only a cheap plastic trophy), there would be no parade down Main Street thronged with cheering masses and beautiful women desperate to sleep with him (if he was lucky Syn might let him try a third position), there was just the satisfaction of having taken control of something in his life and beat it. He bounced the ball a few times, made a visual measurement of the distance to the basket, absorbed the adulation of the miniscule crowd, and readied his shot.

It never came. The ball fell out of his hands, bounced limply a couple times, and rolled out of bounds. At the same time, Cam's body collapsed onto the court. Once on the floor, it curled up into a fetal position. The thumb of the right hand went directly into the mouth and the front of the shorts darkened with the liquid escaping from the bladder. Nobody on the court moved and the crowd went silent. Having to do something, the referee went over to the curled-up man on the ground. He looked conscious and uninjured; the referee thought it was probably just an anxiety attack. Nothing in the rulebook mentioned this kind of scenario. There wasn't any time left on the clock anyway, so he blew his whistle and awarded the game to the Ball Hogs. The victors left the shameful situation and began to celebrate their ringer's hard-earned win.

"Cam! Cam! You all right man?" Boinkman knelt down and shook him without any noticeable effect. He stood up and faced his teammates. "I think he shit himself too, it really stinks down there."

Syn made her way down from the bleachers onto the court as fast as her platform boots would carry her. "What happened? Is he alright?"

R. C. glanced down at Cam and back up to Syn. "What you're looking at here is an epic choke."

Cam sat up and saw Syn and his teammates standing around him. "Hey, what's going on? Did I make the shot?"

"Just the one into your shorts." There wasn't any hint of humor in R. C.'s voice.

An awareness of warm, squishy matter covering his behind and thighs reached him at the same time as the matter's terrible stench. In the entirety of the English language, no grouping of words existed which would help Cam out of his humiliating situation. The only option was to put his head down between his knees and pretend he wasn't there. His teammates left the court without saying a word.

Syn took a look at her phone. "I gotta go, Cam. Go clean yourself up, OK?" Cam heard the clomping of her boots on the hardwood floor fade away while he breathed in the fumes of his defeat.

Cam shoved spoonful after spoonful of his favorite childhood breakfast cereal into his mouth. Its overwhelming sweetness didn't register with his taste buds. His arm, mouth, and digestive system were merely going through the motions.

Dressed for work, his mother came down the stairs into the dining room. "Hi honey. I'm sorry I didn't make it to your basketball game last night, I had to work late. How did it go? Did you guys win the championship?"

"No." A soggy spoonful of cereal went into his mouth.

"I'm sorry. Maybe next time, right?" She searched the pantry for some portable breakfast.

"There won't be a next time."

Cam's mother turned around in surprise. "Why not?"

"I don't want to talk about it." He sipped a spoonful of sugary milk.

"OK, but try not to sulk around the house all day. You have to get out there and get your life back on track. I have to go now, I'll see you later. Love you, bye." She left Cam alone with his empty bowl.

With a heavy feeling of dread he pulled his phone out. It had been turned off since the unfortunate incident of the previous night. His first instinct was to smash it on the dining room floor's faux granite tiles so he would never have to hear from anybody ever again, but it wasn't cheap and without a job he couldn't afford wanton destruction. There were only two messages, a lot fewer than he expected. He supposed his teammates had written him off and were thinking of getting themselves a ringer of their own next season. The first message was from Syn and the other was from Cam's brother. Just to get the inevitable over with, he first opened Syn's message:

Cam,

I've done a lot of thinking after what happened at the basketball game. I've never been so embarrassed for someone else in my whole life. It was so bad that I was embarrassed to be your girlfriend. I don't think I can handle being with someone who loses control like that. I have enough of my own issues to deal with. I don't need someone else's too. I think we should stop seeing each other until you fix what's going on in your life. I'm sorry, but it has to be this way. Good luck with everything and maybe we can get together again someday.

Syn

Again the urge overcame him to smash his phone. Instead, he slammed his fist down on the solid wooden table, bruising his recently healed hand. Angry at injuring himself, he stood up and kicked the nearest chair across half the length of the dining room. After a few seconds of introspection, he walked over to where the innocent chair lie and put it back in its place at the table. He thought he might as well check the news from Paris while his phone was still in one piece. He opened his brother's message:

Hey Cam,

I just heard from Mom what's going on with you. I don't even know what to say. It's hard for me to believe you're doing all this to yourself on purpose. I have to admit I was afraid of something like this happening to you someday. When nothing out of the ordinary happened in your childhood or teenage years, I thought maybe nothing ever would happen and you'd live a normal happy life. I know what I'm saying is kind of cryptic and doesn't make much sense, so I'll try to explain.

I know this is going to sound like something out of a cheesy mystery novel, but I don't know how else to say it—there is a deep dark family secret about you and your early childhood. I was sworn to secrecy about it, so I could never tell you. Even now I can't tell you what it is. I have to leave that to Mom. I think it's the reason all this stuff is happening to you. This secret has been buried deep inside you since you were a little boy and it looks like it's finally coming to the surface.

It's also a big part of the reason I treated you so badly when we were kids. I still feel guilty about that. I hope you don't harbor any anger towards me because of it. I was just a kid too and didn't have the full ability yet to know what I was doing could be so harmful to you. To me it was only innocent teasing, but as I got older I started to convince myself I was toughening you up so the outside world couldn't hurt you. Now I know I was projecting my own anger and powerlessness onto you. I'm truly sorry about that. I should've stayed around to support you instead of taking off the first chance I got. There's nothing I can do about any of this now except hope you can forgive me. I know you're a good person Cam, so keep being yourself and you'll get through this.

Blocko

Cam ran his hands through the stubble on either side of his mohawk and leaned back in the chair. "What the hell is this shit?"

He reread the message three more times. Cam found it unbelievable his brother would drop a bomb like that and not even tell him the make and model of said bomb. And if this bomb has been just sitting around waiting to go off, he wondered why it couldn't have been defused long before it caused so much damage. Cam wanted to immediately call his brother and pry the secret out of him, but he knew Blocko would just blast him with a bunch more cryptic and apologetic bullshit and end up repeating what he said in his message, 'ask Mom'. He'd have to be patient and wait until his mother, the true keeper of the secret, got home from work.

At least the anger from before had dissipated. It was taken over by an agonizing curiosity mixed with a hint of relief - relief that there might actually be an explanation for all the mysterious happenings that had ruined his life.

While waiting for Mom's return and subsequent revelation, Cam's imagination became restless. It jumped the gun and constructed its own stories in which Cam's childhood secret was divulged:

Voice

"Marcus! Stop running by the pool! Blake! Keep an eye on your little brother!" The boys' father yelled from his lounge chair.

Either Marcus didn't hear his father or he ignored his warning (the latter was more probable) and he continued to run near the edge of the hotel's swimming pool. Blake wasn't here on vacation to babysit his little brother, so he disregarded his father's instructions and jumped into the water with some of his newfound friends.

During his run, Marcus didn't see the young boy his own age standing on the edge of the pool, contemplating whether to jump or not. The decision was made for him when Marcus ran into him. The boy's feet went out from under him and the back of his skull slammed onto the pool's concrete lip as he fell into the water. Marcus helplessly watched the small unconscious body slowly sink to the bottom. It wasn't until a couple young girls in bikinis made their way to the vicinity of the collision site that the lifeguard noticed a tiny dark child-shaped object on the bottom of the pool. The boy was pulled from the water and partially resurrected. Breath resumed in the body, but the light didn't return to the eyes. Marcus silently watched the hysterics of the boy's family.

Amid blaring sirens and flashing lights the boy was taken away. Witnesses in bathing suits and towels spoke with men in uniforms and suits. Looks and fingers were aimed in Marcus's direction.

"C'mon honey." His mother wrapped him in a soft towel and carried him back to their room.

"Damn it Blake! I told you to watch him. Now see what happened." Their father had to stop himself from smacking his eldest son in the head.

"But Dad, I *was* watching him," Blake pleaded.

"Obviously not well enough. Let's go home, this vacation is over."

"We shouldn't have brought them here," Mom quietly said to Dad.

To which Dad replied, "They need to see the consequences of their actions."

Mom replied, "But they're only children, they don't need to see this."

Marcus was too young to understand why the little boy from the pool was now sleeping in a grown-up bed in a smelly room with

tubes in his nose and mouth. He wondered if they were still trying to take the pool water out of him. No, the doctors had informed the boy's family all the pool water had been removed along with his consciousness. He would most likely never awaken from the slumber he entered at the bottom of the hotel's swimming pool.

On the day of their visit, it was the boy's grandmother's turn to keep vigil. It was her turn the majority of the time. "Again, we are truly sorry how this turned out and I've brought my boys here to apologize in person for the accident their carelessness caused at the pool that terrible day," Dad told the grandmother.

She nodded and motioned for Blake to come to the

bedside. Nudged by his father, he approached the boy in the bed. Marcus saw his brother whisper into the sleeping boy's ear and then speedily return to the family. Now it was his turn. He would be brave and tell the sleeping boy he was sorry for knocking him into the water. At the bedside the grandmother placed his hand into her grandson's hand. Marcus felt her paper-dry skin squeeze his tiny hand into the other tiny, limp hand. It was starting to hurt, but the harder he tried to release himself, the stronger the pressure became. His panic was momentarily forgotten when he felt a needle stick him in the ankle. He looked down and saw the sharpened fingernail of the old woman's pinky finger in his skin. Two drops of blood escaped his body and streamed down onto his foot. The sight of his own blood caused tears to instantaneously flow from his eyes and a cry to burst from his chest.

His father rushed over and saved his young son from the old woman. "What the hell do you think you're doing?!" Marcus was handed off to his mother for closer inspection and comforting.

The grandmother spoke for the first time. "From now until his end, my precious boy will be a voiceless husk trapped in a world of memories and dreams here in this bed, forgotten by the world. When his end finally does come, your boy's skin will become his lost voice. Forever etched into his flesh will be my boy's unexpressed thoughts and emotions, inescapable nightmares, unanswered screams for help, and visions of a life never lived. He won't be forgotten." She turned to her grandson. "You won't be forgotten."

Dad issued a whispered scream, "You crazy old witch!" and ushered his family away.

In his mother's arms, Marcus watched through tear-blurred eyes the old woman and sleeping boy disappear from his view. "Mommy, what happened?"

Mom gently pushed his head down onto her shoulder. "Go back to sleep honey. You were having a bad dream."

Courier

"I'd like to thank you all for accepting our invitation and coming this evening. Your attendance shows your commitment to your children's futures." His overconfident voice and polished delivery betrayed his genuine concern for their children and exposed him as a salesman hunting out new commissions. Out of politeness and curiosity, none of the parents, mostly fathers, stood up and left, but stayed in the hotel's conference room and listened to the entire presentation. The invitation, printed on pseudo-official government stationary, promised a guaranteed safe method of investment specifically geared for future college tuition fees. No details of the plan were given in the invitation, so attendance to the presentation would be the only way to learn about this important opportunity.

According to the speaker, a government plan was recently put into place designed to assist parents in saving for their children's higher education. This government-protected, minimal-risk investment plan was now open to a limited number of forward-thinking parents. The nitty-gritty of the plan was complicated, but in a nutshell the investments would be part of subsidies for companies needing government assistance. Parents would share a percentage of profits made by these companies. A required percentage of these profits would be kept in low-interest government bonds until the child's eighteenth birthday. Anything made above this required percentage could be used however the parents saw fit. What was the catch? The program sounded almost as if the government were giving away free money. No catch, the government wanted to encourage its youth to pursue higher education.

Blake and Marcus's father thought it was too good to be true. Despite this, he invested the minimal amount possible to test the waters. Over the months he watched his investment grow more rapidly than expected. He even regularly received little surplus checks because the maximum monthly amount had already been put into his sons' college bonds, so he did what any normal guy would do. He invested more. It made his returns higher, so of course he had to invest more. He reinvested his surplus money and made more. He then invested all of his savings and made more. Naturally he took out a second mortgage on his house and invested it. He stopped receiving the checks, he stopped receiving any news on the state of his sons' bonds, and he started worrying.

The bonds didn't exist, the investment company didn't exist, the government program didn't exist, and his money didn't exist any longer either. All this was told to him in a drab office in the back of a police station. The officers involved in his case were sympathetic, but there was nothing more they could do for him. The boys' father was in a state of shock. His life was ruined, his boys' futures were ruined, he would probably lose his house, cars, and anything else of value he had along with his wife. He didn't know what he was going to do.

"Hey, I'm real sorry to hear what happened to you. It's a tragedy when people take advantage of other people who are only trying to help out their family." A plainclothes police officer he didn't recognize had come up behind him and given him more useless sympathy.

"Thanks." He just wanted to get the hell out of this place and go and get smashed on cheap alcohol (the only kind he'd be able to afford from now on).

"I know some people who can help you out of this mess." The officer pulled a creased business card out of his wallet and gave it to the boys' father. "Give them a ring."

He looked at the card he was given. It had a local number and the name above it read: The H.L. Group. Before he could tell the officer he didn't need a lawyer or a financial planner, the cop had already walked away.

"I'd like to thank you both for coming in today and speaking with me. As I told your husband on the telephone, we are not lawyers or financial planners. We are administrators of a cutting-edge education program currently being developed by our government, the details of which I'm not at liberty to discuss at the moment. I know you're asking yourselves, what does an education program have to do with our current financial situation? Well, let me tell you. We need our candidates to have a very stable, almost idyllic home life for the duration of the program. This of course includes financial stability. If one or both of your sons are suitable candidates we are prepared to offer you a generous stipend which I believe would help you to recoup your recent losses." The authority in the speaker's voice and his polished delivery made it difficult to question the validity of anything he said. Blake and Marcus's parents had a million questions they wanted to ask, but before they could, the speaker stopped them.

"Before we get ahead of ourselves, we must find out if your sons are suitable candidates or not. Bring them to this address next Thursday at six PM." He produced a business card from a pocket of his immaculate suit.

"We've finished our testing and it looks like one of your boys is a suitable candidate." The man behind the desk was reading through large stacks of papers through his thick spectacles. His immaculate suit was indistinguishable from their previous contact's immaculate suit. "The results show Marcus would be perfect for one of our new courier programs. Unfortunately Blake's results were not as promising. He is far too headstrong for our purposes." The immaculate-suited speaker produced from behind his desk a thick paper pile contained in a high-quality plastic folder. "This is the contract. Please take your time and read through it, but for confidentiality reasons, it cannot leave this room."

Most of the language in the contract was alien to the boys' parents, but they got the gist of it. They were essentially signing their boy's life over to these people, whoever they were. "I see the phrase 'upon activation' mentioned several times. What exactly does that mean?" Dad asked.

"At any time after your son's eighteenth birthday, we have the right to activate him, if we require his services.

This means all the conditioning and training he has received will be 'activated'. He'll unknowingly be in our employ. Let me assure you of the fact that there will be a minimum of physical danger involved in his potential work." This last piece of information gave no peace of mind to the parents forced to sell their son's future because of a stupid investment.

With a lump in his throat Dad signed and with tears forming in her eyes, Mom also hesitantly signed. "We'll be in touch with all the details." The man in the immaculate suit put the contract into one of many drawers behind his desk and gave each of the parents a handshake with the appropriate amount of pressure.

On their way out of the office, the door thumped against an obstruction. It turned out to be Blake's skull. He hadn't been able to move away from the door fast enough after listening to his parents speak with the well-dressed man about Marcus and himself. Mom pulled Marcus from his contented play with the pile of government-issued Legos and took him into her arms. Dad grabbed the mildly bruised Blake by the hand and led his family away.

Blake stared at his little brother in their Mom's arms and wondered how he'd become activated. Would they give him a magic ring just like those kids had in that superhero cartoon he watched on Saturday mornings? He wanted to get a magic ring too, but they weren't going to give him one because his head was too strong. If it were really that strong, why did it still hurt after being bashed by the door?

Dad was also lost in his own thoughts, not of magic rings but of his tiny son growing up into some sort of mindless superspy-evading KGB agents to deliver stolen military secrets to the CIA. If his son could help keep the U.S.A. safe from the communists then what he'd done to him wasn't all bad. While mentally justifying selling his son, Dad didn't notice the fraudulent investment salesman in his immaculate suit pass him in the hallway.

Vessel

"Dad, I really have to pee," Marcus whined from the back seat.

"Can't you hold it 'til we get to a gas station?" Dad replied.

"Maybe we should pull over. We haven't passed anything for almost an hour." Mom had already become impatient with yet another one of her husband's ill-advised attempts at a shortcut and wasn't in any kind of mood to hear Marcus whine and squirm for another who-knows-how-many miles.

Dad could hear the annoyance in his wife's voice and to prevent it from escalating, he reluctantly agreed to pull to the side of the road even though it meant losing valuable time from his carefully planned journey. One spot was as good as any since nothing but blackness surrounded them.

"Go with him, it's really dark and who knows what's out there," Mom insisted as Marcus got out of the car.

"Fine, I'll find the boy a nice safe spot to drain his little lizard." Dad joined his son on the side of the road. "Just go here." He gestured to the stand of trees lining the road.

"I can't. What if someone drives by and sees me?" Marcus was holding his crotch and hopping around.

"Marcus, we've seen maybe two cars in the last hour,

nobody is going to see you." Now Dad was losing his patience.

"Can we go on the other side of these trees?" Marcus asked. On the other side they found themselves in a neglected field where weeds had overtaken whatever crop had once flourished. Marcus faced the trees and relieved his long-suffering bladder. His father turned the other direction knowing his son couldn't go with anyone watching.

It was a clear night and out here away from the city the stars dominated the blackness and not the other way 'round. One of the stars seemed closer and more orange than the rest. It also seemed to be moving. Dad watched the progress of the star and assumed it was a plane until it abruptly changed direction and stopped. It definitely wasn't a plane, unless planes were now built in the shape of squashed metallic spheres, glowing without any discernable light source, and were able to stop mid-air.

"Dad, what is that thing?" Marcus wasn't noticed as he joined his father in viewing the object. He pulled on his father's shirt. "Daddy, what is that?"

Dad's eyes didn't leave the sky. "I'm not sure." From its great height the object was in some way able to feel it was being watched by the two tiny figures standing in the dark. It rapidly descended towards them. Marcus and his father were momentarily unable to comprehend how or why this thing was coming for them. If Marcus hadn't just purposely emptied his bladder, his fear would have done it for him. His father roughly grabbed his hand and pulled him back through the trees to the car.

Mom was startled by the sudden entrance of her son

and husband and by their pale complexions. "What's going on? Is everything OK?"

Dad's hand was shaking so much he could barely turn the key in the ignition. "We have to go, now!" He was able to start the car, but by then a miniature sun had appeared in the road. Its brilliance blinded the automobile's driver and passengers. Their eyes automatically closed and when they opened again the scene had dramatically changed. All the former occupants of the car stood in a room entirely composed of what seemed to be aluminum foil, not wrinkled after it came off the roll, but still perfectly smooth, shiny, and untouched. Embossed in the foil were countless symbols. Some stood on their own and others were bunched together presumably as forms as writing. Much of it was familiar, but at the same time undecipherable. Four identical figures stood before the family. At about six feet tall each, they had thin greyish green human-shaped bodies, but the similarities ended there. The bodies were completely featureless, except for two black almond shapes where the eyes should be.

To show strength to his terrified family, Dad swallowed enough of his fear to let a few words sneak out of his mouth. "Who are you?" He didn't know if he'd receive an answer since the things in front of him didn't have visible ears or mouths.

The realization that audible speech wasn't their preferred form of communication came immediately. A rapid succession of images bombarded Dad's head. His mind's interpretations of the messages being conveyed to him:

A grandmother, viewed from childhood's eyes, a large open storybook on her lap.

Galaxies, stars, planets, infinite in variety. Earth, but not Earth. Different-shaped continents.

Amalgams of cities from science fiction films of the seventies and eighties. No aliens, but humans with the clothing and hairstyles of the characters of these films.

Egyptian monuments and pyramids, not of stone, but of steel and glass.

A massive group of men and women, eyes closed, dressed in colorful robes sitting cross-legged in a metallic temple. Transparent versions of themselves leaving their bodies.

The transparent people cavorting with fairies and elves in magical forests, conversing with Greek gods on Mt. Olympus, having drinks in *Star Wars'* Mos Eisley Cantina with all the alien creatures, orbiting in space around a giant glowing Buddha figure.

The transparent people hovering in a rusted metallic temple over a floor covered with small piles of bones and disintegrating colored cloth. Transparent tears falling from their transparent eyes.

The not Earth, grey and dead. Mechanized people wandering aimlessly through deserted cities.

The mechanized people immersed in the glow of the transparent people building spacecrafts such as the one Dad and his family were standing in and creating suits to house their transparent bodies, like the four examples standing in front of him and his family.

A group of glowing aluminum-foil-covered ships finding and descending on prehistoric Earth, which is teeming with late-model dinosaurs and various small burrowing mammals.

A group of glowing aluminum-foil-covered ships corralling and hurling a gigantic meteor at prehistoric Earth.

An evolutionary chart of man with the final-stage human immersed in a glowing transparent person.

Famous scenes throughout history straight out of an illustrated fourth-grade textbook, all the historical figures attached to marionette strings held by the transparent suited people sitting in their ships.

Grandma closing the storybook.

Dad looked at his wife and children and understood they received the same bombardment, but most likely interpreted the messages differently. Especially his youngest son, whose face was completely blank. Dad again somehow worked up the nerve to speak. "Nice story, but what do you want with us?"

Another round of images invaded his head.

The evolutionary chart of man with the final-stage human immersed in a glowing transparent person again, this time bigger and brighter.

Earthlings immersed in the glowing transparent

people frolicking in a sunny meadow, eating an immense feast, making love.

A crude model of the human head the size of a small room. On the back of the headroom, a locked toilet stall door. A transparent person attempting to enter the headroom—crawling under the door, climbing over the door, knocking the door down—but the headroom is occupied and the occupant won't let the transparent person enter.

The transparent person coercing, dragging, drugging, killing the occupant of the headroom. Each attempt ending with irreparable damage to the interior of the headroom.

A transparent person dressed as a ghetto gangster vandalizing the exterior of the headroom with a can of black spray-paint. The occupant disgusted by the unrecognizable state of his headroom voluntarily leaves.

On a large stage in front of a studio audience, a game-show host offering the choice of two doors. Behind door one is the transparent ghetto gangster, holding in one hand a can of black spray-paint and holding in the other hand, little Marcus's hand. Behind door two is the ship firing an obliterating ray at the car containing Dad and his entire family.

Dad's outrage at the two choices before him gave him the courage to scream, "I won't let you take my son *or* hurt my family!"

The studio audience bursting into laughter.

Dad wanted to violently kill all four of the things standing so calmly before him and his family, but even if he were given the opportunity it wouldn't have worked. These things apparently hadn't been truly alive for millions of years. His life-or-death choice was merely a joke to them. Of course he'd have to sacrifice his little boy to save his family, what else could he do?

With a grotesque mockery of human movement, two of the suited transparents walked over and took Marcus away. Blinding orange light enveloped the interior of the ship.

In darkness, Dad felt in his hands a familiar vinyl-covered circle. His fingers fit perfectly within the grooves provided for them. He opened his eyes and through the windshield saw a dark, empty road. Next to him, he saw his wife sitting in the passenger seat wearing a dazed expression. He looked over his shoulder and saw his two boys had the same expressions.

Marcus was the first to speak. "Daddy, who were the men in the shiny room? They made a hurt on my ankle."

More violent anger rose in Dad, which had to be suppressed. "You must be thinking of that scary movie we saw earlier about the spacemen. Remember? The spacemen took a little boy and his family to their spaceship and tried to hurt them. But the daddy killed the spacemen and saved the little boy."

It was Blake's turn to speak. "Dad, we didn't see a movie like that, we—"

"Blake, it was a movie and we're not going to talk about

it anymore. It was too scary for Marcus and we shouldn't have let him watch it."

Blake didn't like his answer. "But Dad—"

Mom cut him off this time, her voice shaky and unconvincing. "Honey, listen to your father."

Dad started the car and before he drove off he turned to his boys. "Go to sleep and when you wake up you'll be safe at home in your beds."

Cam was exhausted. What he needed was a hot shower to clear his head. Maybe the steam would seep into his brain and clean away all his recent memories. In fact he wouldn't have minded if the steam burnt them all away. Starting again with a fresh brain would've been a relief.

Unfortunately he stepped out of the shower with all his memories intact. The only thing the steam managed was to temporarily keep him from seeing his reflection in the large bathroom mirror. After removing some of the vapor from the glass, he saw the ink covering his naked body was also intact. It was pointless now to check for new tattoos, his career at the Station was over with and his punk persona was dead. There was no reason to keep up the ruse as a collector of love-inspired body art. Of course if a new one appeared in an obvious place like on his neck or his face it'd be impossible to ignore, but there was nothing obviously different about his marred body this time. The same amount of ruination looked back at him from behind the glass. As he was drying himself off he did notice something slightly different on his torso: faint glowing lines around the edges of some of the tattoos on his chest and stomach. Cam assumed it was just light reflecting off the moisture on his skin.

When he took a closer look he saw that glowing lines were appearing around more and more of the tattoos. The glowing lines were also becoming brighter and thicker. No, not thicker, but deeper, cutting through the layers of his skin. With his towel he tried to wipe away some of the glowing lines, but it didn't work. They were already embedded deep within his skin. Cam watched with horror as one set of glowing lines around a large symbol above his left pec finished its journey and caused the tattoo to fall from his body into the sink with a wet thump, leaving a hole of exposed muscle and bone. The funny thing was he barely felt anything at all; it had the same sensation as a loose tooth falling from the gum.

Before the shock of what had just happened truly had a chance to register, a small tattoo near his right nipple came off and joined its comrade in the sink. Then he heard a low squish behind him and turned around to see a chunk of flesh on the floor. Over his shoulder he looked in the mirror for the chunk's place of origin—it had fallen from just above his right buttock. In the split second it took to turn his head back around, four or five more tattoos had detached themselves from his body.

Just prior to the collision of his mind with the freight train of blinding panic, Cam had a clear thought of collecting the fallen pieces for later reattachment. He could fill the bathtub with ice to keep the flesh fresh. But where could he get that much ice in such a short time? There was only about a bowlful in the freezer. Maybe really cold water would work just as well. He bent over to start collecting the hunks of himself from the floor. Unfortunately the act of bending over caused the tattoos on his chest to fall off at a faster rate.

He caught a couple before they hit the ground. They were still warm on the skin side and damp on the other. He threw them in the sink and while doing so caught a glimpse of his face in the mirror. The tattoo on his temple must have come off while he was bending over. In its place was bloody, exposed skull. Panic had found its opening and smashed its way through.

Cam's idea of collection was quickly abandoned in favor of preservation. In desperate attempts he tried to hold the tattoos in place before they left his body. It was a futile effort. The harder he held a piece in place, the faster it slipped from his grasp down to the ground. It didn't stop him from trying though. Each time a tattoo fell out of his hands he found another to rescue.

By this point chunks of Cam were showering the tile of the bathroom floor so fast he couldn't even get a hold of a piece before it came away. His flesh was piling up at his feet and he was helpless to stop it. "No, no, no, no, no." Cam's brain shut his eyes to block out the trauma of the situation, but his ears still worked perfectly well. The sound of meat cascading down on top of itself seemed never-ending. It eventually lessened to a sprinkling. Then after a couple more drops, it stopped.

Terrified to open his eyes, Cam just stood there, buried up to his shins in tattooed flesh. He knew he had to open his eyes at some point and face what was left of himself, but actually seeing the disfigured creature he'd now become was going to be worse than anything he could imagine.

Thinking it'd help ease him into the presumably horrific view, Cam scrunched his eyes into slits giving himself only blurry partial vision. What he saw was an ill-defined reddish figure standing in front of him. Bit by bit he opened his eyes until clear normal sight returned. A barely begun jigsaw puzzle of a person looked back at him from behind the glass. The figure was composed of visible muscle and tendon with the bones and organs underneath making occasional appearances. Scraps of still-attached skin polka-dotted the body. To his minor relief his genitals were fully intact, but looking the way he did now, they wouldn't be of much use anymore. Parts of mohawk hung to the scalp. His face was no longer ruined by ink. In fact he would've swapped that ink-ruined face without complaint for the face he was left with or in actuality, the lack of face he was left with. Bits of skull peeked through muscle, part of his jawbone was visible along with some teeth, cartilage... it was too much. Before he knew it his fist was smashing into the mirror, shattering it with the sound of a slamming door.

"Hi honey, did I wake you from your nap?" Mom, still holding her work paraphernalia, stood over the couch where a disoriented Cam struggled to sit up.

"No, I was just relaxing." Cam made a subtle but thorough examination of his face and head with both his hands.

Mom dropped her work stuff on the floor and continued into the kitchen. "I'm going to make your favorite dinner tonight, spaghetti and meatballs. How's that sound?"

"Sounds good to me." Cam stood up, gave his body a

once over, and joined his mother in the kitchen. She was already preparing to make her famous meatballs.

"I got an email from Blake today." Cam stood directly behind his mother.

"Oh yeah? How's he doing? I bet he's getting really excited about the baby. It's not going to be much longer now." Her hands were deep in a bowl of raw meat.

"He didn't mention the baby in this particular email. He actually mentioned something much more interesting. He said there's a secret about my childhood he was sworn not to tell me. Is this true?" A pinch of anger peppered his question along with an added dash of accusation.

A just-shaped meatball dropped from her hand. "That son of a bitch."

"So there *is* something! Tell me, I have to know." Cam almost grabbed her.

Hands still covered in meat, she turned around. "Marcus, I think sometimes the past should be left alone. It's not going to do you any good, so can you please just forget about it?"

"No! My life is a complete disaster. This could be part of the reason." He was shaking.

"That's why it's better left unsaid. You don't need any more complications right now. Focus on the future, on the things that can be changed." Her voice was calm and full of motherly authority. She didn't want him losing control.

It didn't work. "Tell me goddamn it!" He lost control and grabbed her.

She broke free of his grip, smearing raw meat on him during the act. To her it was inconceivable he'd dare grab his own mother in that way. His act of disrespect caused a boiling rage in her which in turn resulted in the beans spilling. "Fine! I'll tell you, OK?! I'm not your biological mother. Your real mother is your dead aunt Lana."

"What?" Cam's blood drained from his body into his feet, turning him a light shade of pale.

"Why don't we sit down and I'll tell you the whole story from the beginning." She washed the meat from her hands.

With feet full of blood, Cam found it difficult to move. "No, I'm standing right here."

"OK, whatever you want." His mother sat down. "Where do I start?" She took a moment and mentally readied herself for one of her over-detailed stories. "Let me first tell you a little bit about my younger sister. As a child she never seemed satisfied, no matter how much your grandparents spoiled her. The more she got the worse she became. She started spending all her time alone in the back yard immersed in books from the library. All the dolls, toys, clothes, and other gifts she got just collected dust in her closet. Towards the tail end of her teenage years she found what she thought was the reason for her dissatisfaction. She said we were living in a material-obsessed society without any true spirituality or connection to the natural world. She believed the only people left in this country with true spirituality were the Native Americans. After finishing high school she got a job, saved some money, and took off in the car our parents bought her for her sixteenth birthday. She didn't tell any of us where she was going, I doubt she knew herself. We occasionally received short letters and postcards from out-of-the-way places in Utah, Texas, Arizona, and New Mexico. Of course we were worried sick for her, a pretty young girl by herself on the road. Your grandfather wanted to take time off work and go look for her, but he knew deep down even if he did find her she wouldn't have come back. One day an uncharacteristically long letter arrived from her. In it she told us how she met a Native American boy named Frank. He was Zuni, if I'm remembering correctly. They had just moved into a small apartment together in Gallup, New Mexico. He worked for his father, who owned a housepainting business. Lana told us how happy she was and as a postscript she casually informed us she was pregnant. Your grandparents were furious with the fact she wasn't married to this Indian boy they never even met and let her know in an angry letter they wrote back to her. Lana only ever made one trip out here with you after you were born so everyone could meet you. Frank didn't come. She only came out of a sense of obligation, which she made very clear to all of us. We never saw her again."

Mom had to take a little break to wipe away the tears forming in the corners of her eyes. "Not too long before your third birthday there was a terrible car accident. My sister, Frank's mother, and Frank were all killed. Luckily you were strapped into your car seat and only received a small cut on your head. That's how you got that little scar above your eyebrow. Nobody knows exactly how long you were trapped in that car until help arrived. Frank's only surviving family member was his father, so I decided to take you in and raise you as my son."

The highly anticipated story came to an end and didn't contain any evil curses, government conspiracies, or alien intervention. It was more like the plot of one of those made-for-TV movies shown on the cable channels for bored housewives. There was no explanation for the unexplained multiplying tattoos, unless during that car accident as a child he received physical and/or psychological damage which causes a person to become a self-vandalizing amnesiac as an adult.

Anger reheated Cam's blood and it rose back into his head. "You're telling me you're my aunt and I have no blood relation to that asshole I think is my dad? Basically my whole life is one big lie? Great, just fucking great. Didn't this Indian grandfather of mine want anything to do with me?"

"At the time of the accident he was too devastated to even think about raising a child. Since then I've been regularly writing to him about you and your progress." Her calmness was unnerving.

"So he's cool with this lie I've been living?" Cam began to pace.

"His mailing address is a bar. The man has his own issues to deal with. I think having a well taken care of grandson was the least of his problems." Mom got up out of her chair and attempted to caress her son's head, but he flinched at her touch. "Honey you have to understand that since the day I took you in I've always thought of you as my son and I've always treated you that way. I loved my sister very much and you're a piece of her, so it makes me love you even more."

"Am I the reason that guy I thought was my dad left?" Cam wasn't able to look his mother in the eye.

"At first he did resent the idea of having to take care of a boy that wasn't his own son, but he grew to love you. He and I had problems years before you arrived. We married too young and then grew into different people. We were compatible as teenagers but not as adults." She couldn't get Cam to look at her.

Cam knew his life-destroying tattoo issue wasn't her fault, but the blame had been waiting for a long time to fall on someone and with her revelation it finally found a target.

"Were you ever going to tell me any of this or were you going to let me continue degenerating into even less than I am now? Look at me for Christ's sake! I used to be a good-looking guy with a great life. I had a career that was going places, a beautiful girlfriend who loved me, an awesome place to live with my best friend, and now? All that is gone, I'm gone. My life is over."

"Don't talk like that, sweetie. You still have your family. You'll always have your family." Her second attempt at affection was rebuffed.

"Yeah, a family full of liars. How can I trust any of you ever again? I can't be in the same room as you right now. I'm going." He walked away, bumping into the woman standing in front of him as he passed by her.

"There's no one to blame in any of this. We only did what we thought was best for you!"

Cam stared through the windshield at all the boxes stacked in front of his car. Big blue plastic tubs were the foundation for the multitude of cardboard boxes piled above. The blue plastic tubs contained all the stuff Blocko left behind so he could travel light on his global excursions. He wanted his memories sealed shut and protected just in case he decided to come back for them someday. On top of these were cardboard boxes with faded Marcus's written on their sides. These crumpled cartons contained his childhood: toys, action figures, his keychain collection, ticket stubs from all his trips to Disneyland and from all the baseball and bas-ketball games his 'dad' took him to, love letters from his 5th grade girlfriend Jenny, skeeball prizes from his birthday parties at Chuck E. Cheese's, colorful stones he found on the lake shore while on vacation with his grandparents, a stuffed bear he couldn't fall asleep without… all of it junk, boxes full of useless junk. Stacked above were boxes of his 'mom's' vinyls, records he grew up listening to: The Roll-ing Stones, The Beatles, Queen, Billy Joel, Squeeze. All of it obsolete, only valuable to hoarders of nostalgia. The next level of boxes were marked 'X-mas'. They were full of cheap, chipped and cracked ornaments and frayed tinsel. He'd never cover a dying pine tree in that trash ever again. On top of the stack were brand-new cardboard boxes with freshly written Cam's on the sides. Besides his wannabe punk wardrobe and the car he was sitting in (which techni-cally the bank owned about half of), everything he owned was in those boxes. An entire life encased in cardboard. Was that all he had to show for his time on this planet? Nine boxes? And after he was gone all his boxes would be chucked into a dumpster and then buried in some landfill to rot with the rest of the garbage.

He stuck his head out the window and took a deep breath of the stale air mixed with the carbon monox-ide slowly filling the closed garage. Putting an end to the big practical joke his life had become was the only viable option left to him. His 'mother' kept telling him to leave all his troubles in the past and think about the future. What future? Looking the way he did left him with very few career opportunities. Most of the guys in the world who looked like he did were either tattoo artists or rock stars. His lack of artistic and musical ability was a definite hindrance in pursuing either of those professions. If he were lucky he could get a job at one of the few remaining music stores or at an alternative clothing store. Then what? Begin the punk-rock guy act again while making so little money he'd be forced to keep living with the liar who called herself his mom? No way. Even if he did manage to somehow eke out a living for himself, he'd always be 'that tattooed guy' - stared at, talked about, and pushed to the fringes of society. He didn't want to live that life.

Sitting in a running car in a closed garage was such a cliché, but after reviewing the other choices, it seemed like the best way to do it. He thought about hanging himself, but after they found his body everybody probably would think it was a kinky jerkoff session gone wrong. Cam had enough embarrassment lately, he didn't need any more. Razor blades and guns were too messy. Leaving his blood everywhere for his 'mom' to clean up was kind of a dick move. And he knew he'd screw up a drug overdose and just end up getting sick and stuck in a hospital bed. He heard doing the carbon monoxide poisoning thing was just like falling asleep. If he ever woke up again, hopefully it'd be from the nightmare his life had become.

After a minute or two of fidgeting he stuck his head out the window again and took another deep breath. "How long is this supposed to take? I'm not feeling shit yet. Maybe this garage is too big." He put his head back in the car. "I guess I'll listen to some depressing music to keep me in the mood while I wait." Blocko had left plenty of that when he moved away. On the passenger seat next to him was a small pile of CDs. Blocko had left all his CDs in a separate box in the closet of his old bedroom; he didn't trust his most valuable possessions in the garage. Shuffling through the CDs he'd grabbed from his 'brother's' collection, Cam chose the one he thought had the most depressing cover. It had a picture of a well-dressed man sitting alone in the waiting area of a deserted airport. The album was Limbo Airlines by the band Unlovable. Cam put it in, chose the track with the appropriate sounding name of 'Luggage', and pressed play.

Exit the plane

Make way towards

Baggage claim

Reach the suitcase

Grab for the handle

Changed my mind

Left it behind

Walking down

The carpeted corridor

To another workday

Reach the glass door

Grab for the handle
Changed my mind
Left it behind

Looking through
Home's bright windows
See the expectant family
Reach the front door
Grab for the handle
Changed my mind
Left it behind

Drifting away
From it all
Figure in the fog
Reaches out
Grab for the hand
Changed my mind
Left it behind

Can't press rewind
There's nothing left to find

Little black specks started appearing in Cam's vision.

His head felt lighter, so he didn't understand why his neck was having trouble supporting its weight. The specks grew and connected with each other until the blackness completely enveloped Cam.

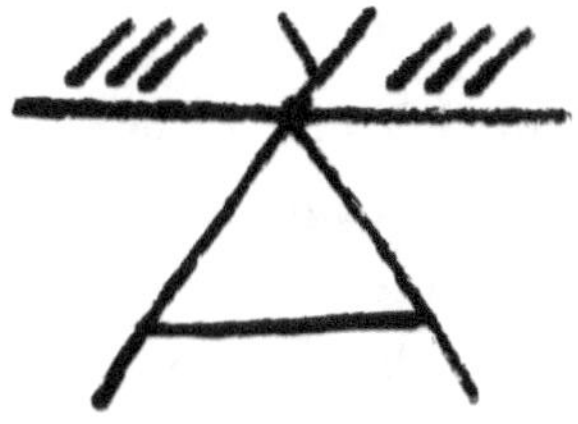

WEAK RED LIGHT invaded the blackness, becoming stronger and stronger, until the black became deep red. Cam understood he was staring at the insides of his eyelids and bright light was shining through the thin skin. All he had to do was open them. To what though? The afterlife? His last memory was purposely sucking his car's exhaust into his lungs. Activities like that usually kill or cause serious brain damage. If he had indeed passed over to the other side, why could he still feel his body?

It was possible his spirit mind was only creating the illusion of having a body so the transition wouldn't be so traumatic. Or maybe his 'mother' found him passed out in the garage and now he was lying in a hospital bed hooked up to a machine keeping him alive. That seemed unlikely as he assumed hospital beds were much softer than whatever he was lying on now. The afterlife it was then. Now he had to force himself to open his eyes and see where he'd be spending eternity.

Blinding light filled his squinted eyes. His hand instinctually came up to shade this light from his vision. Cam saw it wasn't a divine light searing his eyeballs, it was only the sun. He was lying on his back staring up at the midday sky. Patches of blue peeked through the tops of tall trees. Perched on a branch of one of these trees was a large black bird. It looked down at the human lying on the ground and cawed a few times. Then it got bored and flew away. Cam sat up, looked around, and saw nothing but unspoiled forest in all directions. Maybe this is what heaven is, a return to nature, no cars, no buildings, no pollution, nothing manmade. A chance to start from scratch and instead of distancing yourself from the earth, you can work towards becoming one with it.

This beautiful thought stayed in his head until he stood up and noticed he was wearing the same clothes he wore in the car - his leather biker jacket, a grungy black T-shirt, torn jeans, and boots. On his hands were the familiar tattoos he never wanted to see again. And despite it being midday, he felt chilly.

"This isn't heaven, this is just some stupid fucking forest I somehow ended up in," he inadvertently said out loud. Luckily the forest was above those kinds of insults and wasn't offended.

Automatically his hand reached into his right front pocket to retrieve the phone usually sitting there, but this time it was empty. Maybe it was in the left pocket, also empty. He tried the back pockets and again came up empty.

His stomach dropped and in a mini-panic he went through all the pockets of his jacket. Nothing, no phone, no wallet, no keys, not even an old tissue, which he could've also used at the moment.

"GODDAMN IT!"

Internal reasoning kicked in, overtaking his anger and frustration. 'OK, I'm probably just in some sort of big nature park. If I keep walking in one direction I'll eventually reach the edge of it and then I can find a ranger or a park cop and get a ride home.' He spun around trying to decide in which direction to begin his trek. The problem was every direction looked the same. Cam chose the path of least resistance, trees being the perceived resistance.

The sun was closing in on the horizon and Cam hadn't found any sign of civilization yet. Maybe he chose the wrong direction and was walking further into the park. There was no way to know. He found a small outcropping of rocks and climbed to the top. A higher vantage point didn't help at all. It only reinforced the fact he was alone in the middle of nowhere and it was getting dark. The thought frightened him and a panicked yelling session ensued. "HEY! CAN ANYONE HEAR ME?! I'M LOST! HEY, ANYONE OUT THERE?! HELP ME, SOMEONE PLEASE HELP ME."

He continued on and on with the yelling until his voice started to crack. The last of his words followed their predecessors through the air and like their predecessors, became entangled in high tree branches where no rescuer was likely to find them. The prolonged yelling had caused a tremendous thirst and it made Cam realize he had no idea the last time he'd drunk or eaten anything. He saw a small pond in the distance and made his way towards it. Kneeling at the water's edge he cupped his hands, but before they went in to collect the desperately needed liquid, Cam took a good look at what he was about to pour down his throat.

The entire surface of the pond was covered in algae and below this dark green layer he could see nothing but a muddy mess swarming with real and imagined microscopic creatures, each carrying deadly bacteria eagerly awaiting entrance into his stomach. He let out a high pitched "SHIT" as he smashed his fists into the water.

Defeated, Cam slumped down next to a tree where the absurdity of his situation finally set in. Finding himself alone in the wilderness without any idea of how he got there wasn't the absurd part. That kind of shit was his new normal. The absurd part was his attempt at survival and rescue when only this morning (or it could've been yesterday morning, it was impossible to know) he was trying to end it all. Cam had heard stories about the body's overwhelming survival instinct during the last moments of a suicide, but he was nowhere close to death now. If he didn't fall and crack his head open on a rock or if a bear didn't eat him, he knew he could probably survive out here for at least a couple of days. So he asked himself, 'Why did I spend the entire day trying to get back home? Am I in a hurry to get in the garage again for another round of sucking in car exhaust? Wouldn't it be easier to find a nice high cliff to jump from or eat a bunch of poisonous mushrooms than wasting time and energy getting back to civilization for a civilized suicide?'

A possible answer jumped into his brain—If one kills oneself in the forest and no one is around to find the body, did a suicide actually occur? A hiker coming across his scattered bones in a few years wouldn't have the same impact of his 'mother' finding his lifeless body in her garage. If he couldn't die the way he wanted to, then he was going to survive just out of spite. That would show himself, wouldn't it?

During his little life-and-death internal struggle the sun had gone down along with the temperature. He needed to find a place to spend the night. It was getting too dark to attempt to build any kind of shelter, so he went back to the outcropping of rocks. They would at least give him a bit of natural cover. He gathered armfuls of dry leaves and pine needles and built himself a crude nest. It was neither comfortable nor warm. He curled into a fetal position, which made him feel somewhat warmer, but at the same time smaller and more insignificant.

As he stared at the clear night sky almost white with stars, he felt the crushing realization of his place in the universe - a miniscule speck of flesh anchored to a pebble sinking in an infinite ocean. Suburban living had always protected him from these sorts of thoughts. Cities had defeated the night's darkness so long ago Cam had rarely ever seen the unadulterated view of the vast universe surrounding him. On the few occasions he had seen it, he'd been too busy partying with friends and family to let profound philosophical questioning get in the way of having fun. What he was feeling now was almost claustrophobia. He was trapped on a spinning sphere in immeasurable space.

Being lost in the wilderness paled in comparison, but he brought that fear back to the forefront. At least it was a tangible fear that could be dealt with. It was a primal fear, *the* primal fear; the fear of the unknown lurking out there in the darkness waiting to get him. A fire would've been nice. In fact he would've given almost anything for a fire, but he knew that without a lighter or matches it wasn't going to happen. Of course he'd watched countless survivalist shows on TV and seen the many ways those guys were able to make fire. Once he even saw a guy start a fire with a bag of his own piss. Unfortunately Cam didn't have a clear plastic bag or any other handy accessories that would aid him in flame creation. Tomorrow morning he could try to rub two sticks together and hope for the best, but he didn't feel that would be necessary. His plan wasn't to make a camp here. He had to keep moving and find his way back to the real world. Spending hours in the dirt rubbing sticks together for the slim chance of a spark would be a waste of valuable time. Tomorrow morning he'd wake up with the sun and have a full day of light to find the way out.

The problem was he couldn't fall asleep. Every little sound out in the darkness was a bear getting ready to attack. The crunch of leaves could be a mountain lion sneaking up on him. There's were probably poisonous snakes slithering all around him waiting to strike. At least if he had some fire, a knife, or even a sharpened stick, he could defend himself, but he didn't have anything. He was an easy meal for any hungry predator that happened to come along. The feeling of complete helplessness was terrifying and all he could do about it was pray to a god he didn't believe in.

"Please, please let me get home. I never did anything to hurt anyone. I don't deserve this. I don't deserve any of this, I'm a good person. I don't want to become bear food.

I just want to go home. That's all I want, just to go home, please."

Cam noticed he was shivering badly, but he didn't know if it was from fear or from the cold. He curled up even tighter into his nest. Somehow the pine needles were seeping through the leather of his jacket and the denim of his jeans, poking his skin in countless places. Even the rocks he was lying next to were against him. They were radiating cold waves directly through his clothing.

The persistent poking of the pine needles became the legs and fangs of imaginary insects crawling and biting. More and more of them were climbing up his pant legs and heading directly to his crotch. Rolling around didn't crush them, it made it worse. Stripping naked and brushing these things off was the only solution, but that solution was unthinkable. He'd freeze and his exposed body would probably attract the bears even quicker. He had to endure the bugs until morning, when hopefully it'd be warm enough to undress. The problem was he didn't know how long he'd have to wait until morning arrived. Without his phone Cam had no clue what time it was or how much time was passing. Counting to sixty over and over again and then keeping track of the minutes that passed seemed to be a good idea, but after about six minutes his concentration waned and the mental stopwatch stopped working. It didn't matter anyway as he didn't know how many more hours the night was going to last. Waiting in fear, in the cold, and slowly being devoured by insects was beyond intolerable. Morning had to come soon and save him.

Cam felt hours, days, weeks pass without any sign of the dawn. "I remember that whenever I went to bed on

Sunday night, Monday morning would always come so quick. Maybe if I pretend I have a shitty job to go to tomorrow morning this night will end a lot faster. Come on sun, hurry and get your ass up!"

In an apparent response, the black of night began to turn to a dark purple. "Finally."

Cam's relief was short-lived. He'd heard the expression 'false dawn', but thought it was only a saying. He became caught in a state of constant anticipation, waiting and expecting to see the sun pop up, but it never did. "I never knew the morning was such a tease."

Then the unthinkable happened. The sun peeked over the horizon and a ray of light hit Cam in the face. An event that had occurred every single day of his life and presumably every morning since the existence of the planet Earth was miraculous to him. A giant ball of fire rising into the sky, lighting and warming the world was an absolutely incredible phenomenon. He couldn't believe he'd always taken something as amazing as this for granted. For Cam it was now easily understandable why so many early cultures worshipped the sun. He supposed the practice probably died out when God took over the responsibility of guaranteeing the sun would rise each morning. A promise He would keep as long as His followers were cool with Him.

The light and warmth eased Cam into an uneasy restless sleep, but it was better than no sleep at all. His stomach, annoyed at being empty for so long, woke him with a hollow pain. "Don't worry good buddy, I'm gonna find my way out of here today and fill you up with all the chicken soft tacos and Macho Nachos you can handle."

Cam maneuvered his way out of the nest and with

some difficulty stood up. His body was stiff and sore from spending the night on something other than a soft mattress. The urge to strip naked and clean the insects from his skin had faded. Brushing the pine needles off his clothing seemed to be enough. Standing in the sunshine of a new day, Cam's night terrors were replaced with optimism. He had no doubt whatsoever he'd be out of the forest by the end of the afternoon. The only problem now was in which direction to go. Before he had a chance to choose he heard something moving in the trees behind the rocks. It retriggered some of those primal fears about being torn apart with razor-sharp claws and then being devoured by hungry fangs. Maybe it was only a deer or some birds, but he had to be sure.

On his belly, Cam carefully and, as quietly as he could manage, inched his way to the other side of the rocks and snuck a peek. To his relief it wasn't a hungry bear or a vicious mountain lion, but something even more surprising. A young boy of about eight or nine with sandy blond hair dressed in jeans and a dark blue T-shirt was playing alone near some rocks in the distance. Without thinking, Cam jumped up and yelled at him. "Hey kid!"

The boy turned around, looked directly at Cam, and ran away. "Shit." Cam suddenly remembered the way he looked and realized how scary it must have been to see someone as extreme as him pop up out of nowhere, especially for a child.

The kid was Cam's ticket out of the wilderness. His family's campsite couldn't be too far away. They'd have food and know the way back to the civilized world. There wasn't any choice, he had to follow the boy, but the kid was fast, so it became more of a chase.

"C'mon kid, wait up! I'm not going to hurt you. I just want to talk to your parents." Cam really didn't have the energy for a prolonged chase, but the kid was getting farther away, so he increased his pace. It didn't get him any closer. The boy was perpetually fifty to sixty yards ahead of him.

"This kid must've had a shitload of energy drinks for breakfast this morning." Cam was already getting tired and in desperation tried pleading. "Stop please! I'm lost and I need help!"

It didn't work. In fact the boy sped up. Cam's only option was to do the same. He began to run at full speed, which wasn't easy in heavy boots on forest terrain. The ground was full of rocks and exposed roots he had to jump over, bushes he had to avoid, and branches he had to constantly duck under. Dodging obstacles, keeping the kid in view, and maintaining his speed was becoming too much to handle. His thick leather jacket was getting heavier and causing him to sweat profusely. Continuing was only going to cause a collapse and then he'd really be screwed. He eased his pace to a brisk walk and even that was a struggle.

"Gimme a break kid! I know I look scary, but I swear I only want some help from your parents." The words came out between attempts to catch his breath and were barely understandable, but the kid must've registered something of what was said because he stopped and turned around with a coy smile. Before Cam could reach him, the boy hid behind a tree. Using the last of his reserves, he sprinted to the tree, confident he finally caught the damn kid. He wasn't there. Cam scanned the immediate area and saw the boy briefly poke his head out from behind a different tree. Using the real last of his reserves, Cam rushed to the kid's new hiding place and again found no one. He then saw the boy peeking out from behind yet another tree. "That little bastard."

Cam knew he wasn't going to catch this kid by force. He had to outsmart him. With as much stealth as he could muster, Cam hid behind each tree leading up to the boy's hiding place. He was careful to avoid crunching the dry leaves and twigs beneath his heavy boots. It made his progress painfully slow and by the time Cam reached each of the boy's new hiding places, he found them empty. The kid, bored with waiting to be found, had already moved on. After about six hiding places Cam lost track of the boy and sat down to rest on the edge of a large clearing. "Screw it anyway. The little prick is probably lost too."

In the tall grass of the clearing Cam noticed some movement. He assumed it was a rabbit or something, but he then saw a sandy blond head of hair pop up and look around. Cam moved behind the nearest tree and continued to watch. The boy had a stick in his hands and was pretending it was a gun. Alone behind enemy lines, he had to fight his way back to freedom. Bad guys were everywhere trying to kill him, but he was too quick and too sneaky to be gotten. One by one the bad guys were taken out by his super machine gun that never missed its target.

Cam knew the game well, so well in fact he could predict the boy's next moves. The tree line at the edge of the clearing would be the entrance to the boss's headquarters. It would be guarded by at least four men with super machine guns of their own. He would have to switch his super machine gun to silent mode and quietly kill all four guards so as not to sound the alarm. Once inside he'd have to fight his way up to the boss's penthouse. When he was face to face with the big boss himself, he would have to fight him in hand-to-hand combat because all his super machine gun's bullets were gone. With his awesome karate skills he'd deliver a devastating roundhouse kick to the boss's head, decapitating him. On the roof he'd find a helicopter, steal it, and pilot it to freedom. Once home he'd receive a hero's welcome, a parade in his honor and a medal for bravery given to him by the president himself during a nationally broadcasted ceremony. Every girl in school would fall in love with him and every boy would beg to be his friend.

Cam hid himself behind a tree he suspected would be a part of the imagined entrance to the boss's headquarters and waited for the boy to pass. With his stick/super machine gun in hand, the boy shot the guards and ran past the tree Cam was waiting behind. At the right moment he pounced and grabbed the unsuspecting kid from behind by the shoulders, but he was a little rougher than he'd planned and his overuse of force caused the boy to fall forward. Temporarily free from the grip of his attacker, the boy was able to get on his hands and knees and turn around. He looked up at Cam without any hint of fear in his eyes. The only reaction he showed to being caught was the little self-accusing smile that appeared on his face.

"I finally got you, you little punk." Cam directed his comment to the boy, but it was more a self-congratulatory statement. With the little smile still on his lips, the boy shook his head and turned around, readying himself to take off again.

"I don't think so." Cam wasn't going to let the little bastard go, even if it meant tackling him and pinning him to the ground. The boy looked back just before he attempted to flee. Cam had to make damn sure he stopped that from happening and lunged down at him. In mid-lunge a small but strong gust of wind whipped up all the leaves covering the ground, temporarily blinding him. Even though he couldn't see the boy, Cam knew he was right there inches from his grasp. It was a genuine shock when he fell to the ground clutching nothing but handfuls of crumbling dead leaves. He lifted his head from the ground to look for the boy. He wasn't there, he wasn't anywhere.

Exhausted from his seemingly hours of pursuit, Cam had to rest. He found a comfortable spot under a nearby tree. The remaining perspiration clinging to his body and clothing soon chilled as the forest's canopy was preventing the sun from performing its job as evaporator. Cam had spent enough time shivering the previous night and searched out a place in the sun. His perspiration vanished and was rapidly replaced by sweat. Maybe it was the leather jacket making him so warm, so he took it off. It didn't make a difference. Heat, a major deficiency of the night before, was now in surplus and leeching out the valuable little moisture left in his body. "Goddamn it!"

He was forced back into the shade and of course all the sweat again began to cool, bringing his body temperature back down. What could he do but return to an unshaded spot? Finding only a sweltering sense of déjà vu waiting for him, he left to find cooler one.

'Damned if you do... , the grass is always greener... , between a rock and... , Catch 22, out of the fire into the frying'... . Actually that last one didn't apply as both of those places were quite hot, but the rest of the sayings stood out in his head and reinforced his not-so-long-held philosophy that no matter what he did, no matter what choices he made or didn't make, the world, fate, destiny, or whatever was out to screw him as much as possible. Now it wasn't even going to let him rest comfortably for more than five minutes. He couldn't believe it had become that petty.

"Fuck yooooou!!!" Cam yelled to the sky, mountains, trees, birds, to everyone and everything within earshot conspiring against him.

"I'm getting the hell outta here." He stood up, angrily kicked some debris out of his way, and headed off in the direction he supposed would to lead him to the exit. Hours later he found himself in front of a familiar sight, his nest. Mind and body were far too exhausted to produce a strong emotional reaction to the fact he'd spent the entire day going absolutely nowhere. All his body could do was collapse next to a large rock and the only feeling his mind could conjure up was dread. Dread of spending another cold and terrifying night alone in a pile of leaves and pine needles surrounded by the black unknown.

"If I'm going to have to spend another night here I might as well make myself a little more comfortable." Cam's internal dialogue was subconsciously leaking out through his mouth. First he rebuilt the nest, this time without any pine needles. Next he broke off leafy low-hanging branches from some nearby trees. He leaned these against the rock next to his nest and created a roof. For security he found a long straight sturdy stick and sharpened one end as well as he could with a stone. Having a shitty spear was better than not having a shitty spear. During the sharpening process he noticed a good amount of heat coming off the wood. It gave him second thoughts about his ability to make a fire. Second thoughts are second for a reason because they're the runner-up to the first and usually better thoughts. Listening to the frontrunner instead of the runner-up would've saved Cam from destroying his hands with his futile attempts at creating a flame. All combinations of wood and stone were rubbed, spun, and hit. He did succeed in one thing though. He was successful in disproving the saying 'where there's smoke there's fire'. Plenty of wisps of smoke were squeezed from the wood, but nothing more.

Darkness stopped any further tries at producing the warmth and light needed to make the upcoming night bearable. Cam grabbed his shitty spear with one of his filthy cut-up hands and took it with him into his tiny shelter. Without the pine needles digging into his body, the nest was somewhat comfortable and the roof he'd built kept out some of the cold. Having his spear nearby gave him the illusion of safety. These were all huge improvements over the previous night. His mind wasn't consumed by terror, cold, and discomfort as it was the night before. It was free to roam beyond primal fears and into other dark, rarely visited corners.

Not once during his entire life had Cam ever been truly alone. Someone had always been nearby, if not physically then at most only a shout or a phone call away. The company of others had never been out of reach. A buddy to have a drink or a smoke with, a warm body next to him in bed, guys to ball with, co-workers to gossip with, a crowd to get lost in, a family to be a part of - always there whenever he wanted or needed. None of that was available anymore, not now and maybe not ever. All his connections to the people in his life had been severed one by one. Lying in a pile of leaves, stranded in the wilderness was the least subtle way possible of driving the point home he was completely alone in the world.

Without his relationship with his world, Cam wasn't merely alone, but lost. His world dumped him and wouldn't take his calls. Their codependent relationship was over and Cam didn't know who the hell he was without it. He wasn't T's best friend and roommate, he wasn't Crazzee's boyfriend, he wasn't an employee of Reboot Financial or of the Station, he wasn't Ras's buddy and poolhouse mate, he wasn't the best basketball player in the city's amateur league, he wasn't Syn's boyfriend, he wasn't the hot guy the girls all secretly wanted and all the other guys were secretly jealous of, he wasn't the freak everybody stared at, he wasn't Blake's little brother, he wasn't his mother's son, he was only a hunk of cowering cold conscious flesh.

Mother Nature didn't differentiate his hunk of flesh from any of the others around him. Hypothermia wasn't going to question his fashion choices before shutting down his organs one by one. Hunger wasn't going to check his bank account before it deprived his body of nourishment. The bear waiting out there in the dark wasn't going to notice his tattoos while he was tearing through inked skin with teeth and claws.

Unlike the rest of the organisms surrounding him in the woods, he was cursed with the gift of self-awareness.

Cam didn't have the luxury of living moment to moment on pure instinct. He had the ability to look backward with regret and the ability to project forward to the countless possible misfortunes awaiting him. He doubted the birds in the trees above had second thoughts about their nest placement or worried about what they were going to do when their wings were too weak to keep them airborne. Shunned by the world of men and set apart from the realm of nature, Cam was a just piece of organic refuse waiting to decompose. Desolation descended into him and pushed out the awaiting tears. His self-pity continued and multiplied and fueled the continuous stream of water flowing from his eyes. He cried himself to sleep.

A few weak rays of sunshine snuck through the leafy ceiling of the crude shelter and landed on Cam's face, waking him from a deeply disturbed sleep. As he opened his eyes the memory of the vivid and unsettling dream he had been experiencing crumbled away. He was able to catch a few pieces before they were lost. He remembered a group of happy, smiling, but at the same time concerned women standing over him. After watching him experience an intense unbearable pain the women became even happier. An immense emptiness overcame him and those happy faces turned panicked and horrified. He could hear screaming and wailing, but couldn't see anything anymore. His vision had faded away and this, the last piece of the temporary dream memory, left too. What was left with him upon awakening was the immense emptiness inside.

Hunger had left his stomach on the brink of implosion. Having never gone this long without food, it was seriously thinking of resorting to cannibalism. Thirst wasn't doing his body any favors either. He could barely produce enough saliva to keep his throat lubricated and felt he was on the verge of choking to death. Some sort of water had to be found immediately. Cam remembered seeing those survivalist guys on TV sipping the dew off leaves. It seemed an easy way to relieve his thirst.

He left his shelter, saw the sun high in the sky, and realized morning was long over. His plan had evaporated along with all the dew. It didn't stop from him from trying though. After a few attempts at licking seemingly moist leaves and getting mouthfuls of bitterness instead, he gave up. Spitting out the awful taste only caused him to lose more precious saliva. His bungled attempt at quenching his thirst had only caused it to increase and made him even more desperate.

It was this desperation which led him back to the pond filled with its disgusting water. Thirst removed the algae, the mud, and the invisible bacteria from the water and left only an oasis of clean cool liquid refreshment. He bent over the pond and scooped large handfuls of water into his mouth. Cam's taste buds didn't register the horrible stagnant flavor pouring down his throat. He could only feel the magnificent sensation of liquid entering his body for the first time in days. It filled his belly with renewal and hope. He might survive this ordeal and make it back to the civilized world in one piece.

These good feelings rekindled some confidence in his ability to find something to eat. The forest was full of animals that needed to eat to survive. Some of the things they ate had to be safe for human consumption.

Aimless wandering and searching turned up a small

selection of berries and quite a lot of mushrooms, any of which could've been perfectly safe to eat or could've just as easily caused a slow and painful death. Cam closely examined and smelled the berries and mushrooms, but it was pointless. His knowledge of berries included what was available in the supermarket and as for mushrooms, he was only familiar with two types, regular and magic. The question was either to take a chance on eating the bounty provided by the forest and die a slow painful death by food poisoning or not eat and die a slow painful death from hunger.

"Mother fucking Discovery Channel! They make this survival shit seem so easy. I'll bet if any of those survivor guys were in my place right now, they'd be just as screwed as I am. None of those guys are ever in any real danger anyway. When the cameras are turned off they probably go and stay in a hotel and order room service. Then in the morning they…"

An invisible punch to the stomach put his Discovery Channel rant on hold. The punch's pain bent Cam over and all the pondwater he'd consumed earlier violently spewed from his mouth. He attempted to get himself upright and find a place to recover from the shock, but his body wasn't satisfied yet. It wanted to be absolutely sure everything was removed from the stomach, so it blasted him with intense shots of nausea.

"I can't, I can't anymore… there's nothing left inside me." Cam was on his knees, retching up air. But he wasn't as empty as he thought. From somewhere deep inside a fluorescent green slime gushed out of him. He thought he vomited out his soul. If ghosts were made of ectoplasm and ghosts were basically souls without bodies, then it was perfectly logical that the green mess all over the ground was his ectoplasmic essence. Fortunately for Cam the green stuff was only his stomach's unemployed digestive fluid. It meant his soul was still firmly in place in his suffering and ruined body. The tide of nausea subsided, giving Cam the opportunity to collapse.

He returned to consciousness minutes or hours later, he had no idea, but it was still daytime and the sun had heated his leather jacket to the point where it was burning his skin. He quickly got up (quickly at this point was almost two minutes of struggling to stand without passing out again), took off the jacket, and found some shade. One side of his face was caked with dirt and dried bile. The other side reddened from too much sun. Luckily there were no mirrors around. Seeing the added dissymmetry in his face would've only further disheartened Cam's spirit.

Sitting in one spot was never going to get him anywhere. He had to try to find help because it was abundantly clear it was never going to find him. Cam put his still slightly warmed jacket back on and began to walk and walk and walk a little more. Soon he saw a small hill in the distance. It gave him a feeble spark of hope. Maybe if he stood atop the hill he'd be able to see a way out of this nightmare.

His chance of escape came even sooner than expected. A person was sitting on the hill. At least it looked like a person from Cam's vantage point. He rushed towards his salvation. "HEY! Is somebody there?! I need help!"

No response or movement came from the figure on the hill. Cam hoped he wasn't yelling at a bush or a rock. What if someone saw him, they'd think he was crazy.

On reaching his destination he realized the figure was indeed a person and not a bush. It was a young woman with long stringy blond hair sitting alone on a large boulder. What was left of her disintegrated clothing was filthy. Her skin, which her outfit did a poor job covering, was stretched tight over the emaciated body. Nothing of her skeletal structure was left to the imagination. Surrounding her were neatly piled stacks of rocks. Rocks and stones of every shape, size, and color had been assembled into intricate towers. There were dozens and dozens of these structures. Some of them were only three or four stones high and others were almost five feet tall.

"Can you help me? I've been lost for days without anything to eat or drink." Even though she looked in much worse shape than he did, Cam had to ask.

With visible effort, she lifted her head and looked at him. She said nothing.

"Do you have anything to eat or drink?" Cam knew it was another dumb question, but he was desperate.

She looked around at her stone towers and shook her head.

It had been an exhausting day and Cam needed a rest. He sat down next to her on the boulder. She wasn't at all surprised or revolted by his appearance. In fact she paid no attention to him at all. An awkward silence ensued. All the discomfort was firmly on Cam's side. If they were in an Orange County bar together then this kind of situation could've been normal. Cam had been given the cold shoulder by a lot of 'I'm waiting for someone better to come along' bitches in his time. He wondered if she was also waiting for someone better to come by. They were in the middle of nowhere and judging by her appearance she'd been waiting for a while. He had to find out.

"Are you waiting for someone?"

She shook her head.

"So, you're up here all alone?"

She looked at her rocks and shook her head.

Cam blamed his temporary lapse of judgment about the girl on the lack of nutrition his brain was receiving. She was obviously nuts. "How long ya been up here?"

She shrugged.

He knew he couldn't leave her here. She wasn't going to last much longer. On the other hand what help could he give her? A crippled knight in rusted armor on a dead horse wasn't in any position to save the damsel in distress, but chivalry demanded he try. Cam looked at it logically; she wouldn't be any more screwed if he took her with him. "You don't look so good, maybe you should come with me. We'll eventually have to run into somebody out here that will help us. Come on, let's go."

She shook her head.

Cam had a feeling she'd resist, so he stood up and offered her his hand. "Come on. You can't stay here."

She shook her head again. This time more vigorously.

"You *want* to stay here?"

She nodded.

"WHY?"

She looked around at all her towers of stone. "I can't leave them." She spoke in a dry, barely heard whisper.

He knelt down next to her. "You can't leave the rocks?"

She shook her head.

"They're just rocks. You're going to die if you stay here. Don't you know that?"

She looked lovingly at her rocks. "It took me forever to collect them all. Every single one of them is special."

Cam stood and walked over to take a closer look at the rock towers. Maybe they contained stones too valuable to leave behind. Not being a geologist he couldn't say for sure, but none of the stones looked valuable or even special. They were rocks you could find anywhere. Out of frustration he kicked over one of the towers. Immediately the girl rushed over and began to rebuild it. She caressed each stone before putting it back it its place. After she finished the construction she returned to her seat on the boulder. The temptation to kick it over again was difficult to resist.

Instead of further torturing the poor girl, Cam decided he would take her away with him. Even if it meant he had to drag her kicking and screaming. She looked pretty light and probably wouldn't have the strength to put up much of a struggle. He could do it, but which way would he take her? The view from the hill didn't help at all—nothing but trees in all directions. Cam could see the sun was on its downward trajectory to the west. Following it would eventually get him to the coast, which was covered in civilization. Hopefully there weren't any giant mountains blocking his way.

"Come on. We're going." Cam grabbed her wrist, but it was so thin and boney it kept slipping from his grip. He attempted to pick her up, but she squirmed so much he couldn't get a hold. Instead, he knelt down and grabbed her from under her armpits and began to pull. The girl flailed about wildly, trying desperately to return to her rocks.

"Calm down! This is for your own good. I'm saving your crazy ass. Once we get back to civilization you can start a new collection of rocks. I'll even help you, alright?" Cam noticed a golfball-sized stone on the ground the girl must have missed.

He temporarily released his grip, picked it up, and showed it to her. "See, I'm helping already. This can be the first rock of your new collection." He put it in his jacket pocket and continued the dragging. Since she was wearing so little clothing, he had to be careful the way he dragged her. He didn't want to damage her fragile body. Progress was slow, made slower by her flailing and the fact he had to walk backwards while pulling. An advantage of walking backwards was clearly being able to see where you've been in case you needed to retrace your steps back to the beginning of your journey. Of course the main disadvantage was not being able to see the upcoming obstacles in your path. Tired of stumbling over branches and rocks, Cam reversed his grip on the reluctant draggee and was able to walk forward.

Little by little her thrashing decreased until it stopped altogether. "Good. Now will you walk with me so I can stop dragging you? You're heavier than you look."

Cam carefully set her down. He had no clue where the strength to pull the reluctant weight had come from, but it completely drained whatever hidden energy reserve was used. She'd have to walk on her own from now on. When Cam turned around to inform her she'd be traveling under her own power for the rest of the trip, he didn't see her lying on the ground. He saw a large log with two stumpy branch arms poking out from either side of it in her place.

Searching for her was useless, she wasn't here. She wasn't anywhere.

Cam's legs gave out and he collapsed. Despair drove tears down his filthy face. He put his head in his bleeding hands. The fire-creation-attempt wounds on his palms had been reopened by the rough bark of the stumpy branch arms. Everything he'd done so far was meaningless. The outcome of all his struggling and suffering was ending up alone in the dirt.

"I give up." Cam closed his eyes and soon lost consciousness.

To escape from the darkness behind his eyelids Cam opened his eyes, but nothing changed. The darkness remained. He blinked hard a few times and still saw nothing but darkness. He waved his hands in front of his face, but still only saw darkness. Panic set in. He thought he'd been blinded by malnutrition or by something in the pondwater he'd ingested. Then he calmed himself down and assumed it was probably just a moonless and starless night and his eyes hadn't adjusted yet. If he was patient his sight would soon return.

He waited, but the darkness remained. In fact it was increasing. He could feel the pressure of it coming at him from all sides. This darkness wasn't merely the absence of light. It was the absence of everything.

Before it reached him, Cam desperately groped about for some kind of escape or protection and found something familiar, the log with the stumpy branch arms. He wrapped his arms around it, pulled it as close to his body as

he could, and closed his eyes as tightly as possible. Returning to the view behind his eyelids was at least a recognizable darkness, not like the darkness that had surrounded
him. Surrounded wasn't quite the right description since it
didn't have any kind of mass. It was the opposite of mass;
an infinite emptiness. A place where there was no distinc-
tion between things, because there wasn't anything, it was
all nothing. It was a place where time didn't exist. Memories and history couldn't be, because without the past
there's nothing to remember and without the future nothing could ever be planned and nothing would ever grow or
change. It was a place which was in actuality no place at all.
It was where Cam would have never been or would never
come to be.

He clung to the log with all his strength. It was the
only thing preventing him from falling into the eternal nothingness.

All of the log's substantial weight had come to rest on
his right arm, which in turn began to cut off circulation. The
arm filled with vibrating pins and needles. Then it started
to lose feeling all together. Without the proper blood flow
Cam wasn't sure if his arm and hand were getting the message to keep hanging on. He had to roll to the left and get
the log on top of his chest. It took all his strength, but he
managed it with surprisingly minimal damage to himself.
Only a few cuts and scrapes on his wrists and forearms plus
what he assumed was a giant bruise on his chest where the
log came thudding down.

The top end of the log now hovered directly over his
face and its dry bark pressed against his nose. With any
small movement of his head, his nose would scrape against

the bark, flaking off tiny pieces into his mouth. He turned his head to the right and spit out the miniscule wood chips. With such a weight resting on his lungs, breathing became more of an effort than an unconscious certainty, but he couldn't let go. The log was his life raft. If his grip slipped he'd drown in the ocean of nonexistence. No more Cam.

Four pairs of little legs landed on Cam's left cheek. They began exploring the contours of his face. Feeling some heat coming from the mouth, the spider crawled onto Cam's lips, attempting to enter the warm cavern beyond. Cam wiggled his lips and tried to blow the spider off without opening his mouth. Unsuccessful with getting into the cave, it noticed two smaller caves nearby. Strong gusts of wind impeded the spider's entry, but it didn't give up. Some great web-spinning spots might lie just beyond the entrance. These caves had to attract tons of tiny flying insects.

It got itself inside and was disappointed to find the space became smaller and smaller. There wasn't room enough to create a proper web. Cam frantically tried to pull enough air from his lungs to blow the spider out from his nose, but the log on his chest was getting heavier. Unable to get enough air through his nose, he thrashed his head from side to side in an attempt to get the spider out but only succeeded in rubbing the skin on the tip of his nose raw against the rough bark of the log.

Soon after, the spider left on its own accord - off to find a suitable spot to build a home where it could relax and have its meals conveniently delivered, blissfully ignorant of the eternal nothingness and the threat to its existence.

Weakened from days without food or water, Cam's

muscles were already past their breaking point. Only will-power and adrenaline were keeping the log in place on his chest. The temptation to let go was overwhelming. Falling into the abyss would be just the same as falling into a deep dreamless sleep without ever waking up. Sleep was what he needed and the idea of a super long slumber sounded fantastic, but he wouldn't let that happen. He couldn't let his existence be snuffed out. Everything else had been taken from him and he wasn't going to lose the one thing he had left, himself.

Maybe the darkness had already passed. He opened his eyes to check. It hadn't. The darkness was blacker than before. Even though he couldn't see, he could feel his body as an insignificant speck surrounded by the vast ocean of nothingness and his grip on the small wooden buoy of somethingness was slipping.

Cam then became painfully aware of the complete absence of up or down and left or right. It caused vertigo to set in. He tried as hard as he could to ground himself, but it was impossible to get grounded when there wasn't a ground. His failed attempt to find ground caused him to spin, slowly at first and as there's no resistance in nothingness, faster and faster. It was as if he were on an out-of-control carnival ride while drunker than he'd ever been in his entire life. Opposing centrifugal forces were coming from within and without. They were too powerful, Cam couldn't hold on anymore. The log came loose, leaving him without his link to existence. Stranded in the void, his consciousness spun away.

Light, dim starlight and moonlight, but light was what Cam saw when he could open his eyes again. He'd somehow escaped from the darkness, or had he? It all could've been a dream or just another hallucination, but the terror he felt in the infinite nothing was so real. It didn't matter, he was back on solid ground, lost and starving in a dark wilderness, but at least it was somewhere. With some effort he got up off the ground and when he was on his feet again, his body felt very heavy. Lying at his feet was the log. He stared down at it. He had a hard time believing he really spent hours clinging to that filthy hunk of wood thinking it would save his life. The soreness he felt on his chest and in his arms was the painful proof of it. It was embarrassing thinking of himself lying in the dirt petrified with fear holding a goddamned log for dear life. He kicked it. Of course the wood was much more solid than his boot-covered toes and they paid the price. Holding his foot in pain, he was back on the ground next to the log. He wanted to pick up the damn thing and throw it as far as he could, but the reject from the lumber pile had already stolen what strength he had left in his arms. Instead, Cam stood up again, turned his back to the log, and hobbled away.

It was either a continuation of the log-hugging night or it was the following night, whichever one it didn't matter. It was night and Cam had to find a safe and/or comfortable place to wait until the morning arrived. Being able to only see a few feet in front of him as he walked didn't help his search. As he groped his way through the forest he asked himself why he was still bothering. He might get lucky and find another rock to crawl under for the night and then what would he do? He would wait in fear for the sun to rise and then wander around hungry and aimlessly until…

A tiny flickering orange light suddenly grabbed Cam's attention. It was much too low and bright to be a star. There was no doubt in his mind the light had to be manmade. He moved his shattered body as fast as it could go in the direction of the light. Stumbles over rocks and roots and a few branches to the face didn't slow him down, much. Everything depended on getting to the light.

Cam realized as he got closer that the light was coming from a fire. Nearing his goal he saw it was a small campfire on a low hill. A lone figure was sitting in front of it.

"Thank God in heaven and his baby son Jesus." Cam resisted running towards his perceived savior. He didn't want to scare the guy with his abrupt and alarming appearance. The dude might have a gun. It would really suck to survive out in the wilderness this long and then get shot at the moment of rescue. As casually as he could, Cam sauntered up the hill to the campsite, but at the top of the hill there wasn't a campsite in sight. There was only a man draped in an old blanket sitting alone on a rock poking a small fire with a stick. Cam couldn't see if this guy had any kind of supplies with him or not, but he sure hoped he did.

"Do you mind if I sit in front of your fire? I'm freezing." Even in his completely helpless state, Cam didn't want to come off sounding completely helpless. He would ease into the fact he'd been lost without food or water for days and desperately needed help.

Without looking at him, the man gestured with his stick to another rock near the fire.

"Thanks." Cam sat down without hesitation. He glanced over at the man and tried to get a better look at him. A ratty brown blanket covered most of his body including his head. His face was in shadow.

Cam wanted to be polite and wait until he was offered something to eat or drink, but his stomach didn't have time for manners. "You wouldn't happen to have a little something for me to eat or drink, would ya? It's been a while since I've had anything."

The man looked on both sides of his rock and under his blanket. "I have nothing."

Cam thought the guy was probably lying to him. It didn't make any sense that he would be out here alone in the wilderness without anything to eat or drink. If he didn't want to share, that was fine. At least Cam knew he was going to have a warm safe place to spend the night and in the morning this guy could lead him back to civilization. He could do without food or drink for a little while longer.

Cam leaned into the fire to heat up his frozen hands. His heart dropped along with his hope of rescue. "Why isn't this fire giving off any heat? Oh, probably because it's not real. I'm sitting here alone in the dark asking someone who doesn't exist for something to eat. Great, just fucking great."

"I could say the same thing about you. Prove to me that *you* exist."

"What?" Cam felt insulted. He looked at his body and patted it all over. "I can see and feel my body and hear myself talking to you or to myself, same thing. I'm right here for Christ's sake, of course I exist."

"Your proof is you can see and hear yourself, but you can also see and hear me. You just said I don't exist."

"I haven't had any food or water for days and I'm probably delirious. I don't feel like proving anything to a hallucination."

Before he knew it, the hallucination reached over, grabbed Cam by the wrist, and pulled him off the rock. Cam returned to his seat. "That doesn't prove anything. I feel things in dreams. It doesn't mean they're real. My body is probably lying unconscious in the dirt somewhere dreaming all this."

"Then you *don't* exist. Your mind is only dreaming you."

"No, it proves I *do* exist. I have to exist to be able to dream this fascinating conversation. Case closed."

"So now your proof is a sleeping body somewhere out there neither of us can see."

Cam's voice rose in frustration. "This is ridiculous. Why am I wasting my time debating something so obvious? If I didn't exist then I wouldn't be here, but I am here so I do."

The man shrugged and resumed poking the fire with his stick, changing the shape and intensity of the flame. They both stared into the fire in silence. Cam attempted to warm his hands again, forgetting it was of no use.

Usually awkward silences with other guys didn't bother Cam. In fact he sometimes even enjoyed them. He turned them into games of chicken. Whoever could handle the discomfort of silence the longest without speaking, won. But playing this little mind-game with a hallucination wasn't any fun. In essence he was playing against himself. The quiet between them could go on indefinitely.

Cam decided he had to forfeit and restarted the debate to break the silent stalemate. "Do *you* exist?"

"According to you I'm only a creation of your mind, so I exist now. When you wake up, who knows?"

Cam was getting irritated. "In *your* opinion, do you exist?"

"My opinion on the subject isn't important."

"It's a simple question and since you seem to be an expert on the subject, I want to know if you exist or not."

"It's not a simple question. Everything in the universe can only exist in relation to something else." The man gave the fire a good poke. "Look at the light coming from this fire. Would it be here if it weren't for the darkness?"

Cam thought it was a stupid question. "Of course it'd be there, you just wouldn't be able to see it."

"Exactly. Light depends on darkness to exist."

"No, the light is invisible without darkness, but it's still there."

"It would never become visible without darkness, so would it really be there?"

"I'm no scientist, but I know there are many things in the universe that can't be seen, but have been proven to exist."

"They have been proven to exist because of their relationships with other things."

"OK fine, I get it, up needs down, hot needs cold, heaven needs hell, and so on." Cam was tiring of the debate and was ready to concede when a possible winning retort came to him. "What do you exist in relation to?"

The man turned and looked at Cam. The waning light from the fire allowed him to get a glimpse of the face beneath the blanket. Familiar but faded black tattoos marked the deep wrinkles etched into his face. He smiled. "I exist because I don't exist." He turned back towards the fire and knocked it down with his stick until only glowing coals remained. They eventually burned themselves out, taking the little light they gave away with them. The man faded away along with the light, leaving Cam alone in the dark once again.

As the false fire had failed to thaw Cam's hands, he put them into the pockets of his jacket to find some scraps of warmth. One of his hands found something cold and heavy - the stone he'd picked up for the log girl. In his hand he held hundreds of thousands, maybe even millions of years of compressed history. It was unnecessary weight, so he decided to leave it behind.

Without any further reason to stay where he was, he stood up and began to walk. His body on automatic pilot, Cam mindlessly wandered through the blackness until he saw the first light of dawn. False or otherwise, light was light and it meant he could stop. His body broke and collapsed.

'Caw, caw, caw, caw… ' Cam hated to be woken up from such a deep sleep by his annoying alarm, but if it weren't annoying he'd probably never get up and turn it off. He reached over to his nightstand to hit the snooze button (nine more minutes of sleep would be just enough for a full night's rest), but instead of feeling smooth plastic he felt rough dirt. Opening his eyes he remembered he wasn't at home in his nice comfortable bed, in fact that bed and that home were long gone. He was still lost in a forest. High in a tree above him a large black bird was cawing. It looked down at his pathetic body lying in the dirt and continued cawing. Cam's body and mind were completely depleted. All his reserves had been used up. He was done for. There was nothing for him to do but close his eyes again. The sound of the bird's cawing became fainter and fainter.

Cam's eyes opened to an opaque view of the forest. Apparently his windshield had collected a bit of grime being parked for so long on the side of the small dirt road. He looked down. His keys were in the ignition and his wallet, phone, and charger were in the center console. At this point, questioning how he got back to his car was pointless. He was more baffled by the fact no one messed with his car or with any of the stuff inside while he was away. The thought crossed his mind that maybe he wasn't really lost out there as long as he thought. He only had to glance at his dirty wounded hands for confirmation that he was. Then he grabbed the rearview mirror and positioned it to get a good look at himself. It wasn't a pretty sight. His forehead and nose were horribly sunburnt. The tip of the nose was a scab. A light beard surrounded badly chapped lips and his entire face was filthy. Unfortunately his ordeal didn't erase any of the tattoos. They were all still there beneath the damage.

Seeing the dried state of his lips reminded him he

hadn't had anything to drink or eat for a long time. He had gotten so used to being thirsty and hungry he didn't notice right away. Luckily he was somewhat of a slob and usually there were unfinished water bottles and bits of food under his seats. He reached under the passenger seat and found an old plastic water bottle about a quarter full. The stale lukewarm water was the most delicious beverage he'd ever had. Another reach under the seat unearthed the perfect accompaniment, a few rock-hard dirty French fries. Hopefully there were more culinary delights to be found in the back seat.

There wasn't any more food, but on the floor behind the driver's seat was one of his old backpacks filled to the brim with something. He grabbed it and examined the contents. Inside was a hastily packed selection of his clothing and some essential toiletries. Further rummaging found nothing else but a wrinkled envelope. It was addressed to his mother and the return address read: Cecil Deluwanne c/o The Aztec, 1111 E. Aztec Ave., Gallup, NM.

The writing was a barely legible childish scrawl, all in pencil, with some evidence of erasure here and there. Cam opened the envelope sent by the man he assumed was his grandfather hoping to find a heartfelt letter full of concern and curiosity. In its place was a receipt from a drugstore. He thought maybe this guy was making his 'mom' pay for his medication. On the back of the receipt was a short note in the same childish scrawl.

never paint an unprepared surface. sooner or later the dirt and cracks will show through. C

Cam knew he had to go and find him. He needed to know more about his 'real' family. Hopefully this grandfather of his would be coherent and sober enough to fill him in. Someone somewhere had to know why Cam's life had turned to complete shit, maybe this old man would be the guy.

The first thing he had to do though was to get some Macho Nachos. Those melted cheese, refried bean, sour cream, guacamole, ground beef, tomato, and jalapeno-covered chips had been haunting his stomach's dreams for days.

His phone had power but no connection to a network, so Cam prayed his car would start. If he had to go and find help then he'd have to make up some story why he'd been alone in the woods without any supplies for so long. His reservoir of stories was dried up. Luckily the car started on the first try and surprisingly his gas tank was half full. He turned his car around, found the main road, and headed downhill.

ALL ROADS INEVITABLY come to an end, but this one seemed to just keep on going. The desert highway divided the barren landscape into identical halves. Devoid of scenery, it was difficult to judge if any progress had been made. According to his GPS, Cam still had a long way to go until he reached Gallup, but he was determined not to stop until he got there.

He already had plenty of rest and recovery from his outdoor ordeal. A few blurry days in a crappy motel doing nothing but eating and sleeping got him feeling like himself again, whoever that was. Lip balm and lotion were slowly reversing the damage to his face and the numerous cuts and bruises covering his body were already beginning to fade. All his physical injuries would eventually heal, but the mental torment had left open wounds oozing pus onto his spirit. Something inside him broke out there in the woods, something that couldn't be unbroken.

Cam caught up with a slow-moving freight train traveling on tracks parallel to the highway. It was so long that at a certain point it looked as if it were standing still. He couldn't see its beginning or its end. Freight car after freight car began to blend into the monotony of the landscape until he didn't notice it anymore. It came as a surprise when he did finally pass the train because he'd already forgotten it had a beginning.

Gas stations, motels, and fast food places began to sporadically appear along the highway. Soon their numbers increased dramatically, which led Cam to assume he'd entered Gallup. Driving through town he didn't see a city designed and decorated to sell real estate and keep property values high, the kind of city he was used to back in Orange County. Instead he saw a city built by the residents themselves, a no-frills place to live and work. His late-model Camry pulled into a small parking lot covered in poorly laid tarmac. He found a spot in front of a Laundromat and parked his car within a row of much later-model pickup trucks.

Next door to the Laundromat was the place he'd come such a long way to find. It was a squat brick building without any marking expect a small white sign above the door, which in faded yellow lettering read: The Aztec. A couple Native Americans sitting on the curb outside stared at him as he stood at The Aztec's door contemplating whether to enter or not.

The old guy he was looking for was technically his grandfather, but also a complete stranger. Maybe he didn't want to ever see his grandson again. Maybe it would bring up too many painful memories. Maybe it would be better to leave the man in peace. Despite all the maybes, Cam decided this elderly dude owed him some answers. It was the least he could do for the grandson he disowned all those years ago.

Cam yanked the door open and was greeted by a silent darkness. It took a few moments for his eyes to adjust to the bar's sparse lighting and when they did there wasn't much of anything to see. Cam expected to find Aztec art adorning the walls or maybe another kind of an Indian décor, but he didn't. The place was called The Aztec only because it was located on Aztec Avenue. The bar had a bar, a few empty tables, and a bunch of chairs pushed up against one wall and nothing more. About eight older gentlemen sat at the bar. They all wore button-up flannel shirts tucked into well-worn jeans. Each of them had some sort of headwear on. Most of them wore ballcaps and the rest cowboy hats. Not one of them turned around when Cam entered. The men sat together in silence. They had already said everything needed to be said. In their group solitude they sipped their beers.

Cam approached the stoic bartender. "Hi. Do you know where I can find Cecil Deluwanne?"

With his chin the bartender gestured to the man sitting on the stool next to where Cam was standing. He looked at the man who was supposedly his grandfather. An old Denver Broncos cap sat low on his head and even under the shadow of his hat, Cam could see his face was dried leather with age lines cut deep into it.

The old man looked over at Cam and shook his head. "Just what I thought."

"Do you know who I am?"

"Yeah, I know." Cecil took a sip from his beer. "Not a lot of tattooed young bucks come in here looking for me. Might as well sit down."

Cam took the seat next to Cecil and a beer was automatically placed in front of him. He ignored the beer and stared at Cecil expectantly. Cecil leisurely sipped some more beer. "I guess you'll be wanting your wise old Indian grandfather to give you the answers to all your questions."

Cam nodded. "Something like that."

"Well, I'm not wise, just old."

The last part was definitely true. Cam searched his ancient face and couldn't find anything of himself in it, but he did find it unbelievable he was related to this fossil. "Could you at least tell me *something* about my past?"

"Look in a mirror and you'll see everything you need to know."

Cam grabbed the beer in front of him and out of frustration took a big swig. "Can you tell me anything? How about my parents, can you tell me something about them?"

"Coyote stole your parents, Coyote stole my wife, Coyote stole everything." All the other bar patrons including the bartender looked over at Cecil. He took a drink. "But I'm not angry, because that's his way." The bar people resumed their attention on their reflections in the beer.

"Who's Coyote? I thought my parents and your wife died in a car accident." Cam wondered if his mom/aunt had given him bogus information.

"Coyote jumped into their path."

"Are you saying the accident was caused by a coyote in the road?"

Cecil finished his beer. "Let's go." He got up and exited the bar, moving pretty fast for a guy his age. Cam left his beer unfinished and followed.

Cecil waited at the passenger door of Cam's car. "You drive."

After a short and quiet journey—Cecil had only spoken to give simple directions—they arrived in front of a small house. Cecil gave one last direction before getting out of the car. "You'll stay here tonight."

Cam's grandfather opened the gate attached to the rusted chain-link fence protecting his dead lawn. He led his grandson up the path into the unpainted house. It had been painted at one time, but it was so long ago all traces of paint had vanished. The interior walls were also unpainted, but the elements hadn't removed all the evidence of previous paintings yet. Flakes of various shades hung precariously to the upper sections of the walls. The house contained very little furniture, which was fine because there wasn't much house to furnish.

Cam stood in the middle of the living room with his backpack slung over his shoulder. Cecil turned to his uncomfortable grandson. "That bag looks heavy, leave it."

He searched the 1970s garage sale of a living room for a place to leave his stuff, but for some reason was afraid if he did, his bag would be lost in the same time warp the rest of the house was stuck in.

"Just put it down." Cecil was already in the kitchen grabbing a can of generic beer out of his fridge. He sat down at his tiny dining table and opened it.

Cam dropped his backpack at his feet and waited for his next order. It came straightaway. "Come sit." Cecil gestured to the tiny table's other chair. Cam did what he was told.

"Take something to drink if you want." Cecil sipped his inexpensive no-name beer. Cam got back up and looked in the refrigerator for a refreshing beverage. He wasn't in the mood to drink shitty beer or pickle juice, so he found a semi-clean glass and filled it with semi-clear tap water.

The old man and the young man sat at a quiet impasse. The old man stared at the young man's face, which was still sunburnt, especially the nose and forehead. Even after days of constant ChapStick use, traces of his formerly severe chapped lips were still noticeable. "Looks like you spent some time outside."

"I was lost in the woods for more than three days." Cam thought this admission might have some sort of effect on his grandfather, but the man's expression didn't change.

"Who showed you the way out?"

"I don't know. Nobody I guess. I woke up in my car."

"If you got out on your own, you just forgot the way. You weren't lost."

Cecil's accusation almost caused Cam to lose his temper. "I nearly died out there, OK? I didn't have any food or water, I couldn't make a fire, I was out there with nothing. Of course I was lost."

"As a very young man I also spent many days alone in the wilderness with nothing."

"Were *you* lost?"

"No, I was there to find something."

"What did you have to find?"

"My way."

Cam was confused. "You just said you weren't lost, so why would you have to find your way?"

Cecil took another sip of his beer and looked Cam in the eyes. "Not my way out. My way... my path through life. Do you understand?"

"Not really. Why did you have to go into the wilderness alone with nothing to find your way in life?" Cam was still confused. He thought maybe he was just listening to the ramblings of a drunk old man.

"We all have a path we are meant to follow." Cecil carefully set his beer on the table and tapped himself on the chest. "Somewhere deep inside us we know the way, but our eyes and ears only see and hear what our world shows us and tells us. We have to get away from our world, empty ourselves of our world, and then hopefully our eyes and ears will be clear enough to see and hear the way. The most important thing though, is if we choose to follow it or not. Knowing the way and not following it is something a person could regret for their entire life. Sometimes the way is very hard and there are so many easier paths to take." He picked up his beer and resumed drinking. "So, what path did you take?"

"I don't know. I worked a bunch of different jobs so I could pay my bills. Each time I tried to find a better-paying job, if that's what you mean by following a path." Cam took a drink of water; it tasted metallic.

"It sounds like you took the easiest path your world gave you."

"What was I supposed to do? Go to college, get some useless degree, and be in debt for the next thirty years? And then end up making the same amount of money I would've made without the degree, just like most of the chumps I've worked with? Living in the world costs money and my family didn't have much extra to give to me, so I had to go out and make it myself. It wasn't the easiest path, it was the only path."

Cecil chuckled. "No different from your father. Blind to any path that doesn't lead to a fuller wallet."

Cam gave an exaggerated look at the interior of the house. "What was *your* path?"

"None of your business, but I can tell you I'm not on it. I got detoured." For the first time he really looked at his grandson's stained skin. He took a large swallow of beer.

It would make sense if a conversation about paths was going somewhere, but it didn't seem that way. Cam still didn't fully understand what the old man was getting at. His attempt at comprehension brought to mind a video game he used to play as a kid. In the game you had to find your way through a series of lands while collecting treasure and weapons and fighting all kinds of bizarre creatures, but each land had only one way through. The way through became more difficult in each subsequent land and by the last land it was almost impossible to find the way out. Cam didn't know how he was supposed to beat a game he didn't even know he was playing. He thought he could learn something from his grandfather's self-admitted failure.

"I heard you were a housepainter. Was that part of your path?"

"I don't think you're hearing what I'm saying. Any asshole can hop onto a path to make money, a lot or a little, it's the same road. But you were right about one thing, it costs money to live in this world, so I painted houses."

Cam caught him. "So you took a path to make money."

All of Cecil's anger had been used up many years before, so he didn't smack his grandson in the head. "I wonder how much of that ink leaked into your brain. Listen to me. It costs a lot more than just money to follow the correct path. Sometimes it costs more than you can afford to give." His words trailed off and he sat in silence while the past momentarily clouded his vision.

Cam wanted to get to the point. He came here for answers about what was happening to him and felt he was getting a bunch of new-age life-coaching instead. Whatever disaster of a path he was currently on had already cost him everything he had and put him into deep unrepayable debt. "Does that mean I'm now on the correct path? Because I've lost absolutely everything."

"Not yet."

Those two little words troubled Cam. They implied that everything he'd gone through was only a preamble to something much worse, which was almost inconceivable. They also implied his grandfather knew something he wasn't telling him.

"Do you know what's happening to me?"

His grandfather answered without answering. "I spent most of my life covering things with coat after coat of paint. After so many coats no one remembers what's underneath anymore—until those coats can't hold each other's weight and they crack and peel off. Then you're surprised, because you forgot and thought the top coat was the surface. A good painter always starts off with a clean surface. I suppose I wasn't a very good painter." He looked at the flaking walls of his kitchen. "I don't have the energy anymore to put another coat on these walls and forget again. I'm used to seeing what's underneath." He finished his beer. "All this talk made me tired. I need to go to bed. You can sleep on the couch tonight." Cecil got up and patted his grandson on the head.

Cam had one last question. "What am I supposed to do?"

Cecil let his hand rest on his grandson's head for a moment. "You know, you just forgot." He went to bed and left Cam at the tiny table sipping metallic water.

After he was sure his grandfather had gone to sleep, Cam ventured to the bathroom to wash his face and brush his teeth. It was a dingy little room. The only light came from an uncovered low-watt bulb poking out from the ceiling, but it was enough light to see the peeling linoleum under his feet and the nasty rust stain that covered the bottom of the sink. There wasn't a hot water option, so Cam had to wash his face with the ice-cold water that came pouring out of the tap. He looked around for a towel to dry off with, but there were no towels anywhere, not even a towel rack, in fact there wasn't a bathtub or a shower. It made him wonder how his grandfather bathed.

Cam was forced to take off his shirt and dry his face with it. He then looked at his reflection, but he couldn't see much through the cloudy haze of filth covering the surface of the glass. In the blurry soft focus of the mirror the tattoos covering his body looked like a black pox, an irreversible skin disease that people would always think he purposely infected himself with. One of the main reasons he had come here was for a diagnosis and possibly a cure. Instead his grandfather was under the impression Cam himself already had all the answers and had just forgotten. Since Cam never seemed able to find the answers he was looking for anywhere else, he felt he had no choice but to accept the fact his grandfather was probably right.

He looked into the eyes of the tattooed man behind the dirty glass. "I want to remember."

The tattooed man behind the dirty glass stared back into his eyes.

It may have been the lingering thought of skin diseases or just a fresh bug bite, but an overwhelming itch suddenly developed on Cam's left ankle. A light scratch through jeans and sock wasn't going to do the trick. The itch needed some serious attention. He took off his boot and sock, but couldn't pull his jean leg up high enough to properly reach the itch. It meant he had to remove his other boot and take off his jeans. The source of the itch was a tattoo on his ankle, the original tattoo. Cam felt a lifetime had passed since the night he got that tattoo. He scratched the skin raw without relief. Another overwhelming itch sprung up on his right shoulder and then on his lower back. A hand each was assigned to scratching duty. While they were busy working away, Cam noticed the itch on the ankle had completely stopped. He looked down and learned why. The tattoo wasn't there anymore. In fact nothing was there anymore. Empty space replaced the section of the ankle where the original tattoo used to be. Next to his foot was a small pile of black- and flesh-colored rubble. Cam didn't have time to investigate the missing piece of ankle or its apparent fragmented state as his attention had shifted to the itchy section of his tattooed right shoulder. It separated from his body and silently shattered on the stained linoleum. Looking at the place where his right shoulder used to be, he saw a gaping nothing. The itch on his lower back stopped at the same time he felt an irregularly shaped object slip through his fingers. Instead of a lower back, his fingers touched nothing.

Intense itches sprung up all over his body. There were so many he couldn't decide where to scratch next, but he knew scratching them wouldn't bring any kind of relief. Each new itch of course coincided with a piece of himself separating from his body, dropping to the floor and shattering into innumerable pieces that could never be reassembled. The strangest part of the whole thing was his apathy. Cam didn't panic and try to hold the pieces in place or try to catch and save the pieces for later reattachment. All he did was passively watch his body crumble.

When the itching finally reached his face, Cam looked back into the dirty mirror. He watched the tattoo near his left eye disconnect from the surrounding skin. It took the eye with it as it left the body and fell into the sink exploding into tiny ocular fragments. Yet somehow Cam was still able to see. The void where his eye used to be looked into itself and the emptiness reflected back.

The remaining pieces of Cam rained down onto the bleak bathroom's floor, piling on top of the existing dirt. Soon his entire physical form vanished and the nothing that was left stared back at him with nonexistent eyes from behind the mirror. The lack of existence from the space where his body used to be spread throughout the bathroom. When it reached the lone lightbulb poking out from the ceiling, the place where the bathroom used to be could no longer be seen by Cam's nonexistent eyes.

His formless form found itself somewhere which never was and never will be. It was a realm which didn't contain history, so the burden of memories and the anchor of buried emotions instantly evaporated; turning away from this past-less past meant facing forward to a future that would never arrive. All expectations disappeared along with every trace of fear. Fear is the dread of what may or may not come to be and if nothing will ever come to be then there can be nothing to be afraid of. It was a present moment which never began and could never end.

Before two there was only One. By natural process, by accident, or by design, One became many. Those many became everything that ever was and ever will be. Conscious of it or not, it all longed to be One again. The form that used to be Cam had shed all of its obstructions between itself and One. Obstructions it had amassed over eons and drove it further and further from One. At a certain point the internal longing for a return to One grew so strong it triggered a molting process. The lengthy process was finally complete and the form which was once Cam became One.

With violent force, a massive weight crashed down into a bodily form, forcing its terrified eyes open. The first thing they saw was a crusty ceiling polka-dotted with water stains. They lowered a little and the view was of a body spread out on a couch that should've been thrown into a dumpster a long time ago. The body's top half was covered in a decorated leather jacket and the rest was awkwardly positioned in a desperate attempt at comfort. The eyes soon realized they were attached to this body. The attached body was so big, the eyes had no idea how they were going to move it or if they even had the desire to shift its unwieldy mass. Unless they wanted to permanently see the same scene of disintegrating ceiling and worn couch covering, they were to going to have to figure out how to get the body up and moving.

They searched and discovered that directly behind them was a hunk of meat that contained all the instructions needed to control the attached body. They accessed the information they needed and at the same time unwittingly opened a Pandora's Box of memories, emotions, and a shocking amount of trivial knowledge. The eyes didn't understand why this hunk of meat had so much information about how many times tall athletic men successfully threw a ball through a hole.

The form which was once Cam had become Cam again, kind of. When he shrugged off the soreness and exhaustion of sleeping on a terrible couch, he physically felt the same as he always had. Memories of everything he'd ever done and all the people he'd ever known were still bouncing around in his head and all the feelings linked to these memories and people were still there. The difference was he didn't have the slightest attachment to any of it. He knew it was his body and he knew they were his memories and his feelings, but he didn't feel he was the *he* they belonged to. The Cam he was clothed in didn't seem to fit anymore. Who was he then? It was a question that would have to wait for a moment because regardless of any question of identity, the body had to piss very badly.

He rushed into the bathroom and let loose a powerful stream. While waiting for it to end, he glanced into the dirty mirror. It was the face he expected to see, but something was different. It was clean. Not a tattoo anywhere on the exposed skin. He bent forward to get a closer look and the remainder of the stream splashed on the toilet bowl and then onto the already urine-stained linoleum. On closer inspection he couldn't see any trace of the tattoos. He looked at his hands and arms, nothing there either. He took off all of the clothes he was wearing and what he could see of his body was tattoo-free. Even the original tattoo on his ankle wasn't there. The obvious feelings of joy and relief didn't come flooding in, only a trickle of loss. He'd been carrying the ink around for such a long time it had become a part of him and now it was gone. Without it he felt almost weightless. It was an effort to keep from floating away. He'd have to learn how to move through the world with a body of diminished gravity.

He thought maybe Cecil would have some helpful advice for keeping his feet on the ground out there on the road. He peeked into his bedroom, it was empty. He went into the kitchen, it was also empty. On the tiny table he saw a single red apple sitting on a fast food restaurant napkin. The napkin looked as if it had some writing on it. He recognized it as Cecil's childish scrawl.

'gone out. take the apple. don't start off on an empty stomach. C'

Cam took the apple and in its place he left car keys; a car would be too much of a heavy burden. After putting on the backpack that was sitting on the floor, he walked out the door. As nothing in the house could even be given away, he wasn't too concerned that he had to leave the door unlocked. He took a large bite of the apple and began to walk.

It was a glorious day outside. The sun was shining and it was warm enough to wear t-shirts and shorts, if that's your thing. As he made his way downtown he passed some groups of Native Americans. He could've sworn he saw black markings on all their bodies, but their skin was dark and he passed them too quickly to get a good look. He didn't think extensive tattooing was a part of the culture of the tribes in the Southwest, but of course he could've been wrong. On a busy street downtown he found a bus stop. The schedule said the bus wasn't leaving for a while, so he sat down to wait.

Sunshine and warmth detached quite a few people from their TVs and computers and brought them out onto the street. The bus bench was a great people-watching spot. A young guy in shorts and a tank-top passed nearby. His entire body, including his face, was covered in familiar black tattoos. From his seat at the bus stop, Cam nearly stood up and asked the guy where he had his work done, but before he could he saw a middle-aged couple walking hand in hand who were both heavily inked from their baseball-capped heads to their flip-flopped toes. All of their tattoos were done in black ink and had the recognizable theme of odd images and undecipherable writing asymmetrically placed on their skin. From across the street came a mother with her two children. All three of them were tattooed. The youngest child seemed to have more tattooing than her mother or sibling. Not one person on the street was ink-free.

Upon closer observation Cam noticed he never saw duplicate tattoos; every single one was different. Even similar tattoos had a different style and quality. He also noticed that while some people were entirely covered in tattoos, others were only moderately freckled.

Next to him appeared a large muscled jock in a sleeveless shirt waiting to cross the street. His body had relatively few tattoos, but there was something interesting. On his upper left arm was a row of what could've been described as poorly drawn mathematical symbols. These black symbols overlapped the colorful koi fish tattoo clearly placed there with great care and expense. Muscle Guy noticed he was being observed by the dude sitting on the bus bench.

"Whatta you looking at, freak?" He didn't conceal his angry annoyance and crossed the street before he could receive an answer to his query.

The observer was so engrossed with his observations that he didn't realize he had become the subject of scrutiny. Every Gallup citizen who passed gave him a look, either a guarded glance or an unapologetic stare. Some whispered to each other about him and others seemed furious they had to breathe the same air as him. What did *they* see? Did they see someone who had been unburdened of the ink they still had to carry? He wasn't sure, but he did feel sorry they had to carry so much weight.

His thoughts then went out to the carriers who had been closest to him. He owed them at least the consideration of a message before he continued on his way. Where he was headed it was unlikely he'd ever cross paths with any of them again. He pulled the phone from the pocket of the jeans he wore and began to type.

I'm not Cam and I'm not Marcus. They were a habit and that habit has been broken. I was totally addicted to using collections of labels and memories as a me. I looked into the mirror and realized what was really looking back was a shell built from pieces of the past. That covering of fossils has crumbled to dust. I don't know for sure what's underneath, but it's what I have to find out. I do know that whoever Cam/Marcus was, is now gone.

A grouping of words would never be able to express exactly what he was trying to communicate, but since words were the only tools he had at his disposal, the words he'd chosen would have to make do. He selected all the contacts listed in the phone and pressed 'send'.

He saw the bus coming, so he stood up. The phone was still in his hand. It was heavy with the dead weight of all the ink it carried inside it. On the road he didn't want to haul anything unnecessary, so he dropped it into the trashcan next to the bus bench. In the other pocket he could feel more heaviness. He retrieved the wallet from inside. It too was crammed full of ink. Before he threw it away, he remembered what Cecil had confirmed to him the night before, 'It costs money to live in this world.' He removed the wad of cash stuffed inside, shoved it into a pocket, and let the last drops of ink the wallet contained join the other unwanted encumbrances in the bottom of the garbage bag.

The bus arrived and opened its doors for him. He grabbed the backpack, stepped into the vehicle, and bought a ticket. Not many seats were available, so he began to navigate the narrow aisle to find a place to sit. He saw a free seat next to an elderly woman with black deer sketched on her right cheek and the bottom halves of concentric circles peeking out from under her false hairline. The free seat became immediately occupied by her purse. A large gentleman with sloppy Cyrillic written on his face where the right half of a moustache should've been and a simplistic dragon floating above his left set of jowls noticed the man searching for a place to sit. In response he shifted his bulk from the area near the window to the area near the aisle. Every free seat vanished on his approach. The last one was taken by a heavily tattooed toddler who had been moved from his mother's lap into the empty seat.

Without a place to sit, he was forced to stand next to the back door with the backpack at his feet. He stood alone in the crowded bus as it continued along its journey to the next stop.

IT FINALLY HAPPENED. She'd been waiting years and years for this day to come, nearly giving up hope it ever would. Over and over again she read the message on her phone—

"Little Marcel René came into the world this morning at ten-thirteen AM. He and his mother are both healthy and happy. He's looking forward to meeting his grandmother. Love, Blake."

It said grandmother, she was now a grandmother. She wasn't just Mom to a couple of grown men, she was also a grandmother to a presumably adorable little baby boy. When he could speak he would call her Grandma or Nana, but since he was half French he might call her Mamie or Mémé (she'd already looked up the French words for 'grandma' on the Internet). She didn't care what he would call her, just as long as she was Grandmother to someone.

Unfortunately the little guy popped out about a week earlier than expected and her plane ticket to Paris wouldn't get her there for a couple more days. She thought making her arrival date five days before the due date and staying for two weeks would've given her a pretty good chance of being there for the delivery, but the tiny man was apparently anxious to get out into the world. It was OK though. As long she could hold her grandson in her arms she would be deliriously happy. She couldn't wait to have the fragrance of fresh baby fill her nostrils and to feel his vice grip clasp her finger. It was so long since Blake was a baby; she could hardly remember him ever being that small. Luckily there were plenty of pictures. She saw very little of infant Marcus since he lived so far away at that age, but it was a blessing when he arrived to her as a sweet, sad toddler who was in desperate need of a mommy. Despite the fact it widened the cracks in an already collapsing marriage, she became that mommy.

Speaking of Marcus, she hadn't seen him for more than a week. Some of his clothes and toiletries were gone, so she assumed he went to stay with friends. His disappearing acts were a common thing.

Her large suitcase was way in the back of her closet on a top shelf. It was a bit of a struggle to get it down, especially with two Yorkies yapping at her heels. The women across the street had an out-of-town wedding to attend and they didn't want to put their precious angels in a kennel overnight. Lucky for them they knew someone who would never say no to the tiny favor of watching their babies.

Years had passed since she last used that suitcase. The last time was the horrible Caribbean singles cruise she had gone on. It was full of nothing but perverts and creeps, but at least the food was good.

"So ladies, what should I bring to Paris with me?" The two furballs barked so incessantly in response that she barely heard her phone signal to her she had a new message. She thought it was some more news about her new grandson. Hopefully a picture would be included this time.

The message wasn't from Blake, but from Marcus. Even after a few readings it still wasn't clear what he was trying to say. The last line about Marcus being gone played over and over again in her head. A panic overcame her. She knew he was in a bad place, but she didn't think he would resort to ending his life. Immediately she called him and when she didn't get an answer she wrote him a long response telling him how much she loved him and that she would always be there for him no matter what. Her tears flowed freely as she sat on her bed waiting for an answer from her son.

'Holy shit, I'm a father. This little lump of flesh in my arms is my son. How is it possible I made a human being? I didn't even try. I had sex with my girlfriend about nine months ago and that's it. Now another conscious being has entered the world and if he stays healthy and avoids accidents, he'll grow to be a man who could possibly do great things. Where did his consciousness come from? Did he take a piece of mine or a piece of my girlfriend's? But he couldn't have. There's no way each one of my countless sperm have pieces of my consciousness inside them. Sure they have my DNA, but that's it right? I doubt my girlfriend's eggs have pieces of her consciousness either. Then where did the thing that makes this tiny baby a living conscious being come from? From my Buddhist studies I know consciousness or the soul or whatever is constantly recycled until it's ready to move on to bigger and better things. But that doesn't explain where the consciousness originally came from. How did the first bacteria or germ come to be alive? Logically it doesn't make any sense that all life came from some magical explosion billions of years ago. Being alive is scientifically impossible, but somehow I managed to make a new life.'

Blake continued to stare at his newborn son cradled in his arms while he sat at his sleeping girlfriend's side. He looked over at her. Her hair was a mess, her skin was pasty and she was a bit bloated; she looked a lot different from the hot French chick he met three years ago. He still loved her though and he hoped that feeling wouldn't fade with time. Ever since he left home at nineteen, three years was the longest he'd stayed anywhere. Eight months in Yosemite National Park managing the gift shop, about a year on an Alaskan cruise ship working as a bartender, six months as a cook in a Seattle Buddhist center, a year and a half teaching English in Japan, a winter in Vermont running a ski lift… the list kept on going and going until he met the mother of his son while helping to build houses for the needy in Romania. Most of his adult life was spent on the move and he was afraid the urge would come again and his time in Paris would be just another adventure to add to the list. Whatever he'd been looking for all those years, he hoped he'd finally found it here. If he abandoned his son the same way his father had abandoned him, he didn't think he'd be able to live with himself.

A loud buzz came from the table next to the bed, waking up baby and mother. Blake cursed himself for forgetting to turn off his phone. He returned the baby to his groggy mommy. The message was from Cam. He cursed himself again for forgetting to tell his brother about the birth, but then he assumed his mom had already done it for him. In fact she'd probably told the whole world by now.

Cam's message had nothing to do with the birth of his nephew. It seemed it was some kind of a farewell message. Blake read it a few times, walked into the bathroom, and closed the door behind him. His emotions were all turned around. Instead of feeling sadness because he'd probably never see his brother again, he felt a jealousy tinged with anger. He didn't understand how Cam, a guy who used to get depressed on bad hair days, had managed to drop all personal attachment. It could've been that his tattoo fiasco and learning about his real parents had caused him to snap. That had to be the reason. Blake had spent years studying Native American and Eastern religions to find the path to enlightenment, but instead of leaving Blake behind, he built up a rather large collection of Blakes: gift shop manager Blake, bartender Blake, English teacher Blake, Buddhist cook Blake, etc. etc. etc. There were Blakes from all around the world in all kinds of professions who were boyfriends of all kinds of girls. And now he had one more Blake to add to his diverse assortment, Daddy Blake.

He looked into the mirror and decided it was a Blake he didn't want to leave behind. If all the Blakes led him to this Blake then the long road of Blakes was worth it. He'd try enlightenment the next time around.

Crazzee did her research. She checked about three different websites and they all said this was the best place in South County. Still, she wasn't sure she made the right choice until she saw the latest issues of *Vogue* and *Marie Claire* sitting on the real wood table in the waiting room. Her regular doctor never had any recent issues of any magazines in his waiting room. She always had to read the same two-year-old issue of *Cosmo*. Plus you could tell all his furniture was bought from somewhere like IKEA. Not here. The couch she was sitting on felt like real leather and looked designer.

Today was going to be the beginning of her new life, a better life, a life without any embarrassment or shame. Maybe, just maybe she would even get a new name. Crazzee was OK when she was a teenager, but she was a grown woman and didn't want to be seen as some silly little girl anymore. Maybe they would start calling her something like Hottee or Sexxee instead. Today was going to change everything. Today was the day of her first consultation for breast enlargement surgery.

Bigger boobies were going to make everything better. They would make her look more womanly, so people would take her more seriously. Being taken more seriously would help her get better jobs and make more money. So in a way, despite the expense (it was all going on the credit cards anyway, plus she would make her mom help with the costs since it was all her fault she was cursed with small

boobs in the first place) the boobs would be like an investment for her future. And of course guys would pay more
attention to her. She could finally start wearing low-cut
tops and show off some real cleavage, not just the hint of
cleavage she had now.

Little butterflies were fluttering around in her stomach in anticipation of the new Crazzee, or whoever she'd
be. She wished the surgery were today. She wanted to start
shopping for a new wardrobe as soon as possible.

Her phone hand pulsated a couple times, which indi-
cated a message was eagerly waiting to be read. It was from
Cam. She didn't know why the hell he was sending her a
message after all this time. He never once bothered to contact her after they broke up. Maybe he heard about her plan
to get bigger boobs and was trying to get back together. It
was too late for that, he already blew it. She read the message and after reading it a couple more times it still wasn't
clear what he was saying. To her it sounded like he decided
to become one of those new-age hippies who give all their
stuff away and call themselves things like Rainbow and
Leaf and travel the country going to boring music festivals
full of acid heads and weed junkies.

Out of nowhere a drop of guilt plopped down onto
her. In a way she felt it was kind of her fault that Cam
had become a tattooed hippie freak. If only she'd gotten
the bigger boobs earlier, he never would've cheated on her
with those big-tittied whores that made him get all those
stupid tattoos. But on the other hand, it was Cam's fault
she didn't get the boob job earlier. He always told her her
boobs were perfect the way they were, which was probably
just a lie to make her feel better. She should've gotten the

boobs anyway. It was too late now. Cam would just have to be happy with his lame floppy-tittied hippie chick girlfriend with hairy armpits that smell like patchouli oil. It was his loss.

"You can come on back now." The large-breasted receptionist let Crazzee know it was her turn to see the doctor. She deleted Cam's message and walked through the door where her new life awaited.

The apartment hadn't been this clean since the day he first moved in. T didn't want his new roommate to think he was a slob, which he wasn't. He just never had time to straighten the place up. Working full time tires a guy out and who wants to waste their weekends cleaning? This weekend was an exception. It sucked, but it had to be done. The worst part was cleaning Cam's old bathroom. It was pretty damn demeaning cleaning his dried piss off the toilet and floor. Selling all of Cam's furniture was also a pain in the ass, but he had to make some money to pay the other half of the rent. Living alone was nice, but expensive. OK, he had to admit he did sometimes miss having someone around to shoot the shit and smoke a fat bowl with.

His new roommate was a pretty cool guy and had an entirely different group of friends (which included a lot of females). It was going to open up a whole new social world for him. Plus, and it was a big plus, he had all the latest and best audio/visual equipment. He said he was bringing all of it with him and would set it up in the living room. T had some good stuff, but this guy had stuff T had only read about in magazines. It was going to be awesome. No more watching movies and playing video games on inferior equipment.

When Cam moved in he didn't bring shit. His crappy TV went straight into his bedroom along with all his other stuff. He used T's couch to sit his stinky ass on, watched T's TV, and left marks all over T's coffee table. What did he ever contribute? T even had to twist his arm to get him to pay his part for the bud they smoked. What a shitty roommate. He should've kicked him out sooner and could've avoided all the shit that went down in Vegas.

"Speak of the devil." T saw he had a message from Cam. "He probably heard someone new was moving in and wants his furniture back. Well too fuckin' bad, it's all gone. In fact he should be thankful I didn't take his ass to court."

Cam's message didn't make much sense and T was about to read it again when he heard a loud banging on the front door. Excitement flashed through his body; it brought back the childhood memory of the moment just before the first glance of all the presents under the tree on Christmas morning. On his way to the door he stuffed his phone back into his pocket and while doing so unintentionally deleted Cam's message. Two Mexicans, one medium-sized and the other extra-large, were on the other side of the door and at their feet was the biggest TV T had ever seen.

"What's up Chuy?" T gave a firm sideways hand-grab to the medium-sized Mexican.

"Hey T, what's happening?" Chuy motioned his head to the extra-large Mexican behind him. "This is my cousin Angel."

"Sup." The word didn't actually come out of Angel's

mouth. Instead a deep vibration emitted from the top of his neck.

"Come on in guys." T was in awe of the jumbo TV the Mexicans carried between them. "That thing is a lot bigger than I thought it'd be. I hope there's room for it."

"That's what all the girlies say." Chuy gave a little laugh as he and his cousin set the TV down in the living room. T supervised while they brought in the rest of Chuy's stuff.

"OK guys, sit down. I want you to meet someone very special to me." T went into his bedroom and brought out his three-foot glass bong. "This is my girlfriend."

"Damn." Chuy's eyes widened and his cousin's stoic expression imperceptibly altered. "I'm going to be stuffing that bitch every night."

T smiled. "You're such a prick, Chuy."

The Station needed a new employee with a mohawk and tattoos and in an unorthodox bit of hiring, Burn found a girl to fill that role. Her name was Lolli and her mohawk was pink. All of her tattoos were candy themed. Her arms were nearly sleeved with old and obscure candy logos and characters and above her generous cleavage were two crossed rainbow swirled lollipops. Where she would've had dimples, each cheek was pierced with a little pink ball. She wore a short girlie dress covered in pink polka dots. It was Syn's job to show her the ropes.

"You look familiar," Lolli told Syn shortly after they were introduced.

"You probably saw me in *Cyber Noir* magazine. I

had some pics in there not too long ago." Syn led her to the section of the store she would have to keep stocked and organized.

"No, I haven't read that magazine in years. I didn't even know it was still around." Lolli took a look at her section. "Do people really still buy DVDs? Hey wait, now I remember where I've seen you before. I think you used to like make my coffee at Bean Breakers."

"Maybe, it's been a while since I worked in that shithole." Syn didn't want to discuss her barista past so she changed the subject. "So, what kind of music you into?"

"Huh? Oh I don't know. I like all kinds of stuff." Lolli's attention had shifted to her tongue, which was playing with the piercings in her cheeks, but since it was her first day, she made a conscious effort to stop and be polite. "You?"

"Me? Yeah, I like a pretty wide range of stuff. I'm into Victorian anarchtronic music like The Nun's Hood, Midnight Fang Kiss, and Stigmata Splinters... ." Before Syn could finish, Lolli took her turn to speak.

"I liked that kind of stuff when I was like twelve or thirteen, but these days black bubble pop is what gets me off my ass. You should check out Hooded Entry, you'd probably dig 'em."

Syn had never heard of Hooded Entry. "Yeah, I've heard 'em before, I think at a club or something. They're OK. Do you know Dryck Fläder or Talanglösa Rövhål? Swedish dark ice trash is what gets *me* off my ass."

"Once you've heard Finnish sugar core, that Swedish stuff sounds tame. Tikkukaramelli blasts my hearing holes with such a sweet sonic noise that the threat of going deaf is totally worth it."

Syn had no idea there was such a thing as Finnish sugar core. "Sounds heinous, but my eardrums don't always feel like getting annihilated so sometimes I give 'em a break with some electro-ambient folk. Jam Hoarder is great for that."

"Oooh I can't stand folk. Having to listen to that shit would really kill my ears. But I know what you mean about giving the old sound tunnels a breather. A little glamgazer does the trick for me, especially when I put on some Dolly Cancer. Those guys could give your hearing some serious rehab." Lolli began to aimlessly flip through the DVDs hoping to find some interesting movies she could download later at home.

It had only been a short while since Burn had given her the assignment to train the new girl, but it was already becoming annoying. Syn glanced at the clock to see how much longer she'd have to spend with this pink puke. "What do you think of bossa no wave? A lot of new bands are coming onto the scene worth checking out. The New Death Frogs, Three Point Maneuver, and Van Gogh's Crotch Locket are a few I've been listening to lately. They all sort of have a retro-futuristic vibe that makes all that mainstream nonsense sound like music made for drunk children."

"Yeah, bossa no wave is like really trendy right now. I saw a thing about it on Tunes TV while I was flipping through the channels the other day. It seems alright, but I don't really follow trends. I'm keen on more subterranean stuff like puckered pre-pronk. If you want to hear the future of music forty years ago then you have to listen to Dour Snatch. Wow, you'll wish you could send one of their albums in a time machine to like the seventies and save the world from the suckfest of music we have now."

The clock wasn't moving fast enough. Syn was tired of listening to this wannabe blabbing on about genres and bands she either made up and/or only read about on underground websites. "I don't know if you go out much, but you should really come to Squalid sometime. I go all the time and if you want I could even bring you with me. Lipgloss Holocaust played the last time I went, they were fucking amazing."

"I used to go to Squalid. It was cool back in the day, but it's too commercial now. Having Lipgloss Holocaust play only proves it. No, these days you'll usually find me slumming it at Asthenosphere. You know how like all these people pretending to be rich bought big-ass houses they couldn't afford, well the bank took 'em back and now they're empty, so a couple kids I know use 'em for some ferocious parties. They try to keep it pretty exclusive so it doesn't get too out of control and the oinkers get woken up, but if the bacon does start sizzlin' there's always an Asthenosphere B somewhere waiting to be revealed. That's where shit gets rabid. If you want to tag along sometime I could probably get you in." Lolli had already forgotten about Syn's invitation by the time the last word popped out of her mouth.

Syn kept her hands busy re-alphabetizing DVDs to stop them from strangling the pathological liar she was being forced to listen to. As she glanced at the clock once again a deep rumbling shook the Station's entire glass-fronted exterior. All heads rotated in the direction of the rumbling. A custom chopper made to look as if it were spun by a metallic spider whirred outside, revving its motor. In the saddle sat the kind of fellow you'd expect to see revving an engine of an oversized motorcycle for no apparent reason.

His facial hair was so abundant his age was difficult to ascertain. He could've been anywhere between the ages of twenty-five and fifty-five. The sun had turned his tattoo-sleeved arms into faded messes of color. "Thank god." Syn exhaled. She turned to Lolli. "It looks like my boyfriend's here to pick me up for lunch."

"Nice bike." Lolli tried to get a closer look at the motor-cycle and its rider while trying not to look like she was try-ing to get a closer look at the motorcycle and its rider.

"I know. See ya after lunch." On the way out Syn picked up her purse from behind the counter and automatically took out her phone and checked it for messages. Cam's was the only message. She read it and then erased it. "Whatever poopy-pants." When she got outside she kissed the rider on the cheek, popped on a purple sparkly helmet she grabbed from the saddlebag, and jumped on the back of the bike. Her arms encircled the rider's waist as the chopper sped off.

●

In the waning hours of the night a motorized vehicle in a state of shameful disrepair considering its considerable age ceased its nocturnal jaunts and reappeared from whence it came. The location of the motor-coach's reappearance was a manor under the ownership of the forbearers of the operator of said coach. Heavily bearded and clothed in a greatcoat despite the temperate temperature, the operator removed himself from his conveyance and traversed the expanse of the estate's anterior grounds to the property's posterior. Situated in the posterior was the modest dwelling he presently inhabited.

On entering his humble habitat, he took notice of the recent cleansing by the chambermaid, as was her bi-weekly duty. It pleased him on one hand to have such a tidy residence, but alternatively it disturbed him knowing a migrant laborer earning a paltry sum was performing lowly chores which he himself could have very easily accomplished. A minuscule fraction of the mass of banknotes he removed from an interior compartment of his greatcoat was in all likelihood greater than her total earnings for a day's travail—monies which meant naught to him, monies which he had no need of to obtain sustenance or settle a tenant's fee. Every material good he fancied was in his possession and yet he unfailingly found himself wanting. All his efforts at combating his perceived hollow existence resulted in defeat. He conjectured if he conducted an austere life, contentment would promptly arrive; luxuries were whittled away, his transport was as meager as would allow, his garments were few, he found menial employment in a doomed retail establishment, he even took on the persona of a monk. It was all to no avail and his melancholy increased. He next surmised it was the long shadow of the wealth of his parentage, which must be blotting out the sun of his satisfaction. He commenced peddling medications, which relieved the ills of troubled minds and bodies in order to sire a nest egg of his own which would one day hatch into financial autonomy. Rather than hatching, the egg swelled and expanded; the green-backed embryo became fearful of abandoning the security of the ever-thickening shell. Joy and bliss, whose companionship he continually courted, were as elusive as ever. As he extracted his surplus of tablets and capsules from compartments ingeniously hidden in the hem of the greatcoat, the irony of his predicament was in no way lost on him. For his trade was in a tonic which was the remedy for the very malaise he suffered.

Before retiring to his bedchamber, he deposited the communication apparatus he employed in his pharmaceutical enterprise in the location where it received its required re-energization. Subsequently the contraption utilized exclusively for social intercourse was inspected for missives which may have been transmitted by relations or acquaintances wishing for a correspondence. It appeared a former comrade, one who had of late betrayed the confidence so generously bestowed upon him, had made contact. Perhaps it was a plea for forgiveness. The brief communiqué was not an appeal for amnesty; it was a farewell of sorts and its content struck at the very core of the reader's being. A core, the reader realized, which had been concealed by layer upon layer of falsehood for an inordinate span of time.

He was a perjurer in a trial where he himself was judge, jury, and executioner. What luxuries had ever been whittled from his life? In stark contrast to ninety-eight percent of the population, he lived in opulence. His transport was meager and his garments were few for the one simple truth of his life. The wealth which he had always been associated with was a shameful burden. As a rotund schoolboy he was incessantly harassed, but when word of his family's prosperity was ultimately divulged, the selfsame persecutors were first in line to pursue friendly relations in order to gain access to his swimming pool and costly and abundant playthings. Every childhood friend was suspect. In his adolescence he grew a veil of hair to hide beneath and shrouded himself in oversized coats to avoid these false social interactions. His resemblance to a certain Russian monk was noted and his present-day persona came into existence, a persona which had swallowed him whole. His menial occupation as a retail clerk was to spite his parents. Long hours of toil and drudgery did not necessarily result in financial stability. Pushing pills was done out of spite as well. Creating massive quantities of cash was an effortless enterprise; any immoral ignoramus willing to take advantage of the inherent weakness of others had the ability. The tragic fact of the matter was his parents were so absorbed by their own labors, they hadn't the slightest inkling of the malice directed towards them by their son.

He viewed his visage in the looking glass above the basin. The man who returned his gaze was an utter coward. In actuality it was not a man at all, but a frightened boy playing dress-up. A boy desperate to procure interest from disinterested parents, yet fearful of the negative consequences which may result from that interest, a boy too afraid to exit through the unlatched door of his gilded cage. It could not continue in this manner any longer—the boy had to be eliminated! Sharpened shears were retrieved from the kitchen and once again he faced the boy in the glass. He held the razor edges to his bearded neck and proceeded to cut. Matter from his neck cascaded into the sink. Ras was gone. The boy behind the glass looked out into the eyes of a barefaced individual with a familial resemblance. The boy realized his hiding place had been destroyed and resigned himself to the fact that he must at long last grow the fuck up.

O

THE MAN STOOD on the edge of a deep canyon. A new day was just beginning and the sun was rising up from some far off place, possibly from within the canyon itself. Its illumination eventually revealed the river that wound its way along the canyon's base. The man watched as the river changed from a sliver of platinum to a thread of silver to a string of gold and back to a sliver of platinum. He looked down on a river that had spent millions of years carving its way through the earth's floor, exposing its hidden history layer by layer. A process neither the river nor the earth can stop and will only end when the river finally reaches the earth's foundation. The man shouldered his backpack and began his descent into the canyon.